Secret Dreams

Secret
DREAMS

a novel

Elizabeth Ann Thompson

Visit elizabethannthompson.net & pursueyourdreams.net to contact the author.

Publishing Consultant: AuthorPreneur Publishing Inc.—authorpreneurbooks.com
Editor: Mary Rembert
Cover Designer: Zizi Iryaspraha Subiyarta
Interior Designer: Amit Dey—amitdey2528@gmail.com

ISBN: 979-8-9916199-0-5 (paperback)
ISBN: 979-8-9916199-1-2 (ebook)
ISBN: 979-8-9916199-2-9 (audiobook)

*To my niece, Mary "Mel" Lesch (1983 – 2023) who
dreamed big dreams and whose light continues to
shine in this world and beyond.*

CHAPTER 1

Sweat from his arm dripped onto the ivory, heavyweight paper and smudged the embossed business envelope as Hank yanked it from the stack of letters in the mailbox. His heart kickstarted as he locked on the address in the upper lefthand corner: Johnson, Smith, and Clark, Attorneys, Cheyenne, Wyoming. His free hand, calloused from farm work, adjusted his black Stetson, his auburn ponytail grazing the collar of his short-sleeve shirt.

His worn cowboy boots felt heavy, like bricks, as he trekked the quarter-mile driveway to the house he would soon share with Miranda, his new wife. On his way, Hank tossed a couple bills addressed to his mother-in-law, Justine, on the back porch of her white farmhouse perched at the front of the property. Hank and Miranda's house had been built in the back, next to the barn, overlooking the cornfields. He was relieved Justine was at school, teaching her kindergarten class. He didn't feel like talking.

Hank barely noticed a flock of crows landing on the cornstalks in the field beside the driveway on this warm August afternoon. Their sharp beaks jabbed at the sweet kernels beneath the silks on the husks. When Hank reached the end of the driveway, he glanced up and inspected the new house next to the restored barn he and his buddies from Farm and Fleet had built over that summer. His sloping shoulders raised, and his chest puffed as he noted how well it turned out.

Hank had waited all summer to surprise Miranda. She'd been away on a three-month internship studying with Dr. James Harriot, the infamous veterinarian in Yorkshire, England. Harriot had written several books about his life as a country vet. It had been a dream come true for Miranda to work under his tutelage. Hank had been thrilled that she could fulfill her dream, but it didn't take away his longing for her while she was gone.

Along with his job as a farrier, Hank had worked overtime on the house to finish it by the time she returned. All their savings had been spent, except for a few dollars he'd set aside after he'd completed the construction. He hoped it was worth it and that she liked the house. He'd built their home, but his heart felt homesick for Miranda.

He lingered for a few moments studying the blue, ranch-style home, black shutters on the windows, and a walnut front door that he handcrafted himself from a tree at the back of the property. Miranda's cousin, Larry, had poured cement for the porch and sidewalk. Her mother, Justine, planted peony bushes lining the front of the house that would bloom into yellow and orange blossoms next spring.

Hank's heart danced inside his chest as he envisioned picking up Miranda from the airport the following day on her return home from England. He cast a glance at his hand clenching the envelope. They'd only been married six months. Their future looked bright, and he hoped this one incident wouldn't get in their way. How would he tell her that his past had caught up with them?

He took one last look and flung the letter from the attorneys. It scraped the inside of the burning barrel behind the garage as he headed toward the barn. Their horses, Mandy, a grey Arabian mare, and Rocko and Red, both chestnut Quarter Horse geldings, needed to be fed and groomed.

When he reached for the metal door handle, he heard the low rumble of a car in the driveway behind him.

Who was *that*? He didn't need any more surprises. Hank sighed heavily and fixed a stare on the taxi puttering down the driveway. He squinted and blocked the sun with his hand. The driver got out of the yellow car, took a couple steps to the trunk, and hauled out two large suitcases. A breath of air caught in his throat, and his mouth fell open as Miranda popped out of the taxi's passenger side.

He sprinted to her. Miranda dropped her handbag, and they wrapped their arms around each other. Their lips pressed together, long and hard, Hank relishing the taste of her kiss. Holding Miranda in his arms was something he'd dreamed about every day since she had left for England at the beginning of summer.

Miranda's glistening blue eyes bore into Hank's, tears streaming down her face. "Hi, husband."

Hank's heart felt like it would burst from his chest. He brushed a lock of long blond hair away from her chin and kissed her again, on her ear, her cheek, her eyes, and her nose.

"Ahem."

Still holding each other, they turned to look at the cab driver.

Hank chuckled. "You need to get paid." He reached for his wallet and pulled out a fifty. "Keep the change."

The taxi driver scooted to his vehicle, got in, and left, leaving a trail of dust.

Hank took Miranda's hand and squeezed. "Come on. I want to show you something." They strolled for a few steps, hand in hand, and stopped, facing their new house.

"Oh." Miranda covered her mouth with one palm. "It's beautiful." She squeezed his arm. "I love the color. And the door."

"I made the door myself."

"You did such a beautiful job. The ornate carving around the edges." She bounced a couple inches off the ground and tugged him toward the house. At the door, she curved her fingers around the grooves and slid her hand across its smooth panels.

"The walnut is from a tree on our property. Larry showed me how to do the woodworking and let me borrow his sander."

She took both his hands in hers. "You did an amazing job." She laid her head on his chest and hugged him tightly. "I missed you so much."

Hank breathed in the familiar rainwater scent of her shampoo. He bent his head and meshed his lips with hers; she tasted like fresh strawberries. Miranda leaned into him, responding to his desire. He scooped up his wife, and she let out a whoop. He held her in his arms and grinned. "I need to carry you over the threshold of our new home to bring us good luck."

She giggled. "You're such a romantic."

CHAPTER 2

Being held by Hank felt like a blanket of love wrapped around her body, permeating her heart. An ocean of waves rolled throughout Miranda as Hank carried her over the threshold, waves of missing him, loving him, and knowing that she was finally home after being homesick for three months. She had arrived in his arms. She was. Finally. Home.

Ben, Miranda's German Sheperd from childhood, met them at the door, tail wagging ferociously. He let out an excited yip, jumping up on them. Then Ben ran back and forth in the room, jumping on Miranda and barking and whimpering.

Hank lowered Miranda to her feet as she greeted her dog. "Hey, buddy." She crouched, and he licked her face. "I'm glad to see you too." He flipped on his back, and she rubbed his belly.

"He goes between your mom's house and ours. He likes hanging out at the barn too." Hank reached over to take her hand, and she got to her feet. "You know who has become inseparable?"

Miranda tilted her head. "Who?"

Ben rolled over and seated himself, leaning against her legs.

"Ben and Petey."

Ben gazed adoringly at Miranda.

Her crystal blue eyes widened. "The *neighbors'* donkey?" She rubbed Ben's smooth black and tan head.

"He gets loose, trots over here, and follows Ben everywhere. I load him in the horse trailer and cart him back. The Browns are apologetic about it, but that donkey is so smart he figures a way out even when they lock him in a stall." Hank shook his head. "Darndest thing." He pulled Miranda close to him and kissed her softly. "I missed you a lot."

"Me too, babe. I'm glad I'm home." She took him in. This brawny man. His slow smile, chipped front tooth. His sea green eyes. She remembered the first day she met him at Farm and Fleet. She'd gone in to get supplies for her horses. Hank had melted her heart then, and he still did with his kind eyes and the way he listened to her. He was truly present. It took her breath away and made her feel like she was the only thing that mattered in the entire world. "I don't want to be away from you that long ever again." They held each other for a few moments and then she placed her palms on his chest. Her eyes caressed his face. "The house looks amazing." She gestured. "Give me a tour."

Hank threaded his hand into Miranda's and led her into the kitchen. She stopped abruptly, and her mouth gaped as she took in the panoramic view of what Hank had built while she was in England.

"When I left home, you had guys helping mud and sand the drywall and painting. This is amazing." There were round, white handles on each of the oak cupboards and forest green tile on the countertop and backsplash. Brand new white appliances stood next to the white ceramic kitchen farm sink. Large beige tile adorned the kitchen floor, butting up against brown shag carpet in the living room. Miranda's eyes followed the edge of the carpet to an oak table in the dining nook. "Is that …?" She pointed, and her stomach flip-flopped. "That's my parents' table, isn't it?"

"Your mom thought you'd like some of your family's heirlooms in our new house."

Miranda liked the table, but not in her house. It was old and had been in the family for generations. She didn't want to think of all the family dinners and her dad every time she ate. She also didn't want to think about her mom's sad face sitting at the table for months after her dad died. And she didn't want to think about her ex-fiancé, Dylan, and the fights they had at that table. Nope. She wanted a fresh start.

"What's wrong?"

Miranda forced a smile. After all, her husband had done a beautiful job on the kitchen, and she didn't want to spoil the mood. They'd talk about the table later. "I love what you've done with the kitchen. It's gorgeous." She gave him a hug. "Thank you, babe, for everything." She turned and looked at the living room and gestured toward the terracotta orange leather couch. "Is that new?" Next to the couch stood a matching La-Z-Boy chair. "And that?"

"I got those at an estate sale near my grandma's house in Clinton. The furniture was practically new." He took her hand. "Enough of the main part of the house. I want to show you the most important room." His eyebrows wiggled as his eyes flashed fire at her. "The bedroom."

Miranda's lips formed an alluring smile as she followed him down the hallway. When she entered the bedroom, she sucked in a quick breath. Hank had painted the walls powder blue, and he'd made the bed with a white bedspread. A white canopy draped over the bed, and yellow roses stood in a tall vase on the dresser. The room looked just like the one she'd shown him in a magazine before she'd left for her internship. He'd remembered what she wanted. She felt so lucky to have Hank as her husband. She squeezed his hand and kissed him, slowly, tenderly showing her appreciation as she leaned against his chiseled body. Heat radiated between them. Hank wrapped his arms around her and lifted her onto the bed.

CHAPTER 3

"**B**oys. Time to sit down in circle time." Justine glanced at the two five-year-olds throwing wooden blocks at each other as she picked a book from her desk and perched on a chair. Her class of fourteen kindergarten children gathered in front of her on the navy carpet, sitting cross-legged in a half-moon, anticipating a good story. She breathed in the familiar smell of paste, tempera paints, soap, and cafeteria. It smelled the same as when she had taken Miranda to kindergarten twenty years before.

A little girl dressed in a princess outfit scooted from the playhouse in the corner of the room, leaving behind scattered plastic dishes and pots and pans she'd set up in pretend play. Crayons, paper, and Play-Doh covered the top of a large table on the opposite side of the room. Pictures of letters; shapes of bright colored squares, triangles, and circles; and adorable animals donned the light green cement block walls.

The two boys throwing blocks shoved one another and then scrambled to sit next to the other children.

Justine scanned the children facing her and raised the book in the air so the children could see. "This is a book I used to read to my daughter when she was your age."

A girl in front of Justine shot her hand up, fiddling with the bow in her red hair. "You have a daughter? How old is she?"

"She's married and takes care of sick animals."

"My cat's sick. She threw up this morning."

"That's too bad. I hope your cat feels better soon." Justine opened the book in her lap. "This book is called *A Apple Pie,* and it's about learning the alphabet."

Another girl popped her hand in the air. "Mrs. Graaf? What's an eltabet?"

A freckle-faced boy in the back stood up, his finger twirling in his ear. "I *love* apple pie."

Justine smiled. "Ok, children, let's wait until after the story before we ask any more questions."

Ever since she filled in for a sick teacher at Sunday school two years prior, Justine had been determined to pursue a career in teaching. Thirty years ago, she received her degree and married Stanley. But when his father died, they both put off their vocations to keep the family farm going.

Justine had just finished her refresher courses for her teaching degree when she was offered a full-time position at Central Elementary in Davenport. She accepted the job immediately. Only two weeks into her new job and she loved it. Teaching children exhausted her, but Justine felt like she'd walked into her dream career.

She glanced at the children quietly awaiting the story. Warmth radiated throughout her body, and Justine began reading, starting with "A apple pie ..."

CHAPTER 4

After a three-hour nap, Miranda rose from her comfy bed and padded out to their new kitchen. She rubbed her eyes. "Jet lag really got to me." Through a yawn, she said, "What a welcome home earlier." She hugged Hank from behind as he poured tea into glasses full of ice.

He turned around and held her close. "As much as I want to keep you all to myself, I'm sure your mom would like to see you."

Miranda lumbered over to the living room window and peeked outside. Looked like Justine was home from work. "You tell her I'm home?"

The cubes clanked against the sides of the glass as he took a sip of iced tea. "I wanted to leave that up to you."

Miranda checked the clock on the stove. "I'll change and then we can walk up to the house."

Before she left for her trip, Hank and Miranda had lived with Justine. They had stayed in Miranda's childhood bedroom. Hank liked Justine, but he wanted their privacy and was glad they had a home of their own. Still, he knew it would be selfish of him to make Miranda wait to see her mom.

As they walked hand in hand on the pathway leading to Justine's house at the front of the property, the letter from the Wyoming attorneys flashed in Hank's mind. A bolt of adrenaline swept through his body. What if Justine had dumped some trash to be burned when she got home from work? She'd see the letter and ask him about it.

The early evening sun began to set and cool the August heat. A few yards away, several monarchs circled the butterfly bushes in front of Justine's porch. Miranda said, "I hope you've looked after Mom while I've been away."

Deep in thought, Hank murmured, "Hmmmm."

"Hank? Honey?"

His thoughts still focused on the letter as they continued walking. Hank recalled the sharp pain in his hand after punching the drunk in Wyoming, causing him to worry if helping someone had ruined his career as a farrier.

"Hank?"

"What … Sorry, what'd you say?"

"Are you ok?"

"Yeah, sorry, just thinking about something."

"Anything you want to talk about?"

Hank tried to shake off thoughts of the incident two years before in Wyoming when he helped a waitress in a bar fight with her drunk ex-boyfriend who had accosted her. And how ridiculous the whole fiasco was and how attorneys could make mountains out of molehills. "No. It's just stuff at work."

How could he lie to Miranda? He didn't mean to, but the thought of telling her made his breath catch in his throat, and he exhaled slowly, trying to calm himself and clear his mind before they went into Justine's house. How would he explain it if Justine had seen the letter?

At Justine's back porch, a squirrel scrambled along the railing, jumped onto the grass, and scurried up a nearby maple tree. Miranda asked again, "Have you looked after my mom?"

"I've tried, but she's pretty independent." Hank added, with a slight smile, "Much like her daughter. I really haven't seen much of her. She's been gone a lot taking refresher courses at the college."

Hank put his hand on her back as they stepped onto the porch, and Miranda opened the door, stuck her head inside, and yelled, "Mom, I'm home."

They entered the corridor, shoving off their shoes. Hank noticed a pair of men's black boots he didn't recognize. He thought Justine had gotten rid of Stanley's clothes a year ago. He shrugged it off and watched the reunion between the two women.

Justine scurried down the stairs into the kitchen and put her arms in the air. She'd had her blond hair cut into a bob. "Miranda, you're home." She rushed to her daughter and gave a tight hug, tilted her head, and inspected Miranda. "You've lost weight. Didn't they feed you in Yorkshire?"

Miranda rolled her eyes. "Mom, I'm fine." She fluffed her mom's hair. "Cute. I like it."

"Thanks. I had it cut at the beginning of the summer when it got so hot." She ran her hand through her hair. "I thought you were arriving tomorrow." Justine released her hold on Miranda. "I'm thrilled you're home."

The childhood smells of butter, cinnamon, and vanilla frosting grounded Miranda and made her mouth water as she scanned the kitchen: coral cupboards and an olive refrigerator and stove complemented the white and green checkered linoleum floors. Flowered curtains framed each of the three windows. "I took an earlier flight and thought I'd surprise you."

Miranda's eyes halted in the middle of the kitchen, where she noticed a 1950s rectangular white and green laminate table with matching chairs. "That's new."

"I wanted a fresh start."

Miranda's thoughts traveled to earlier when she saw the old oak table in her new dining area. Apparently, nobody wanted that table and its memories.

Justine looked between Miranda and Hank, holding hands, their faces beaming, and said, "Looks like you surprised someone else as well." Her blue eyes sparkled. "First things first. I know I play second now. And that's ok." Justine gave each of them a hug again. "Mothers worry. Even if you are a grownup, I'm happy you made it home safely."

CHAPTER 5

Through the screen door, Miranda caught sight of a vehicle moving down the driveway and parking. A man got out of a light blue Cadillac and headed toward the back door. Her brows knit. "Who's that?"

Justine bit her lip as she looked out the kitchen window. "Good, he made it. I wanted you to meet someone I've been spending time with." She fiddled with the collar on her pink cotton blouse, and her eyes darted from side to side.

Miranda followed her mom to the window and eyed the stranger up and down, observing that he was of medium height, a couple inches taller than Justine. He had a tan, not a farmer's tan, but the kind you'd have spending time in a tanning booth. He had short, salt-and-pepper dark brown hair. He wore a tan cashmere sweater vest and a cream shirt. His dark brown trousers accented the brown flecks in his silk tie. She guessed he was around sixty, and the skin around his brown eyes crinkled when he smiled as he knocked on the screen door.

Justine scooted to the door and opened it. "Hi Richard, come in, come in."

The stranger entered and kissed Justine on her flushed cheek.

Miranda's mouth dropped. Who was this guy? And why was he kissing her mom? At that moment, she wished she

20

could do a somersault out of the kitchen and onto the porch and run back to her own house.

"Miranda, Hank, this is Richard Baker." Justine wrapped her fingers around Richard's tanned arm. "Meet my daughter, Miranda, and her husband, Hank."

What … her mom was seeing someone? Her dad had only been gone two years. What was her mom thinking? Miranda squeezed Hank's hand as she eyed this new person in her mom's life. Yep. Definitely. A somersault into the air, onto the lawn, and escape into the barn. The next time she saw her best friend, Tanya, she'd ask her to teach her some gymnastics moves.

Richard stepped into the kitchen and held out his hand to Miranda. He smiled a salesman's smile. "Your mom has told me all about you and your great adventure overseas."

Miranda stood with her mouth gaping. Her mom hadn't mentioned this man in their phone calls when she was away. How long had she been dating him? Her head felt fuzzy, and her ears started ringing. The second hand on the large round wall clock tick, tick, ticked as it circled the numbers on the face of the clock.

Hank glanced at Miranda, standing frozen. He shook Richard's outstretched hand. "Nice to meet you." His gaze bounced between Justine and Richard. "Quite a surprise, for sure."

Miranda took a long glance at Justine, and, in drawn out words, as if she'd had a stroke and was learning to speak, said, "Yes, it is a big surprise." She looked at Richard and said stiffly, "Nice to meet you."

Justine gave a nervous laugh. "Why don't you all go into the living room, and I'll bring out some refreshments."

Miranda's mouth felt as dry as sawdust. She blurted, "I'll help." She glanced at Hank and motioned toward the living room.

Once they were alone in the kitchen, Miranda whispered, "What are you doing, Mom?" She grabbed a Tupperware full of chocolate chip cookies, flipped off the lid, and plunked the cookies on a plate, breaking two of them in half.

"What do you mean, what am I doing?" Justine's lips pursed. She picked up the plate of cookies and tipped them back into the Tupperware, snapping the lid. "Is that really any of your business?" She retrieved a long knife from a drawer. "I met Richard at the farmer's market this summer. I was selling vegetables from our garden, and he was standing in line waiting for coffee and pastries at the Sweetie Pie Bakery stand next to mine." She cut a piece of lemon cake with vanilla frosting and placed it on a dessert plate. "They make a delicious blueberry apple crescent. You wouldn't think the two fruits would go together, but it's amazing."

"Mom!" Miranda measured coffee and dumped it into a paper filter. She poured water into the coffee maker. Her face grew hot as she said louder than a whisper, "I can't believe you would get involved with someone so close to dad dying."

The aroma of hot coffee swirled through the stone-cold atmosphere.

Justine kept slicing and filling plates. She ignored Miranda and went to the freezer. "Cake is better with vanilla ice cream."

She shoved aside frozen peas and carrots and plucked a gallon of ice cream out of the freezer. Justine opened the cardboard container and then took a scooper, dug in, and plopped a dollop next to each piece of cake. She handed two plates to Miranda.

In a sugar-sweet voice, Justine said, "Honey, could you please take these out to the guys."

Miranda's eyes threw daggers at her mom as she grabbed the plates. Heavy-footed, she trudged into the living room. She handed a plate to Richard, then Hank, her manners overwhelming her anger. Her throat felt dusty, and she croaked, "My mom will be out soon."

In the kitchen, Justine took a few deep breaths. She had known it would be hard introducing Richard, but Miranda had taken it harder than she imagined. It's not that she had forgotten her husband, Stanley. She thought about him and had missed him every day for the past two years. She never even dreamed of getting involved with another man. But she started talking with Richard every Wednesday and Saturday morning at the market. He had lost his wife five years prior and understood what Justine had gone through. And then, in the middle of summer, they went out for coffee, which led to dinner, movies, and walks in the park. Would she rather have her Stanley back? Of course. But she was growing fond of Richard.

He was different than Stanley. He was a CEO of a bank in Chicago, not a farmer. Richard wore pressed slacks and polo shirts. Stanley had worn overalls and John Deere baseball hats.

The first time she spoke with Richard, the wind had fluttered through leafy plants on her flapping tablecloth, and the aroma of basil floated through the air from the table next door. She was wrapping asparagus into bundles, and Richard smiled at her and struck up a conversation while he waited in line to get his coffee.

"What is that?" When she told him, his nose wrinkled. "You mean that mushy stuff in a can?"

She laughed. "That stuff is awful. If you cook asparagus right, it's a delicacy. It's one of my favorite vegetables."

"Mmm. I'll believe it when I see it. You should give samples. People will buy more."

"Thanks for the tip."

The following week, she had samples of grilled asparagus with lemon and garlic.

Richard came up to her stand and tried one. "You're right. This is good. I'll buy all the bundles you have left." He took a piece of paper out of his pocket. "Could you write down the recipe? I'm a novice chef."

She smirked and wrote down how to cook the asparagus.

"Could you jot your number too?"

"I don't know you." Justine looked up from the paper and rested her hand on her hip. "Why would I give a stranger my number?"

"Because I'd like to get to know you."

She studied Richard for a few moments. He stood there in his light blue polo shirt and tan golf pants, flashing perfectly white teeth and a radiant smile that she couldn't resist. He was different than most men in their town. He was polished and eloquent, smoother than the straightforward bluntness of the Dutch farmers she'd known her whole life. His charm flattered her and ignited a glimmer of light that she hadn't felt in a long time.

"Tell you what. When I'm done today, I'll meet you at the bakery a block over. We can sit down and have coffee."

That afternoon, they had talked for hours. Justine learned that Richard was a widower, and his wife had died five years prior. He had twins, a son and a daughter. His son, Jason, was an attorney who worked for an international company and spent a great deal of time overseas. His daughter, Jenny, was a pediatrician and had just landed a job at St. Luke's Hospital in Davenport as chief of pediatrics. He had a house in the suburbs of Chicago, where his children grew up. And he had just bought a newly renovated condo in Davenport so he could visit his daughter while in town.

For the rest of the summer, they went out to dinner, movies and the theatre, mostly in Chicago. Justine tasted the high life, and it was like nothing she'd ever experienced before. Her life had always been simple, down-to-earth, and wholesome. Her husband, Stanley, had been the one true love of her life. She cherished her marriage but had felt lonely since he died.

Justine turned off the coffee maker and plucked a pitcher of lemonade from the refrigerator. She put it on a tray with some glasses, taking a deep breath. *After all*, Justine thought, *I'm only in my fifties. I don't want to live the rest of my life alone. Miranda is just going to have to get used to it. I'm not replacing her father. I'm just getting on with my life.*

Her stomach flip-flopped as she anticipated more flak from Miranda before heading into the living room to join them. She wanted to be strong and live her own life, but her daughter could trigger her insecurities in decision-making and how to live since Stanley had passed. It had been a struggle without him, and she continued missing him but knew he'd want her to be happy.

Justine reminded herself that even though Miranda was an adult, Justine had been alive a lot longer than her daughter. Even though she had raised a girl who grew into a confident woman, Justine could be confident too. She patted her hair in place, held her head high, and walked into the living room. She placed the tray of drinks on the coffee table in front of the brown upholstered couch and gestured. "Help yourself, everyone."

Miranda scowled. "Want me to get the coffee, Mom?"

Justine threw her a look. "I turned off the coffee maker. It's too late in the day."

Richard rose from one of the brown suede chairs opposite the couch and scooted over to the table, picked up a glass of lemonade, and took a couple of swallows. "Justine, you didn't tell me your barn burned down a year ago. Hank told me what happened and that it had been a close call with the animals, but they all made it out. Wow. That's something."

"It was quite a day. Thank God no one was hurt. The neighbors came and helped rebuild a few days later."

Richard dug into the cake and ice cream. "Justine, this is so good, really moist."

Justine, Hank, and Richard started eating their desserts. Miranda sat next to Hank on the couch and didn't eat or drink anything.

Miranda remained silent, her chest tightening as she watched the conversation taking place. *Was Richard Justine's boyfriend? Or maybe just a friend that she did things with?* She certainly hoped that was it. The idea of her mom being involved with him romantically churned her stomach.

Justine interrupted her thoughts by saying, "Miranda, honey, tell us about Yorkshire. I want to hear all about it."

Miranda waved her hand through the air and said sharply, "I'll tell you later. I'm sure Richard doesn't want to hear about caring for animals in England."

"Miranda, you're being rude."

Hank's eyes darted between Miranda and Justine. "I think she's had a long day. Miranda, let's head home." He rose and held out his hand.

She took it and got up, then gave her mom a brief hug. "I'll call you later."

Hank nodded. "It's nice meeting you, Richard."

Richard flashed a smile like a salesman closing a deal. "Likewise. Miranda, it was nice finally meeting you."

She glanced at him and gave him a fake smile before heading toward the door.

Justine squashed the last piece of cake on her plate with a fork. Her mouth was dry as a bone. How could her daughter be so closed-minded? How would she convince Miranda that it was a good thing for her to have Richard in her life? She watched them leave, heading toward their house at the back of the property. She had been looking forward to Miranda's return home. But now she felt even further away from her daughter than she had when Miranda was overseas in England.

CHAPTER 6

The air was rich with the scents of grass and warm earth as they left the house and crossed the backyard on the path to their new home. Miranda held tightly to Hank's hand and pondered the last hour. A slow murmur and climb in pitch to a multiplying buzz of cicadas engulfed the night air.

How could her mom start dating someone while Miranda was out of the country on the other side of the world? Justine never once mentioned Richard while Miranda was away. They used to be so close. Sure, they had their squabbles, but they always talked it through. But this was different. Miranda felt like she didn't even know her mom anymore.

"I know you're upset, but you're crunching the bones in my hand."

"I just don't see how she can have somebody in her life so soon," Miranda said through gritted teeth. The sun was setting, and a harsh gust of wind blew across the farmyard. She shivered.

Hank started to speak, then stopped.

"What ... What were you going to say?"

"I know you don't want to hear this." He paused and then took a breath. "But it has been two years since your dad died."

Miranda halted, let go of Hank's hand, and turned. She spat out the words: "I know how long it's been since he died, but he *was* my dad. It doesn't mean I'm over the loss of him." She marched forward, leaving Hank standing there.

"Wait up." He trotted to catch up. "I know you're mad, but you can't blame your mom for not wanting to be alone."

They walked side by side in silence and then, when they reached their front door, Hank wrapped his calloused hand around Miranda's arm and said softly, "Sweety, you haven't been here all summer. Your mom was in a bad space and seemed depressed when you left."

Miranda's eyebrows furrowed and she scanned his face, listening to what he had to say.

"She was busy, but when I did see her, she didn't smile much until she met Richard at the market. Then something shifted in her. Her mood seemed to brighten."

Miranda eyeballed the night sky, stars beginning to shine, forming feverish constellations. She thought about Hank's words for a few moments. Her stomach tightened. She had no idea that her mom was in such a bad place. On their phone calls, they typically talked about the farm, Justine's classes, and her produce sales at the market. How could she have kept her depression from Miranda? She was Justine's only daughter, and she'd listen to anything. Her gaze floated from the sky to Hank.

"I don't want her to be sad." Tears filled her eyes as she said, "It's just so hard to see her with someone other than my dad."

Hank took her hand and drew her inward. "It's got to be hard. I know you miss your dad."

Miranda melted as Hank enveloped her with his strong arms.

"What do you say we get into bed and pretend it's just you and me in the entire world? Leave all our troubles for tomorrow?"

"But. My mom …"

Hank cradled Miranda's face in his hands, and his eyes fixed on her eyes. She felt him look deeply into her soul. He whispered, "Until tomorrow. Just us."

He kissed her on the cheek and then her mouth. Fully. A deep longing kiss. And right then, at that moment, she let herself be carried away inside his love for her.

CHAPTER 7

The next morning, Miranda settled on the edge of the deck attached to the back of their house and swung her legs as she sipped coffee. A trail of steam drifted upward from her mug. She felt she was the luckiest woman in the world. She had a wonderful husband and a beautiful farm where she was about to make her lifelong dream come true and open her practice as a veterinarian. She'd passed her national and state licensing exams before she left for Europe in the spring, so she was ready to go. It was a warm late August day, and the cornstalks swayed in the soft breeze, rustling lightly. Harvest was around the corner. She fixed her gaze on the bounty in front of her.

Miranda heard the slider open behind her, and Hank strolled across the deck. A comforting warmth spread throughout her chest as he sat beside her and wrapped his arm around her, his embrace like a soft blanket once more. He brushed his lips across the sweep of her cheek.

Miranda turned her head to look at him. Hank tousled his sun-lightened auburn hair, wet from the shower, and the curves of muscles on his bare chest glimmered in the morning sun. Her eyes trailed down his faded blue jeans that hugged his long legs, bare feet crossing at his ankles. Miranda's pulse quickened as she drank in the sexy man who was her husband.

A steady beat hummed in her chest and radiated throughout her entire body, reaching the tips of her toes.

She wanted to drink in once more the taste of their nightlong closeness yet knew that they both had lots of work to do that morning. The edges of her mouth turned upward. "Hey, handsome."

Ben hopped on the deck and padded over, lying down beside them. Miranda buried one hand in the fur on Ben's back and held Hank's hand with the other. "Got my two favorite guys right here." She flashed a radiant smile at Hank and then nestled her head against his shoulder. "This is heaven."

"That it is, my love, that it is," he murmured. After a few moments, Hank grasped Miranda's empty coffee mug, got up, and set it on the deck table. He reached down and scooped her hand, helping her stand.

She studied the quirky grin he had on his face.

"What are you up to?"

Ben jumped to his feet, leaning against Miranda.

Hank's sea green eyes sparkled. "Wait right here." He rushed inside the house and came back, holding her cowboy boots in one hand and his in the other. "Put these on and then come with me." He squeezed Miranda's hand. "Now close your eyes."

"What …?"

"No questions. Keep your eyes closed until I say you can open them."

Miranda trusted Hank like no other. She felt safe even with her eyes closed. He led her down the steps of the deck.

"Be careful here. Ok. We're on the ground now." His hand collected her elbow as he guided her onto the dirt. He wheeled around, gently gripping her shoulders, guiding her from behind. They walked across the bumpy earth.

"Where are you taking me?" she giggled. "The suspense is killing me. I'm going to open my eyes."

He covered her eyes with his hand. "Not yet. We're almost there."

He released his hand from her shoulder as he leaned forward. She could hear the grating woosh of a barn door opening.

Hank guided her forward a few more steps. "Open your eyes, babe."

Miranda gasped. Their horses, Mandy and Rocko, were saddled and ready to go riding. Her eyes bugged. "When did you do this?"

Mandy, her gray dapple mare, nickered. Miranda wrapped her arms around the horse's neck. The mare nuzzled against Miranda's shoulder.

"When you were sleeping in this morning. I knew you hadn't seen these guys yet. What better way to get reacquainted than to go for a ride?"

She beamed and stroked Mandy's face. "I'll get my riding clothes."

"Already got them. Everything you need is in the tack room."

"You thought of everything." Miranda eased over to him and slid her arms around his waist, kissing him on his neck, chest, and then his lips. "You're the best husband a girl could have, you know that?" On her way to the tack room, she stopped by Rocko's side. She rubbed his nose. "I missed you guys."

Hank watched Miranda greet their horses and thought about the secret he'd kept from her. Would his wife still feel that way if she knew about the letter from the attorney and that he had a criminal background? He focused on a yellow barn cat running across the cement floor and leaping onto a bale of straw.

Mandy bobbed her head up and down, snorting.

"Let's get going before these guys get too antsy." Hank grabbed the mare's reins off the pummel on the saddle.

After changing in the tack room, Miranda mounted Mandy and slipped her riding boots into the stirrups. "It's been way too long." She lifted her chin toward Rocko. "I'm surprised you're riding him. What about *your* horse?"

"I've ridden Red a lot this summer, and I thought ole' Rocko could use some exercise."

When they emerged from the barn, Hank viewed the back of the property. His chestnut quarter horse roamed the pasture, getting some well-deserved grazing time. Over the summer, Hank had imagined filling up the large pasture and starting a business raising horses. He'd thought about this idea since he'd worked in Wyoming for a rancher, shoeing quarter horses. The idea excited him. Since he and Miranda got married Hank was trying to figure out his place and wasn't sure how his dream would fit in on the farm. After all, it had been Stanley and Justine's for years. Hank was the man of the family now but, at the same time, he didn't want to overstep his bounds. He'd bring that up later after Miranda got her practice going.

The horses' hooves thumped like a muffled drum against the grass as they covered ground on the trail that threaded through their cornfields. Miranda and Hank moved forward into the rhythm of horse and rider, trotting side by side.

The morning sun beamed down on them as they rode. Sweat dripped down the nape of Hank's neck onto his back.

Miranda wiped her face and neck. "I've forgotten how hot it can get in Iowa during the summer. England is much cooler."

Hank lifted an eyebrow and smirked. "Follow me." He squeezed Rocko's sides, and they quickened into a canter.

Miranda whooped and urged Mandy to follow.

They rode toward the edge of the woods lined by oak, white pine, red-flecked maples, and the occasional walnut like the one he used for their front door. Squirrels scattered as the horses entered the shady forest. Dragonflies circled in front of them, and their wings glistened in the sun, peeking through the trees as they made their way deeper into the woods.

Hank's brain buzzed with the sensation of floating on a cloud from Miranda finally being home again and then grew murky under the dark cloud of his legal troubles. He managed to tuck those heavy thoughts away and focus on the here and now. Reaching across the distance between their horses, he scooped Miranda's hand in his, and they rode toward one of their favorite spots: the pond in the center of the woods.

When they arrived, Hank jumped down from Rocko, let go of the reins and started taking his clothes off. A light breeze chilled his damp skin. He darted into the water, naked.

Miranda dismounted, following suit, already tugging her top off. She laughed. "Wait for me." She hopped out of her boots, pants, and socks and threw her clothes in the grass.

The horses took small steps as they munched on grass near the shore, their reins draped across their withers.

Hank turned back and grinned. His body heated from head to toe in the cool water at the sight of his slender blond wife wading toward him. Her body had curves in all the right places. And then he dove into the pond and swam toward her. He tried to grab her from underneath as she approached before coming up for a breath. But Miranda sidestepped him. Hank came to the surface, let out a throaty laugh, and treaded water.

She paddled away. Over her shoulder, Miranda called out, "See if you can catch me, hot stuff."

Hank swam toward her and nuzzled up to her back as he embraced her from behind. She shrieked with laughter. He pulled her closer, kissing her neck. His pulse raced, and fluttery electric shocks danced on his skin. He closed his eyes and breathed in the scent of her.

She whipped around and took his face in her hands. "You're brilliant. You always have such great ideas."

They embraced and he pulled her closer, kissing her forehead, her nose, then her lips.

"Look." She pointed to the opposite side of the pond. "We've got company." From the shore, the horses jerked their heads up from eating. A large coyote, about forty pounds, perched near a log, watching them.

Hank's chest tightened. He took Miranda's hand. "We should get the horses out of here."

They quickly swam through the water and jogged onto the shore. Hank eyed the coyote as they put their clothes back on. Mounting their horses, he looked back, and the coyote was gone. "I don't think he'd hurt the horses, but better to be safe."

As they rode through the woods on their way back home, they smiled at each other and held hands for a stretch of the pathway until they reached the cornfields. Hank thought, *I am a lucky man.* On the rest of their journey, his jaw tightened as he chewed on how he'd tell Miranda about the letter he had received. *I hope I don't screw things up.*

When they reached the barn, they dismounted and slipped the saddles off the horses, hoisting them up on the fence railing. As they walked the horses, cooling them down, they chatted about the days ahead.

Hank said, "Remember my buddy Nash from Wyoming? The guy I worked with on that ranch?"

Miranda nodded as she led Mandy around the outside corral.

"He called the other day and said he was coming for a visit. His boss wanted him to look at some quarter horses for sale here in Iowa."

"That'd be great. It'd be nice to meet him." She glanced at him. "You've told me very little about when you worked out west."

Uneasiness crept throughout Hank's body. His chest tightened. "There's not much to tell." Another lie. Why did he compound things? He should just tell her all about the letter from the attorney. Miranda loved him. He knew that. She would understand. She was a good person. Would she forgive him this discretion? He swatted the thoughts away. "Nash wants me to come with him to see the horses. In Des Moines."

She studied him for a moment, and then they walked some more until the horses had cooled. Hank followed Miranda, leading Mandy into the barn.

They gave their horses a good rubdown, fed and watered them, putting them in their stalls.

Hank took Miranda's hand and pulled her into an empty stall, laying her gently on the straw. "Let's finish what we started in the pond."

CHAPTER 8

Later, they held each other, and he picked a piece of husk from her hair. "Welcome home, wife." Beneath the sweet smell of straw, she breathed in the earthiness of their damp bodies lying together, their love filling up the empty stall.

She kissed his salty lips, saying, "I'm glad to be home, husband. I was away too long."

"Copy that, babe." He wriggled his eyebrows. "And … I like practicing making babies."

"You're thinking of having babies? We just got married."

"We'd make beautiful babies." He smiled and stroked her face with his finger. The green in his eyes sparkled like water flickering from the sun on the surface of the ocean. "If we had a girl, she'd be beautiful, just like you."

She giggled. "A boy wouldn't turn out ugly, that's for sure."

"So. Let's have a girl."

She sat up and gathered her shirt and jeans. A curtain dropped across her face. "I'm not quite ready for that yet. Let's slow down some."

He stood and held out his hand. She pulled herself up. He wrapped his arms around her waist. "I've been thinking about it since the day we got married."

Miranda scooped her hands around his arms, tilted her head, and hesitated. Her eyes lowered to the floor of the stall. "I'm not ready to have kids. I'm sorry. But I haven't thought about it at all."

His green eyes which had sparkled only a minute ago suddenly clouded over. The hurt in them filled her chest with a thick gray smokiness.

"You don't want kids?" Hank dropped his arms to his sides. He shifted from one foot to another and leaned on the back of the stall. "I've always imagined us as parents, raising a family. Ever since we got married."

The yellow barn cat drifted inside the stall and did a figure eight around Miranda's ankles. She bent to pick up the cat, and it started purring. Her speech stutter-stepped: "I'm not saying never. But I want to get my career going first." Her face felt hot as she held the cat and stroked his back. Her eyes searched his. "I thought you knew that."

"I guess we never really talked about it, did we?"

Miranda set the cat on the floor, and it scurried out of the stall. As they got dressed, her chest filled with a gray murkiness, making it hard to breathe. She wanted to get away from this conversation about babies and clear her head. She gave Hank a quick kiss on his cheek and put her hands on his chest. "We'll talk about this soon. I promise." She glanced toward the door. "Right now, I'm going to call Tanya. I promised her I'd call when I got home from England."

As Miranda walked toward their house, she remembered that Tanya was on the road competing in gymnastics. So, instead of calling her best friend, she went inside and took a shower.

CHAPTER 9

Two states away, on August 23, Tanya was competing at the 1987 Pan American Games in Indianapolis, Indiana, one of the rungs on the ladder leading up to making the Olympic team. She and her teammates stretched out on the gym floor to warm up, and Tanya's nostrils detected the signature smell of sweat, rubber mats, and hard work combined into the scent of her home away from home. This competition was important because it was Tanya's last chance to fulfill her ultimate dream of a gold medal in the 1988 Olympics. If she waited until the next Olympics, she'd be too old.

Across the gymnasium, one gymnast at a time barreled the length of a runway and flew onto a pommel horse, practicing their skills: pikes, twists, and handsprings. Other gymnasts hurled their bodies through the air, performing somersaults, arabesques, and triple turns soaring above a 40 x 40 mat. On the uneven bars in the opposite corner of the gym, gymnasts patted their hands in a chalk tray, white dust clouding the air, and warmed up with jumps, handstands, and straddles.

The massive room echoed the buzz of spectators finding their seats. Thumps of gymnasts' feet landing on apparatuses and mats as they warmed up prompted cheering from the fans. Music with a beat played in the background as athletes

40

practiced dance moves and twists, backward flips, and forward passes.

Tanya's calves felt tight, and her left knee throbbed. Aches and pains were normal for elite athletes, and Tanya had gotten used to sore muscles and injuries in her sixteen years as a gymnast.

She remembered when the only gymnastics coach in the Davenport area came to all the elementary schools and auditioned girls in the third, fourth, and fifth grades to be on a community gymnastics team. Mr. Barnes marveled at how easily Tanya could do somersaults, cartwheels, and backbends as if she were gliding across the room. He saw talent in her and a feisty, brave attitude. Tanya didn't have any fear when it came to learning skills. She'd fall off the beam and hop back up and try again. Mr. Barnes picked three girls from each school and made up a team of thirty.

The gymnasts met every day at 3:30 in the largest elementary school of the area. Tanya loved it. From third grade on, she practiced all the time, at home on the lawn, on the living room carpet, and in her bedroom. She was always bending, twisting, flying through the air, and balancing. Sometimes, she stood on her hands for minutes at a time. Doing tricks was second nature to her, and she was always moving. Plus, gymnastics gave her an outlet away from her fighting parents.

In high school, Tanya trained at gymnastics camps during the summer. After graduating, she made the gymnastics team at the University of Iowa in Iowa City and her career took off. She was well on her way to competing in the Olympics and having her lifelong dream come true.

The MC boomed on the loudspeaker: "Gymnasts, you have thirty minutes before competition begins."

Tanya's scalp prickled, and she trotted to the balance beam, her favorite. She got in line behind other gymnasts. When it was her turn, Tanya executed her entire routine beautifully, but on the roundoff tuck double back, she landed too far backwards in the dismount and fell on her butt. She bounced back up from the mat, and as she passed other competitors on her way to join her team in the corner of the gym, her face, neck, and ears felt hot. She shook her arms, and, in her mind, laser focused on all the times she'd done her landing perfectly in the past. Tanya didn't want to dwell on the mistake she'd just made, so instead, she sat with her team, closed her eyes, and visualized the perfect landing over and over.

When she opened her eyes, Tanya spotted her boyfriend, Daniel, in the bleachers amidst the crowd watching the meet. He waved and gave her a thumbs-up, and it felt like her insides were vibrating. She had thought Daniel would be so preoccupied with his own competition that he wouldn't come. Her lips parted, and she sent up a small wave.

Tanya and her teammates gathered in their designated area for the U.S.A. team. She pressed her hand to her heart when she found out she had been picked first in the lineup. That way, she could get it over with and relax with the rest of the team, cheering them on.

It was Tanya's turn to perform her beam routine. She walked toward the beam and stood a few feet away, closed her eyes for a moment, and visualized her routine. She took a deep breath and then did a roundoff onto the springboard into a back flip tuck onto the beam. Her feet felt solid as they gripped the four-inch wooden rail, four feet from the ground. Power cascaded throughout her body, feeling like nothing could stop her. She conducted her entire routine perfectly except for a slight waver on one of her turns. Tanya ended with a roundoff tuck double back and stuck the landing. The crowd clapped and cheered. Her teammates hugged and congratulated her when she returned to their huddle. She'd get a deduction for the turn, but overall, she was happy with her performance.

Tanya canvassed the seat where Daniel had viewed the competition, but he had gone. Ice stabbed through her heart. Did he see her perform? Was he still in the building? Why had he come if he was going to leave before she had finished? Her mind raced for explanations. They'd only dated a few months, but she thought he loved her.

She bent forward and stretched, trying to sluff off the feeling that her heart was shrinking. As a sigh escaped her lips, Tanya sat next to the other gymnasts and tried to focus on the competition.

CHAPTER 10

Back in Iowa, at the Graaf farm, Hank finished leading the horses out into the pasture for the day. His brain felt waterlogged as he thought about the discussion he and Miranda had about having children. He hooked the lead rope on the peg in the tack room. What if she never wanted kids? Could he be ok with that? He'd always wanted the chance to do a better job than his own father, who'd deserted them when he was eight. Four years after his dad left, his mom died, and he was raised by his grandma. He loved Miranda more than life itself. His heart sank in disappointment at the thought of never having children with her and having a family of his own.

Hank sighed and headed for the house to make lunch. He'd have to set the idea of having children aside and hope that someday Miranda would want kids as much as he did.

CHAPTER 11

The hot water cascaded down Miranda's head as she lathered her hair. What was Hank thinking? Having children after they'd only just gotten married?

Over the last few months, a few people in England had asked her if they were going to start a family. She didn't know what she thought about the subject. The more people asked, the more she got irritated. She wished people would mind their own business.

Miranda thought it was strange that she and Hank had never had that conversation before they got married. She assumed it would work itself out, and when the time was right, they'd talk about it. She had been so focused on her career that children were at the bottom of her list. Oh, who was she kidding? It wasn't even *on* her list. Even as a girl, she'd never dreamed about having a family like many girls did. Her dream had always been to be a veterinarian.

She finished her shower and dried off with a towel. If this was something Hank wanted, she'd consider it. But would she *ever* want children? That remained to be seen.

After she got dressed, Miranda came out of the bedroom and gave Hank a kiss, trying to soften the conversation they'd had earlier. Hank smiled briefly as he finished making tuna sandwiches and then set two plates on the table. The air was thick, like heavy moss hanging from trees in a southern marsh, as they ate their lunch in silence.

CHAPTER 12

The next morning, Miranda opened her eyes after a restless night's sleep. She'd only been home a few days, and already their marriage was shaky. She searched Hank's eyes as he lay in bed next to her, *his* eyes fixed on *her*. Worry lined his forehead. Thoughts swirled in her mind. Were they ok after last night's discussion about having children? Should they talk more about it?

His eyes slowly circled her face. He then reached out and barely touched her lips. A flock of butterflies took flight in her stomach and her chest tightened. Normally, when he touched her, she melted and wanted to get closer to him. But she felt herself become rigid, and her mind raced, searching for answers.

Just then, Hank grabbed her hand and kissed it. "Come on. I want to show you something." He flung out of bed. "Get dressed. I set the coffee timer last night. Coffee is already made." He pulled his blue jeans on, threw a black T-shirt over his head, and left the bedroom.

What was going on? Why was Hank acting so weird? She got out of bed and donned a pair of black jeans and a light blue blouse.

They shoved their boots on. Hank handed Miranda a mug of hot coffee. He took her hand and led her outside.

She really didn't need coffee as she was wide awake, but she took a few sips anyway. Her eyebrows squished together. Even though it was a cool morning, she felt sweat trickle down her back. "I know I was away all summer, but you're full of surprises. Where are we going?"

"A little faith, please. We're almost there." They approached the side of the barn. Hank took hold of a doorknob and turned.

"What? Wait a minute." She put one hand on her hip. "There didn't used to be a door on this side of the barn."

He beamed. "There is now." And then he opened the door and stepped inside. "Come in."

She followed him and entered a room filled with medical supplies, a desk, chair, and lab equipment. Her mouth fell open. She breathed in the smell of steel, fresh paint, and new linoleum. She walked around the room and stroked several white cupboards above a long countertop. "This is amazing." The butterflies bouncing on the inside of her stomach were suddenly set free. She did a happy dance and then ran into Hank's arms and squeezed. She looked into his eyes. "Thank you. Thank you."

Hank's eyes brightened, and his husky laugh echoed in the room. They stood a few moments holding each other.

"This space used to be the storage room for feed and supplies. You did *all this* while I was gone?"

"Me, your cousin Larry, and one of his builder friends." He stepped away from her, swooping his arm through the air. "I'm glad you like it."

"I love it. I can't wait to get started in my practice." She went over to one of the cupboards and opened it, looking inside. "How did you know what supplies to get?" She eyed a centrifuge and other lab equipment. She scooted over to the microscope. "This is a nice one. I would have picked it out myself."

"Doc Tanner helped me out. He picked out all the medical stuff. The rest was Larry and me."

She ran her hand through the air. "Can we afford all this?"

"We had some money left over from the loan to build our house." He smiled. "All the labor was donated. And that's the biggest expense."

She scanned the wooden desk in the corner of the room, made from cedar. She ran her hand over the smooth top. "It's beautiful. Almost too nice for a vet's office." Above it, a picture of her and Stanley next to a mare and foal. "You framed this?" Miranda had helped Doc Tanner by going onto the floor, stroking the mare's head, talking to her when she fretted during labor. "That's when I knew I wanted to be a vet."

At the other end of the room was a stainless-steel exam table, and medical supply cabinets lined the wall. She ran her hand along the table's smoothness. Miranda was glad she didn't have to come home and do everything Hank had already done to start her practice. It was something she had been dreading. Picking out equipment and designing her office wasn't her thing. And because he got professional advice, her clinic turned out perfectly. "You've thought of everything."

"I'm happy it meets your approval."

"That and more." She smiled. "Thanks, babe. I can't wait to get started. I've learned so much from Dr. Herriot, and I'm anxious to use my new skills."

"I'll be back in just a minute. Don't go anywhere." He held up his hand before he left. "And don't peek. Leave the door closed."

"What? Are you kidding me? What are you doing?" She slumped in her chair and said, "Augh. This is torturous."

He opened a door leading to the rest of the barn and slipped through, closing it behind him.

Her mind swirled with confusion. What is he doing? Why is he taking so long? Her knee bounced up and down. Maybe she could take a peek. But no. He'd be disappointed if she didn't wait. She could hear thumping and footsteps in the other room.

Finally, Hank opened the door to the office and came inside, shutting the door behind him. He smiled. "You ready?"

There was a clunk on the other side of the door outside her office in the barn. "What's that?"

"Why don't we go and see?"

Hank led Miranda into the barn area, and she gasped.

"Surprise!"

She scanned the familiar faces and placed a hand on her chest. Her cousin Larry and his wife and kids, her neighbors, the Browns, the VanBurens, Pastor Bob from their church, some friends from college, her uncle Rex and his boyfriend, Rodney.

Justine came to her side, slipping an arm around her waist. "Welcome home, honey."

Miranda flinched. They hadn't spoken since Maranda met Richard the evening she got home. She had tried not to think about her mom having a man in her life other than her father.

Justine gestured toward a table packed with desserts, salads, sandwiches and casseroles, and turned her head to face the group. She announced to those in the room, "Please help yourselves to the food."

This was a joyous occasion, and Miranda was happy to see all her friends. She shoved away the conflicted feelings about her mom's life and tried to focus on having fun at her welcome home party.

Larry approached and gave her a hug. "It's good to have you back." He looked downward and then said, as his eyes darted, "I know you just got home but could you take a look at my lab, Beauty? She's out in the car. Something's wrong. She's the kids' dog, and I'd hate it if something happened to her."

Miranda exhaled the breath she'd been holding since Justine had spoken. "I'd be happy to. Let's go see what's up."

She had to admit, as the reality of practicing veterinarian medicine sunk in, she liked the idea of being the town's only country vet. Doc Tanner had retired the year before, and the only small animal vets were in town. The closest large animal vet was in Iowa City. It made her feel needed and that all her hard work in school had been worth it.

Miranda waved at the group. "I'll be back shortly. Duty calls."

Hank glanced at Miranda following Larry through the main door that opened to the backyard. He frowned, saying "What the …?" He just wanted to give his new wife a welcome back party and for people to let her relax for an hour. Was that too much to ask? He shrugged and took a plate from the table behind the line of people gathering food.

iranda fell into step beside Larry. He opened the tailgate of his station wagon, and Beauty was stretched on the back seat, facing them. She lifted her black head, tail thumping against the Naugahyde.

Miranda approached and scratched behind the dog's ears. "Hi Beauty. What seems to be the matter?" Miranda then gently palpated the dog's abdomen, searching for bumps or tender areas that indicated abnormalities.

Beauty whimpered and licked Miranda's hand.

"Let's get Beauty into my office, and I can examine her more thoroughly."

Larry scooped up Beauty and carried the dog across the dirt path leading to the barn. Miranda stood holding the door open in front of a sign nailed to the barn that read *Dr. Miranda Graaf, Veterinarian.* The corners of her lips turned. She thought, *This is my first patient in my new office.* Nerves swirled around in her belly as she thought about the responsibility that she held in opening her practice. Before, she'd always had someone to help or supervise her, yet this was a whole new chapter to her life. Her chest felt like it might explode with emotion. She gestured toward her exam table.

Larry gently laid Beauty on the table, and the dog stayed still while Miranda examined her. She pressed the chest piece of the stethoscope on Beauty's abdomen in different areas and then listened to her heart and lungs. She noticed the dog's breath smelled of outhouse ammonia.

"I'd like to do some blood work. She been eating or drinking?"

Larry shook his head. "She just lays there most of the time for the better part of a week. She'll drink a little water out of my hand. That's 'bout it."

Miranda located a syringe in her medicine cabinet. She wiped an area on Beauty's leg with rubbing alcohol. "This will sting a little bit, girl." As she drew blood and filled the syringe, she said, "You're such a good girl."

Beauty dry swallowed.

Miranda collected urine from Beauty with a catheter and then she ran a blood chemistry and urinalysis using her brand-new equipment. She looked at Larry. "It may take a while to get the results from all these tests. Go ahead and join the party. I'll come find you when everything is done."

Fear flashed in his eyes. "I'll wait here if you don't mind."

Miranda placed the tube of blood into the centrifuge and then turned toward the exam table. She placed her hand on Larry's forearm. "I'm going to take good care of Beauty."

His eyes blinked rapidly. "I've no doubt, Miranda. You've always been good with animals."

"Could you do me a favor and go tell Hank I'll be here a while?" She gestured. "You can go through that door into the rest of the barn."

He nodded and went to the side door. He grabbed the handle and turned his head. "I'll be right back."

Miranda thought about a time in Yorkshire, England, when a call came to Dr. Herriot's surgery from a farmer with an ill cow. Normally, farmers didn't think of cows as pets, but this particular animal had been with this farmer for years. When Dr. Herriot tried everything and nothing helped, he eventually had to euthanize the cow. The farmer was devastated. You'd have thought he lost his best friend. Miranda knew after accompanying Dr. Herriot on that call that not only would she have to deal with the pain of animals but the losses of the pet owners as well. She only hoped there would be a brighter outcome for Beauty, her first patient. And family.

Hank spotted Larry coming through the side door. "Everything ok in there?" The hum of guests chattering filled the air and, in the corner, Pastor Bob's rotund belly jiggled when he let out a raucous laugh as he talked to some of Miranda's friends.

"Miranda's doing some tests on Beauty. She asked me to let you know that she'd be a while."

Hank sighed.

"Sorry, I didn't mean to take her away from her party. I just didn't know what else to do."

"Don't worry about it. It's what she does. Helps animals." He thumped Larry's back. "I've got to get more pop. Tell Miranda I'll be at the clinic in a few minutes."

"I can help if you want. The least I can do."

"Sure. Follow me to the house."

They left the barn just as the mailman drove down the driveway toward them. He got out of his mail truck and came over to Hank. "I need you to sign something for me, Hank." He handed over a certified letter and pointed. "Sign here."

Hank signed. The mailman took the card with the signature and returned to his truck. The letter was from Johnson, Smith, and Clark, Attorneys. Hank's shoulders sagged. They just sent him a letter a few days ago. A guy can't catch a break.

"Everything ok?"

Hank shoved the letter in his pocket. He nodded at Larry. The last thing he wanted to do was let Larry in on his secret. They headed for the house to find more Coke and Mountain Dew.

After Larry left, Miranda perched on the stool next to the counter where she ran the labs. She dragged her palms down her pant legs. Beauty's pale gums, mouth ulcers, and chemical breath she had noted while she conducted the exam told her it was bad news before the labs were completed.

While Miranda waited for the centrifuge to finish spinning, she got up from her seat and stroked Beauty's face. Beauty looked up with brown, doting eyes. Miranda said, her voice cracking, "Are you going to be my first heartache?"

Why couldn't she have started her practice with something simple like fleas or immunizations? She knew this was part of being a vet, but it was also the hardest part: when your patient had a serious disease, and you couldn't do a whole lot about it. There was a hollowness in her chest.

Miranda's thoughts were interrupted by Larry and Hank coming through the side door. Hank approached her. "Babe, your guests are waiting."

"I can't leave my patient alone right now." She folded her hands in a prayer gesture. "Can you give my regrets and thank you's for coming?"

Hank gave Miranda an incredulous look. In a gruff voice, he said, "You'll miss your coming home party."

Larry blinked rapidly and cast a glance at Miranda, then at Hank, and back again to Miranda. "I'll be here with Beauty."

At the sound of her name, Beauty let out a yelp.

Miranda patted Beauty on the back and then followed Hank out the front door of the surgery. She closed the door behind her, and they stood outside on the steps. His face darkened. The wind carried sounds of muffled conversations coming from the barn. It's not that she wanted to miss her party. It was her professional responsibility to care for sick animals. She couldn't ignore Beauty while the dog needed medical care.

Miranda's voice rose a bit. "You had to know that this could happen. Things are unpredictable with animals. They're just like people. They get sick or hurt." She touched Hank's arm. "I can't believe you're upset about this."

His eyes were stormy, and his voice could've turned water into ice cubes. "It's something else."

Goose pimples ran up and down her skin. "Honey, what is it?"

He marched away from her, and she followed him toward the main entrance of the barn. Over his shoulder, sour words fell out of his mouth: "Don't worry about it."

Miranda shivered. And it wasn't because of the unexpected August wind. She had never seen this side of Hank. She couldn't tell if it was because of the sick dog or something that had happened to him before they came into the clinic. Whatever it was had happened within the last half hour.

Her stomach rolled. She forced her anxious thoughts into the field of cornstalks. For now, she'd focus on her guests in the barn.

Inside the barn, Miranda stopped a moment, and her chest thawed as she took in the low rumble of the guests talking with one another, the occasional uproar of laughter, and the aroma of coffee coming from the tall urn on the table. Bits of luncheon meats, cheeses, and breads were scattered on empty platters. The chips and dip were gone. A few cookies remained on the plates of desserts.

Miranda scooped up the last brownie and walked toward Justine, who was talking to Pastor Bob. The large gathering of people in the small area drove the temperature in the room upward, and he took out a handkerchief, wiping the beads of moisture from his forehead.

Just then, Richard approached, a cup of coffee in one hand. He wrapped his other hand around Justine, claiming his turf. Miranda quickly veered off, looking for someone else to talk to. The last thing she wanted was to be involved in a conversation with Richard. She didn't like that her mom had found someone only two years after her father's death.

She wanted to talk to Justine about Richard, but in the few days she'd been home from England, Miranda couldn't seem to find a moment without him by her mom's side.

Miranda popped the last bite of brownie in her mouth and walked over to Mr. and Mrs. Brown, the farmers next door, standing at the edge of the room, holding Styrofoam cups.

"I heard your donkey's been pestering my dog."

"Oh, that darned donkey." Mrs. Brown guffawed and ran her hand through the air. "Petey just loves Ben. It's like they're attached at the hip."

Mr. Brown, thumb hooked through his denim Carhartt suspender, said, "It's not just Petey. We've seen Ben at our place a couple times too. They're pals, for sure."

Miranda smiled. "Sounds like Ben is a bad influence."

Hank walked toward her, his face grim. "Larry came and got me. Said his dog's passed out. Won't come to."

She wanted to stay and visit with her guests. Plus, Hank was upset. She didn't know why, but if it had anything to do with her skipping out on the party, she didn't want to make him more unhappy than he already was. Something wasn't right. He was usually understanding about her profession and forgiving when it came to helping animals. But today, he was acting strange.

Miranda felt caught between her veterinarian's oath and appreciating the time it took to put this party together for her. She didn't want to be rude to her guests and didn't want Hank to be upset, but after all, this was why she had gone away for the summer. Her friends would understand. She scratched the side of her neck and struggled to find the right words. Finally, she pivoted and waved to the neighbors and friends mingling in their barn, having a good time. "Thank you everyone for coming. I have a sick animal to tend to." She headed to her office.

✳

Back in the clinic, Miranda donned her stethoscope and listened to Beauty's heart and lungs. She studied the results from the urinalysis and blood tests. Her shoulders sagged. She motioned for Larry to sit on a chair near her desk. When they were seated, Miranda saw the bags under Larry's eyes. He slumped forward and bit his lip while Miranda talked.

"Larry, I'm sorry to have to tell you this, but Beauty has kidney failure."

He turned his face away and looked down at the floor. "That's pretty bad, isn't it?"

She nodded slowly. The quiet pause in their conversation seemed like an eternity. What she had to tell him next would hurt them both, though she knew this was part of her job. She'd had to help Dr. Herriot care for critically ill patients when she was in Yorkshire. But why did it have to be her first patient in her new practice? She had looked forward to opening her doors and caring for the people she knew in this town and their pets. But this was horrible. A horrible beginning for her and a horrible day for her patient and those who loved her.

"It looks like Beauty may have accidentally ingested some poison."

Larry's face paled. "What? How could that have happened?" He shook his head. "I'm always really careful with anything I use on the lawn or in the garden."

"Beauty could have wandered down the road." She hesitated. "I can keep her as comfortable as possible. But I think you need to make a difficult decision."

"You mean, putting her down?" Larry swiped a hand over his face. "What am I going to tell the kids?"

With every bit of strength Miranda had, she tried to stay strong for her patient, for Larry and for his family. It was the hardest thing she'd ever done in her career, thus far. Harder than the hundreds of hours she studied. Harder than recouping after the fire that burned their barn. Harder than leaving her husband for the summer a few days after she married him. Right up there with grieving for her father. To kill another living being was hard no matter how you looked at it. The one solace was knowing she'd be ending Beauty's suffering.

In a gentle voice, Miranda said, "Just be honest with them." After a few moments she added, "I think they need to say goodbye first."

He nodded slowly. "I'll go get my family. I'll be back within the hour."

When Larry left, Miranda exhaled and then went into doctor mode, not allowing herself to feel what was about to happen. She located the phenobarbital solution from her doctor's bag and prepared it in a syringe, which she set on the counter. Then she stooped over Beauty, petting her, feeling the dog's staggered breaths, waiting for her family to come say their last goodbyes. As Miranda perched beside the black lab, it brought back memories of her dad's final hours and how difficult that was for her and Justine. But they got through it, and so would Larry and his family. It was a difficult part of loving someone for sure. And with pets, loving them was so short-lived.

A half hour later, Larry and his wife, with their three teenagers, came into the clinic. They swarmed their beloved dog, petting her and crying.

"I'll give you all some time. Let me know when you're ready," Miranda said. She walked to the other end of the room and plopped in the chair at her desk, pretending to look through some papers, her heart heavy.

After a few minutes, Larry said, "Ok, Miranda."

She took hold of the syringe. "I'm so sad to have to do this. Beauty's already unconscious. This will happen quickly."

Not wanting to view any of their faces, her eyes focused on the task at hand.

She looked at Beauty for a few moments and stroked her head. She then got to work and injected the shot into a vein in one of the dog's front legs. Beauty quickly became still. Miranda palpated her heart with the stethoscope. There was no sound. She looked at the family before her and said, "It's all over now. She's no longer in any pain."

Larry covered Beauty with a blanket and scooped the dog up in his arms. His family followed him as they all walked out the door, closing it behind them.

Once they left, Miranda put her head in her hands and wept. She knew this would be part of the job when she began veterinary school. But it didn't make it any easier. She knew that it was one of the ways to help animals and put them out of their misery. Yet she didn't know if she would ever get numb to the sadness of having to put an animal down.

CHAPTER 14

Miranda closed the door behind her when she left her office. She breathed in the afternoon air, unusually cool for late summer, and sat in the grass just outside and let the solid wood of the barn support her as she leaned against it. All the cars were gone: the guests had left. She scanned the freshly mowed lawn in the yard and took note of the bounty in the garden full of tomato, cucumber, and green bean plants. The growth in front of her sent a cascading warmth of gratitude throughout her face, neck, and heart. She felt appreciation for the Dutch ancestors' lives before her, all the way from the Netherlands, working hard to leave this piece of land for Justine, Miranda, and now Hank. It was so peaceful. The heaviness she'd felt after euthanizing Beauty dissipated, and a lightness came over her the longer she sat there.

"Mind if I join you?" Hank was walking toward her. "Heard you had a rough go of it." He sat next to her and put his arm around her shoulders.

She leaned her head on his shoulder. "Pretty rough." They sat quietly for a few minutes, taking in the pinks, yellows, and oranges of the Iowa sky.

Miranda broke the silence. "What happened this afternoon?"

He moved his arm off Miranda's shoulder. "What do you mean?"

"You had a look on your face earlier. Something happened."

He had to tell her something. They had always been in tune with each other and able to tell when something was wrong with the other. He took a breath and began. "There was a bar fight in Wyoming before I came to Iowa. An attorney sent me a letter in the mail. Nothing to worry about." He plucked grass from the lawn and tossed it aside. That's all he wanted to say for now.

She studied him for a moment. "I trust that you'll let me know if there's more to talk about."

He exhaled. "If there's something you need to know, I'll tell you."

The sky came fully alive before settling in for the night. A flock of starlings swirled in a figure eight pattern above them before landing on the barn's roof. A gust of wind blew a plastic bucket across the yard, landing a few feet away. Hank stood and put his hand out. "Let's go inside."

Miranda glanced upward as stars began to come out of hiding and sparkled in the early dusk. She took her husband's hand, and they walked to their house. Before she opened the door, she heard a bark and turned to see Ben with Petey following close behind. Ben ran up to her and she bent down, rubbing his ears. She laughed. "You guys escaped again?"

Hank's eyes floated upward, and he let out a sigh. "I'll drive Petey back to the Browns."

"I'm going to take a shower." She patted her leg. "Come on, Ben. Enough carousing the neighborhood."

CHAPTER 15

On his drive to the Browns, Hank mulled over what had happened over two years ago in Wyoming. Hank had never told Miranda the story of the bar fight or that he went to jail for a few nights. Cleaned out his savings to pay the fines.

And.

That he had a felony for assault on his record.

Hank grimaced and rubbed a hand over his face as he thought about the incident in Wyoming that continued to trail him. He had partied with his buddies from the ranch where he worked as a farrier. A few nights per week, they'd blow off steam at the local bar in town. That fateful night, they took a load off around a big table, when a drunk guy the next table over started harassing their waitress. The drunk grabbed the waitress, and she fell toward him, and he tried to kiss her. She pushed him. He persisted. Hank rose to help her and grabbed the drunk's arm to pull him away. The waitress thanked Hank. But the drunk came after Hank and punched him. A huge brawl started, and several guys were involved. The men had to spend a couple nights in jail.

In the trailer behind the truck, Hank's thoughts were interrupted by Petey braying, pining for his buddy, Ben. Hank chuckled and murmured, "Knucklehead," as they continued their travels toward the Browns.

A couple days after the Wyoming bar fight, during their hearing at the courthouse, Hank was charged with assault because the drunk's nose was broken, and he knocked out a couple teeth in the fight.

The bar waitress happened to be the drunk's ex-girlfriend. She didn't testify on Hank's behalf because she was afraid of backlash from the drunk.

He had left Wyoming and moved to Iowa to be near his grandma who had raised him and to get away from his past and make a fresh start. He thought this was all behind him, but now it was all resurfacing, and he wasn't sure how to handle it.

While Miranda had tended to Beauty and Larry's family, Hank had opened the certified letter, knowing that the attorneys would keep hassling him if he didn't. Attorneys representing the drunk man in the bar were suing him for damages from the injuries the man sustained when his nose had been broken. The drunk claimed that he had sinus pain, and he was suing for $20,000 for medical expenses to have sinus and nose surgery.

Hank's teeth ground as he thought of the drunk. Such a jerk. He had been mean to women, rude, and according to people who knew him, a slacker on the job as a construction worker. Hank knew this lawsuit was a ploy to get money and that people could sue for anything. The whole situation was because he had tried to help someone. But it just kept following him.

The whole ordeal embarrassed him. And he didn't want her to think less of him. But now they were married. Dylan, her ex-boyfriend, had kept things from Miranda and had secrets. Hank didn't know if Miranda would forgive him for not telling her about this secret.

After driving about a mile, Hank turned into the Browns' driveway. At the door to the trailer, he said, "Come on, Petey. You're home." He clipped a lead rope on the donkey's halter and backed him out of the trailer. Hank rubbed Petey's forelock. "No more of this, ok? You can come for a visit once in a while. But this is getting to be a bad habit." He could swear that Petey smiled as his lips turned upward slightly.

Hank shook his head while he led the donkey back to the barn and his stall. Hank had done this so many times that he didn't even bother to knock on the Browns' door. They were probably sleeping anyway.

On his drive home, Hank returned to his predicament. What would he do about the letter? How would he tell Miranda?

CHAPTER 16

The following week, Miranda cleaned out the cages of two dogs and a cat in her office. She'd quickly acquired patients from Dewitt and from the neighboring cities of Davenport and Bettendorf in the two weeks since she'd been home. Since she was the only country vet in the area, she'd been getting quite a few calls. Some calls were from Doc Tanner's practice, and some people called her because they wanted a vet close to home rather than traveling to Davenport or Iowa City. She took in a deep satisfying breath.

The door cracked open, and Justine peeked inside. "Mind if I come in?"

"It's open to the public, Mom."

Justine tiptoed to where Miranda scooped out a black cat from his cage. He meowed.

"Wow." Justine's eyes bugged. "He's huge."

"He's a Maine Coon. They're notoriously big. This guy got caught in some barbed wire." Miranda stroked the fur on the cat's back. "Landis weighs twenty-five pounds." She lowered him onto the metal exam table and inspected his bandaged foot. "You're a sweety, aren't you?"

The cat licked her hand and purred. Loudly.

"I was wondering if you and Hank would like to come for dinner tonight?"

Miranda glanced at her mom and scratched an eyebrow. She hesitated for a few moments. "Can we bring anything?"

"Richard's going to be there too. He's bringing steaks and apple pie from the bakery in Davenport."

Miranda's hand stopped in midair, holding a tube of antiseptic. "You're inviting *him*?"

"He is a part of my life. I wish you'd get to know him better."

"Don't you think it's a bit soon?" Miranda unwrapped the bandage on Landis' paw. "Dad just died."

"It's been two years, Miranda. I'd think you'd want me to move on with my life and be happy." She pivoted on her heel and headed to the door.

Miranda yelled as Justine was leaving, "Mom. Mom, come back." She secured the cat on her exam table. "We can discuss this."

Justine slammed the door behind her.

The big black cat put his healthy paw on Miranda's arm. He meowed and his yellow eyes stared into hers.

She cradled his large round face in her hands. "I bet you agree with me. Don't you? It's too soon." Miranda cleaned the animal's wound and wrapped his paw with a new dressing before gently placing Landis back in his cage.

CHAPTER 17

That evening, Miranda and Hank plodded to Justine's house at the front of the family farm. She shuffled a basket of hot, homemade rolls from one arm to the other and grumbled, "I can't believe she's having Richard over. I haven't even had time alone with my mom." Her hand circled in the air. "He's always here. He was there when I got home from Europe. He was there at the party. And she went the following week to the house he owns in Chicago." She tripped over a garden hose. "She's either with him or at school, teaching her kindergarteners."

Hank squeezed Miranda's hand. "I know this is tough. Another guy in your dad's place."

"It doesn't seem like she even cares about my dad. Like he never existed." Miranda stomped her way toward the back door.

Hank halted on the dirt path to the house, grass trying to push through but flattened by footprints. "Honey?"

She exhaled a jagged breath.

"I know you're upset." He gave her shoulder a gentle squeeze. "I don't know if I like Richard either, but let's just try to enjoy the evening."

"There's something about him that I can't quite place."

"I just don't know him well enough yet to have an opinion."

"But you'll admit, there's something off about him?"

"Maybe. But I want to give your mom the benefit of the doubt." Hank smirked. "Plus, I'm the new son-in-law. I don't want to get on her bad side."

"Oh. That's it." Miranda chortled. "You'd pretend to like him if it meant my mom liked you."

"Got that right. I'm the new guy."

Miranda kissed her husband's cheek. "I don't know anything you could do to get on her bad side. She loves you."

A glimpse of the bar fight in Wyoming flashed in Hank's memory. He shrugged. "I don't know about that. But I'm supporting her choices, just the same."

They arrived at the door and knocked, then stepped inside. Miranda yelled, "Mom, we're here." She carried the basket of bread to the counter and shoved Richard's apple pie toward the back. She placed the rolls in front, took the towel off the top of the basket, and threw it on the pie.

Justine came into the kitchen, smoothing her hair. Her lipstick was slightly smeared. Richard followed close behind.

"The table's set and the steaks are on the grill."

"Hello, Miranda. Hank," Richard said. "I'll go check the meat. It should be done."

"Richard brought a nice bottle of red wine. Could you get it from the counter? I'll see if we have a bottle opener somewhere around here." She shuffled through a drawer.

Miranda stood looking at her mom. She hadn't remembered her mom drinking wine before. What was this guy doing, trying to change Justine? She recalled Hank talking about having a nice evening, so she stuffed her feelings deep in her belly, muttering, "What can I do to help?"

"You two can put the silverware and plates on the table." Justine reached into the fridge. "Here's an ambrosia salad." She handed it to Hank. "The twice-baked potatoes are staying warm in the oven. When Richard comes back in, I'll take those out."

Miranda thought, *Twice-baked potatoes? Since when had mom stopped making just regular mashed potatoes? What was this new guy doing anyway?* She scrunched her nose. "When did you start making those?"

"I got the recipe from the chef at a restaurant we went to in Chicago."

Miranda did an inner eye roll. "Hmmm."

Richard returned, carrying a platter with giant steaks. The aroma of grilled meat filled the kitchen.

Hank scooted toward Richard. "Let me help you with that." He grabbed one end of the platter, and together, they placed it on the table.

Miranda finished setting the plates and silverware on the table.

Justine plopped a potato on each of the plates. "These are hot."

Richard said, "Careful, sweety."

Miranda's stomach rolled. She'd have to get through this dinner somehow. "You said there's wine, right?"

Justine handed Miranda a corkscrew, and she opened the bottle, pouring some into each of the wine glasses on the table.

"Everyone sit down before it gets cold," Justine said.

They all placed linen napkins on their laps.

Richard cleared his throat and held up a glass of wine. "I'd like to make a toast." He focused on Justine. "I never thought I would find someone after my wife died. I pictured myself living alone the rest of my life." He tilted his glass in the air. "Until I met this beautiful woman."

Miranda's throat felt as dry as the dusty driveway outside. She shot a glance at Hank. He fidgeted with the napkin in his lap, rolling the white material around in his fingers.

Justine blushed. She leaned into Richard and kissed his cheek. "Thanks, sweety." She sipped her wine, then set her glass on the table. "Let's eat before it gets cold."

Hank reached for the breadbasket and nudged Miranda. "We made these from scratch today. They're still warm. Everyone, please, help yourself." He took one and tapped Miranda's frozen wrist planted on the table with the basket.

She glanced at him and grabbed the basket, taking a roll and dropping it on her plate. She passed the basket back to Hank.

He said in a low voice, "Pass this to your mom."

Miranda continued to stare at Justine and Richard, breadbasket in midair. Thoughts reeled in her mind. *What was her mom thinking?* Her eyes roamed the kitchen as she tried to get her bearings. *Was that a suitcase in the corner? Was he spending the night? And what about Chicago? What else didn't she know? This guy was taking over Stanley's place.*

Justine cracked an opening through Miranda's thoughts. "I'd like to try those rolls, honey."

In an attempt to pass the basket to her mom, Miranda bumped her glass, and red wine splashed all over the white linen tablecloth and onto Richard's white polo shirt. "Oops." She grimaced. "Sorry."

Richard tsked, jumped up from his chair, and grabbed his napkin, blotting his shirt. His lips formed a straight line.

Justine helped him dab the wine from his shirt. "Why don't you go change, and I'll put this one in the sink to soak."

Miranda knew it was bad to enjoy seeing Richard flustered, forced out of his car salesman composure, but she had to admit it was nice to finally see the real him. Richard grabbed the suitcase in the corner and rolled it into the bathroom.

After he had left the room, Miranda stood and cleared the dishes, put on fresh linen, and reset the table.

When Richard returned, he had on another polo shirt, light yellow this time. He had plastered on a smile and was ready to resume his role as her mom's controlling boyfriend. He sat and Justine put his plate in front of him.

"Let's eat, everyone."

When they finished eating dinner with long silences and no more spilled drinks, Hank and Miranda cleared the table. Dishes clanked as Miranda stacked the plates in the dishwasher.

Justine said, "Honey, that's ok, we can do that later. Let's go into the living room and have a slice of the apple pie that Richard brought."

Miranda closed the door of the dishwasher. "I think we'd better get going. I've got an early day tomorrow with patients."

"You can surely stay a few more minutes for a piece of pie?"

"Sorry, Mom. I have a practice to run. And the animals in the clinic need me to be there early."

"How 'bout I cut you a couple slices to bring with you?"

Miranda sighed. "Fine, whatever."

Justine quickly cut two pieces of pie, putting them in Tupperware. She glanced at Miranda and then handed the container to Hank.

Richard approached Miranda and Hank. He leaned in to give Miranda a hug. She stuck her arm out for a handshake. His Adam's apple bobbed as he swallowed and shook her hand.

Hank offered his hand. "Thanks for the steak dinner. Nice flavor in the meat."

Richard returned the handshake. "It was a special garlic rub I put on beforehand. Seems to keep in the juices and bring out the flavor."

Miranda hugged Justine and then they left, stepping into the muggy August evening. In silence, Miranda stomped down the drive to their new house, Hank jogging to keep up.

When they walked inside, Ben greeted them, tail wagging and nuzzling their hands. Miranda stooped to pet Ben.

"I'm going for a walk. You wanna come with me?"

Hank's eyebrows raised. "Looks like you could use some alone time. You go." He began taking off his shoes. "Why don't you take Ben? He could use some exercise."

CHAPTER 18

An hour later, Miranda strolled the length of the driveway after her long walk, hands on her hips, beads of sweat rolling down her face. She had kept an eye out for the coyote they had seen a few days ago while riding their horses. Ben followed close behind, panting. "Come on, buddy. Let's get a drink."

Miranda turned on the faucet at the edge of the main house. Ben trotted to her and lapped the water streaming from the garden hose. Miranda bent to drink the cool water herself. And then looked up at the stars peeking through the clouds.

She heard a voice behind her: "Beautiful, aren't they?"

Miranda turned to find Richard. He got up from his seat on the back porch and walked down the steps toward her. Ben circled and then sat in front of Miranda. His ears perked, and a low growl rumbled in his throat. His brown eyes focused intently on Richard.

"Will he bite?"

She rubbed Ben's ears. "He never has before." She looked down at her dog. "It's ok, buddy."

Ben's front paws shifted, and he leaned into Miranda's legs.

"You don't like me very much, do you?"

She continued holding the hose and water streamed onto the ground, puddling in the grass. The small lake was moving toward Richard's loafers, and he backed up. Miranda hoped he'd leave her alone and she could avoid this conversation, but he remained, studying her.

She didn't want to hurt her mom's feelings by being rude to her boyfriend, but he was right: Miranda didn't like him. He was moving in on her dad's position in the family, and it bothered her. The more she thought about it, the more her blood boiled.

"If you had kids, you'd know how hard it is to welcome a new person into their lives."

"It just so happens I do. I have a son and a daughter. They're both grown and living on their own. They're happy that I've found someone. I wish you could feel the same way."

She glared at him and turned off the water.

"Your mom just wants you to be happy for her."

"How do you know what my mom wants?" Miranda plowed past Richard and stormed toward her house. Ben trotted closely beside her.

Justine peeked outside the kitchen window and watched Miranda as she huffed and marched home with Ben right behind. Richard turned on his heel as he charged in the opposite direction.

Justine met him at the back door. "What was that all about?"

Richard relayed the conversation that they'd had outside as he poured himself a glass of iced tea and they went into the living room.

"Why did you talk to Miranda about us? It's just made things worse."

"I want us all to get along." He sipped the tea. "Miranda is being selfish. Hank seems fine with us being together. Why can't she?"

Justine turned and picked up a towel on the couch she'd taken from the dryer and snapped it, hard. Heat burned Justine's cheeks, and her voice rose: "Don't talk about my daughter that way. You don't know what we've been through. When Stanley died, she stepped in and took care of the farm while I was holed up in my room, grieving. She cared for me and made sure I ate and got my basic needs met." Justine stomped her foot. "She's been a good daughter. So don't push *us* onto her." She folded the towel and picked up another one.

Richard stuffed his hands deep into the pockets of his khaki suit pants. "I'm sorry. I was just trying to stick up for you." He glanced at the pile of clean wash. "Let me hire someone to help you with the housework."

Justine shook her head and took the corner of a bedsheet. "Don't be ridiculous." She turned to face him. "You leave Miranda to me. I don't interfere with your kids."

"I know. But they have taken a liking to you quickly."

She lined up two corners of the white sheet and shook it. "Your wife passed away five years ago. Stanley has only been gone two."

"But still …"

Justine tossed the folded sheet onto the couch. "Let's leave this conversation for another time." She tented her fingers and looked at him. "Let *me* talk to Miranda."

ater that week, Miranda answered the clinic phone. "Dr. Graaf. How can I help you?" She filled a jar with 4" x 4" cotton bandages.

A familiar voice on the other end made Miranda smile. "It's so cool you can use the word doctor now."

"It's so good to hear your voice, Tanya. It seems like forever since we've talked."

"Not since you've been back from England. Are you all settled in your new digs?"

"It started out rough, but it's going well. I've got two cats and a dog staying a few nights. The word's out and I keep getting busier. Soon, I'm going to need a vet tech to assist." A dog in one of the cages started whimpering. Miranda scrunched the cordless phone between her shoulder and ear and walked to him. She opened the cage door. "Want to quit gymnastics and work for me?" She reached in, scooped up the Pomeranian, and held him.

"That sounds fun. Best friends working together. Us against the world of sick and injured animals." Tanya snickered. "Sometimes, when I get really sore after a long day of practice, I wonder why I'm spending my life flinging my body through the air."

"Because you're such a great athlete. That's why." Miranda was so proud of Tanya. Her best friend had so much talent, and Miranda was thrilled that she was pursuing her career in gymnastics. She had a great chance of securing a position on the Olympic gymnastics team. She looked down at the small dog she was petting and put him back in the cage with a treat. "When do I get to see you? How did Pan Am go?"

"I won a silver. It went great. I miss you. What I wouldn't give to go riding with you like we used to do."

Miranda smiled. "I hear that. The next time you're home, let's go." She pulled out an index card with addresses of her patient's owners and set it next to a pad with veterinary invoices for billing she'd send out later today.

Tanya hesitated. "That might happen sooner than you think."

Miranda perched on a stool. "What's going on, Tonny? What aren't you telling me?"

"I have someone I want you to meet."

"Who?" She jumped up and down, and her voice went up an octave. The Pomeranian began yipping in his cage.

Tanya giggled. "I met someone while I've been on the road competing." Her voice cracked. "He's pretty great."

"I'm so happy for you."

"I've had my share of duds, that's for sure."

Miranda thought about all the guys Tanya had dated over the last few years. None had been good enough for her. Some had been abusive, verbally and physically. She hoped Tanya had finally found someone worthy of her, deserving of such a wonderful person.

"When can I meet him?"

"How about next month? I have a break after the last meet." Tanya snorted at Miranda's burst of giggles that echoed through the phone. "I was wondering if you could pick us up from the airport? I don't want to go to my parents when I get home."

"Absolutely. We'll be there. I'm *sooooo* excited. You are going to stay with us. I'll get our guest room ready for you."

"I can't wait. I gotta go. We're boarding. Next stop is Denver. I'll call in a couple weeks with the flight details."

"See you in a month. Safe flight."

As Miranda hung up the phone, she thought about how much she missed having her best friend nearby. They'd known each other since elementary school when they would ride horses together, and Tanya practically lived at the Graaf's. Tanya's parents were always fighting, and she would escape the turmoil by staying with Miranda. They became like a second family to her. Miranda and Tanya had been as close as sisters.

Tanya set the receiver into the cradle of the pay phone and leaned against the wall. The last time she'd seen Miranda was at her wedding in the spring. A lot had happened in Tanya's life since then. She'd dated one of the trainers on the gymnastics team for a couple months. He'd gotten rough with her and gave her a black eye when she stopped his advances. Fortunately, when she reported the incident to her coach, the trainer was fired.

Tanya felt proud that she did something about the abuse to prevent it from happening again. She had learned from other women on the team that this type of behavior had happened before with this same guy. But Tanya was too embarrassed to tell Miranda because it seemed she always picked the wrong guy. Tanya witnessed her own father abusing her mother. But she wasn't going to put up with that kind of behavior herself. She hoped this time it would be different with Daniel, her new boyfriend. And she hoped that Miranda liked him and approved. *Because*, Tanya thought, *he might be the one.*

A month had gone by since Miranda had returned home from England. It was late September. The corn was almost ready to harvest. Streams of yellow, orange, and red began coloring the leaves in the forest. Miranda fell into the routine of caring for her patients. Hank went about his days as a farrier, traveling to various farms. They both took care of the animals on their own farm too. Justine juggled the responsibilities of teaching kindergarten and seeing Richard on her days off, traveling to Chicago when she could.

Miranda missed her mom's company and was angry about this new man taking Stanley's place, but she couldn't do anything about it, so she avoided her mom as much as possible. Miranda hoped Justine would come to her senses and break up with Richard. Corn harvest was coming soon, so she knew she and Justine would have to work together to feed and accommodate the team of guys arriving to do the job. But she didn't want to think about that now.

After the afternoon chores of cleaning the cages, calling back patients' owners, and sweeping the floors, Miranda turned off the lights in her clinic and hurried home to her house. This was a day she'd been waiting for—to see her bestie, Tanya. She wanted to get the guest room ready because Tanya was arriving later that evening, and Hank and Miranda were picking her up at the airport. Tanya was bringing her boyfriend, and Miranda was anxious to meet him.

She reached the back door and felt ill suddenly. She swung the door open, rushed into the bathroom, and threw up in the toilet, barely making it. She sat on the floor, her back against the bathroom wall, and wiped off her mouth with a towel. Was it something she'd eaten that made her feel bad? Maybe the tuna on her sandwich had spoiled? But then she remembered feeling nauseous the last two mornings and she shook it off. She'd had a tuna sandwich, which was her favorite, for lunch the past few days. She'd have to try something different tomorrow. Maybe she was becoming allergic to tuna. She'd remembered a classmate having an allergic reaction to shrimp when they'd all gone out to dinner to celebrate the end of the semester. Hives had covered her entire body, and when she went to the doctor's office, she found out it was a food allergy.

Maybe the same thing was happening to Miranda. She shrugged, stood up, and looked in the mirror. While she brushed her teeth, she noticed her face was pale, so she put on some blush and brushed her hair.

Stepping into the living room, she found Hank, who had just come home from work. He wrapped his arms around her, kissing her on the top of her head and then again on her mouth, a long and passionate kiss.

She responded with openness, eager to see her husband after the hours apart. Suddenly, she felt a wave of nausea and turned her mouth from his. She ran into the bathroom, barely making it to the toilet, throwing up once again.

Hank stood in the doorway of the bathroom. "You ok?"

She wiped her mouth with the back of her hand.

He took a washcloth from the cupboard and ran cool water on it. He twisted out the water and then placed the cloth on her forehead as she sat against the wall, her head leaning back.

"That's the second time today. I don't know what's going on with me. I think it might be the tuna sandwich I had at lunch. Bad tuna, I guess."

"Hmm, that's strange. I had tuna too, but I feel ok." Hank held a hand out, and she took it as he helped her to her feet. "Why don't you lie down? I can make you some tea."

"Thanks, sweety. That'd be great." She went to the couch and leaned back on a couple throw pillows, stretching one leg on the couch. Ben wiggled his way around the coffee table and plopped on the floor near her other leg. She stroked his head and smiled weakly. "You always know when I'm feeling bad."

Ben licked her hand and whimpered.

Hank brought over a mug of steaming Earl Gray tea and set it on top of a coaster.

"Thanks." She took a sip. "You brew a good cup of tea."

"Learned from the best."

"Your grandma?"

"I've watched you. Remember the first time you made me tea?"

"After my dad's funeral." She rubbed her queasy belly. "You brought over that plethora of Tupperware filled with food the ladies at the church made."

"Yep." He plastered on a smile. "That was our first tea party."

"I was so hot for you then."

"Was?"

"Still am baby, still am." Her voice took on a low, sexy tone. "You're hotter now more than ever." The nausea she felt grew stronger and tired her out. She let out a deep sigh. "I'm just going to close my eyes for a minute."

He squeezed her hand. "I'm going in to take a shower."

She slowly nodded and fell fast asleep.

Twenty minutes later, Hank returned to the living room, bare-chested and rubbing a towel through his wet hair.

Suddenly, she clasped her hand to her mouth. "What time is it?"

Hank glanced at his watch. "5:30, why?"

"Tanya is flying into Quad Cities airport at 6:30. I told her I'd pick her up." Miranda scooted into the kitchen and set her tea mug in the sink.

"Are you feeling well enough?"

She still felt a little woozy but didn't want to let Tanya down. She grabbed keys off the kitchen counter and tossed them to Hank. "You drive."

As they traveled in Hank's truck, she said, "We're picking up her boyfriend too. We'll have to sit four in the front." Miranda took a fleeting look at the fields of corn that flanked the highway.

Hank glanced at her. "Do we like this guy?"

"He sounds nice. She's had so many losers before. I hope this one treats her good." They passed an Oscar Mayer plant. The stuffy air from the putrid smell of processed meat wafted through the window, and Miranda gagged. She plopped some Doublemint gum in her mouth and offered a stick to Hank. "We'll have to see for ourselves when we meet him."

She took long, deep breaths as they crossed the bridge over the Mississippi River and into Moline, Illinois, and drove on 69th Avenue into the Quad City International Airport. Hank parked and they walked through the airport's main doors and headed for the baggage claim, where Tanya said she'd be waiting.

Miranda spotted Tanya facing the suitcases ejecting out a half door onto a moving belt. Next to her stood a tall, handsome man with a lean physique dressed in a red, white, and blue tracksuit. His medium-length brown hair matched the color of his neatly trimmed moustache.

Miranda came up behind Tanya and tapped her athletic friend on the shoulder.

Tanya shrieked. "Ran. You're here!" She flung her arms around her best friend, her brown ponytail bouncing. "I'm so happy to see you."

When they released their embrace, Miranda said, "I've missed you so much."

"I hated that I had to leave for training right after your wedding. Six months is way too long." Tanya switched her focus to the man standing next to her. "Where are my manners? This is my boyfriend, Daniel." Her dark brown eyes glistened as she glanced at Miranda. "Daniel, this is my best friend, Miranda." And then, "This is her husband, Hank."

They all shook hands.

A flicker of a smile passed Daniel's lips. "I've heard a lot about you both. Tanya thinks the world of you." He glanced at Tanya as he held her hand as if he'd never let go.

After they got their bags and headed for the truck, Miranda asked, "What sport are you in, Daniel?"

Daniel shuffled the red, white, and blue gym bag on his shoulder. In the other hand, he held the handle of a suitcase that rolled behind him. Walking beside Daniel, Tanya rolled a similar suitcase.

"I run the 400-meter hurdles and the 4x4 400-meter relay. I also do the high jump."

Hank's eyes widened. "Wow. Impressive."

They threw their bags in the truck bed and crammed into the cab.

Miranda scooted tightly next to Hank. She glanced at Daniel and Tanya. "Sorry we're so scrunched, but my mom was using the station wagon, and I also have a truck, so this was the only option."

Daniel's shoulder was jammed against the passenger-side window, and the knees on his long runner's legs pressed into the glove compartment. "Hope we don't pull a muscle just sitting here."

Tanya tsked and playfully smacked his thigh. "Babe, you'll be fine. It's not that far."

He had a scowl on his face and kept stroking his mustache.

Miranda wondered about this new prima donna boyfriend. Did she like him? She could tell he liked things his way. She just hoped he wasn't controlling like Tanya's other boyfriends. Maybe he was nervous meeting them for the first time. She'd give him the benefit of the doubt.

By the time Hank parked in the driveway, Miranda felt nauseous again. She barely made it into the bathroom, where she threw up once again.

Tanya watched her friend rush into the house. As she pulled her bag out of the truckbed, she asked, "Is she ok?"

"Miranda said she ate something that disagreed with her," Hank said. "It's weird because she'll be fine and then get nauseous suddenly."

Tanya crooked one of her eyebrows upward. "I'll go check on her." She trotted to the front door of their house and opened it as she said, "I'm coming in, Ran." Before she entered, she turned and yelled, "Your new house is awesome, Hank."

Hank nodded and then looked at Daniel. "I can give you a tour while the girls are catching up."

Daniel chewed on his bottom lip. "If you don't think we'll be too long?"

Miranda slumped on the couch, head hung low and palms resting on her knees. Tanya sat next to her, holding a glass of cool water. Miranda said, "I can't believe I'm still throwing up. That's the third time today. I wish I hadn't eaten that tuna sandwich."

Tanya gave Miranda the water and examined her as she drank. "And yet, you felt good enough to come get us at the airport." She put her hand on Miranda's knee. "Ran, I don't want to alarm you, but if you had food poisoning or the flu, you wouldn't be able to move, let alone get us."

Miranda slowly lifted her head and looked at her friend. She tucked a strand of blond hair behind her ear. "What exactly are you saying? You think I'm making this up?"

"Have you considered that you might be pregnant?"

Miranda's mouth opened wide, but no words came out. She clasped her palms around her belly. "But. I just got home a few weeks ago. We've been so careful ..." She stared straight ahead. "Oh no." She gasped, and her face suddenly turned ashen.

Tanya hugged Miranda. "Ran, this is so exciting. You're going to be a mother."

"We don't know that yet. I'll have to take a pregnancy test first to confirm."

"Have you missed a period?"

Her belly felt squeamish but not from nausea. "I am a couple weeks late. I chalked it up to traveling and the stress of a new practice, being newly married ..." She couldn't be pregnant … Or could she? Tanya's words bounced inside her head like ping-pong balls. This couldn't be true. They'd only been married a few months. She just started her vet practice a couple months ago. Tanya was exaggerating. She wasn't pregnant. Besides, she was on the pill. She'd taken it every day, hadn't she? Everything had been such a whirlwind when she got home. Seeing Hank after being away, new house, new practice. Not to mention jet lag.

"Maybe you're not pregnant." Tanya took Miranda's empty glass from the table and stood. Her eyes panned the room. "You guys have done a beautiful job with the house. I love the open layout and the cathedral ceilings." She ran her arm through the air like she was a model on a game show, showcasing a prize. "It's so modern."

"That's Hank's doing. He did all of this when I was away."

"You've got a keeper. I hope I can be that lucky." She glanced at Miranda. "Do you want more water?"

Miranda shook her head. "Thanks for your praise on the house." She rubbed her belly and then mumbled, "I really don't think I'm pregnant. I still think it's the tuna." She heard the guys talking outside. Looking at Tanya, she narrowed her eyes. "Not a word to anyone." She stood and pressed her fingers to her lips.

"But."

"Not. A. Word." She pointed a finger at Tanya and stretched out the last word for emphasis. "Proooomise?"

Tanya went to the kitchen and placed the glass in the sink. "I promise. If that's what you want." She nodded at the door. "Not even Hank? You're not going to tell Hank?" She returned to the living room and sat cross-legged on the couch.

Miranda shook her head firmly as the guys came inside.

Hank slid a curious glance. "What are you ladies talking about?"

Miranda waved her hand through the air. "Nothing really." She took a quick glance at Tanya. "She was just telling me about her latest gymnastics competition at Nationals."

Hank motioned for Daniel to sit. He settled next to Tanya on the couch and wrapped his arm around her shoulder, bringing her closer to him. He began rubbing his thigh.

"Daniel hurt his quadricep jumping over a hurdle in his last race." She flashed a smile. "He came in second."

"I didn't warm up enough." Daniel's chestnut eyes and thick eyelashes blinked rapidly as he justified his predicament. "I could have beat the guy in first place had I not pulled a muscle."

Miranda's mind wrapped around this comment: That's probably why he had acted like a prima donna earlier. He was worried about his career as an athlete. She could understand that. His body, just like Tanya's, was a tool in the same way medical instruments and equipment were important to Miranda in her career. She exhaled and lowered herself into a chair near Hank. She wanted to know more about this guy who seemed to have caught Tanya's eye and grabbed her best friend's heart. She hoped he was good to her. She looked at each of them. "Tell us how you guys met?"

Daniel started in, cutting off Tanya. He jiggled his thigh as he said, "We literally bumped into each other coming out of the men's and women's locker rooms."

Miranda wasn't sure if his leg was bouncing because he was nervous, bored, or loosening his tight muscles.

Daniel looked downward at Tanya and smiled, his teeth forming a perfect white smile. "She dropped her gym bag, and I bent to pick it up. I handed it to her and then she dropped it again and we started laughing. I teased her, saying she was pretty clumsy for a gymnast, and she said I should have been able to get out of the way since I was a hurdler. We'd both watched each other compete that day. I have a friend on the men's gymnastics team, so when I was done with my event, I hurried over to watch him at the gym."

"One of our teammates has a boyfriend who is a sprinter, so a bunch of us went to watch him run, and I caught sight of

Daniel." She turned to Daniel, and her face lit up as she spoke, "I thought he was cute."

"I laid eyes on Tanya and knew I wanted to date her."

Miranda couldn't place what it was, but there was something about Daniel that she didn't like. He was handsome, athletic, and seemed to really care for Tanya, yet her best friend seemed stifled and not her spunky self. She seemed to go along with everything he said. Miranda wondered if, even though she knew he had to think a lot of himself to maintain a competitive edge, he seemed too possessive. She looked at how he was holding Tanya's hand. And how he answered questions, interrupting her friend and controlling the conversation. She knew she had to trust that Tanya could make decisions about who she shared her life with. *Just give him a chance*, she told herself. "You guys want something to drink?"

Hank added, "Daniel, how 'bout a beer?"

"That'd be great. Don't tell my coach. He'd make me run more sprints. He's a taskmaster."

Tanya sat straight up on the couch. "I'll have one too, Hank, please."

"Think that's a good idea, babe? Beer is fattening."

She leaned back and shrugged. "You're probably right. I don't need any extra weight when I'm flying through the air, doing a back layout on the beam." Her cheeks flushed a slight pink color.

Miranda shot a look back and forth between the two guests. What was Tanya doing? That wasn't like her, backing down to anyone. Anyway, there wasn't an ounce of fat on her friend. What could one beer hurt? Daniel needed to back off.

Hank interrupted her thoughts: "Want anything, Miranda?"

"Um … I'll just have water, thanks." She pressed her hand to her mouth. Maybe that's why Tanya backed off about the beer. She thought Miranda was pregnant and couldn't drink.

Tanya and Miranda exchanged looks. Tanya had a smirk on her face.

Miranda narrowed her eyes slightly and moved her head slowly from side to side, warning Tanya not to say anything. When Daniel glanced at Tanya, Miranda ran her fingers over her mouth and threw an imaginary key over her shoulder.

Hank brought over a beer and a glass of water, watching their exchange. He set the drinks for Tanya and Daniel on the coffee table and then stood for a moment, looking back and forth. "What's with you two?"

Miranda's face flushed. "Just talking girl stuff."

Hank grabbed another beer from the refrigerator and after he opened the bottle, took a swig. He brought Miranda a glass of water and studied her face as he gave it to her.

Tanya reached over, snatched one of the beers, and took a sip.

Daniel grabbed the beer. "I'll take that, thanks."

She rolled her eyes. "I just drank a little."

"I don't know how you do it, stay on such a strict diet and training schedule," Miranda said. "That's one of the reasons I run. To burn off calories. That, and it's a stress reliever."

Hank chuckled. "You *do* have a sweet tooth."

Tanya laughed. "I remember when Ran used to eat all the chocolate out of the bag before we'd get home from trick-or-treating. Then she'd have a stomachache the rest of the night."

She smiled. "That's cuz my dad liked chocolate too, and he always took the good stuff while I was sleeping."

"You're right. Stanley had a sweet tooth too. That's who you got it from." She rubbed her belly. "I even look at a Snickers bar and I gain two pounds."

Daniel drained his bottle of beer. "This has been great. But we have to get up early and go to the gym." He stood and took Tanya's hand. "Come on, babe, we've got to get to the hotel. It's been a long day."

Tanya jerked her head toward Daniel. "I thought we were staying here. We talked about it before we left home."

Miranda whined, "We hardly had a chance to catch up."

Daniel cocked his head, his long, lean body towering more than a foot over Tanya's petite frame. "I wanted to surprise you."

Tanya shrugged. "Daniel's right. We have to work out." She wagged her finger. "No days off for us."

"Why don't you guys at least spend tonight here," Miranda said. "The guest room is ready. I put clean sheets on the bed."

Hank nodded. "You're more than welcome. We both get up early for work. We can wake you so you can go to the gym."

Tanya pleaded with Daniel. "Please, babe. That'd be fun. Miranda and I have lots more to talk about. We've hardly had much time. And it's been so long since I've seen her. We can go to the hotel tomorrow morning."

Daniel stayed firm, his jaw setting with determination. "Maybe next time. But we've rented a hotel room in Davenport. There's a 24-Hour Fitness gym next door." He took Tanya's hand. "Come on, babe. Let's go." He turned toward Hank. In a stilted voice, he said, "I hate to ask this, but could you take us to the car rental place? It's in town."

"You can just use my truck while you're here," Miranda said. "I can use my mom's station wagon if I have to make a house call."

"Are you sure, Ran?" Tanya said. "We don't want to put you out."

Miranda grabbed the keys off the counter. "Don't be silly. Glad to help. Then you don't have to pay for the rental."

The guys shook hands. Miranda and Tanya hugged at the door. Tanya whispered in Miranda's ear, "Your secret's safe with me."

CHAPTER 20

After their guests left, Miranda and Hank walked to the barn to check on the horses. The night had darkened except for the stars. On their stroll, Miranda stopped and pointed to the sky. "Look at that. You can see the Milky Way." Hank held her hand, and they both stood for a few moments gazing at the wonder of the night sky.

As they continued walking, Hank said, "My buddy, Nash, from Wyoming, called. He said he wanted me to help him pick out some horses for his boss. I just wanted to give you a heads-up. He'll be here in a couple days."

"Sounds great. I'm excited to meet him and learn more about when you lived in Wyoming."

Hank's stomach rolled over in a spin. He was grateful Nash was a quiet guy without many words.

They reached the barn and Hank looked in his quarter horse's stall. The horse was munching on hay. Hank glanced over to the stall next to him and leaned inward. "Well. Look at that." He chuckled. "Sweetie. Come here."

Miranda walked to where Hank was standing. She peeked inside the stall and spotted Ben and Petey lying next to each other, fast asleep. "What is it with these guys? They're besties for sure."

"Speaking of besties." He gave her a sidelong glance. "What's with you and Tanya?"

"What do you mean?" Miranda wasn't sure how she felt about being pregnant, if that was why she was sick. She still thought it was something she ate. Or maybe she got something from one of the animals at her clinic. It happened. She didn't want to tell Hank anything until she was sure, one way or the other.

"All that whispering between the two of you."

"Like I said. Just girl stuff. Like periods …"

He put his hands up. "Ok. Ok. I get it." He bent toward the animals. "Ok, you two. Time to go home, Petey." He scratched behind Ben's ears.

"Why don't we just leave Petey? We can call the Browns and let them know he'll be staying."

They left the two buddies in the stall and returned to the house for the night.

CHAPTER 21

A couple mornings later, Tanya drove Miranda's truck as it bounced over the rutted road leading to her friend's house. The night before, at the hotel, she'd fought with Daniel. They'd spent the day together working out, dining at the hotel restaurant, and going to the cinema to watch *Coming to America*, starring Eddie Murphy. They held hands during the movie; they laughed and had a good time. When they reached the truck after the movie, Daniel opened the passenger door for Tanya. She snuggled over to his side, and he draped his arm over her shoulders. On the ride back to the hotel, they chatted about the movie they'd just seen.

Then Tanya changed the subject. "I'd really like to spend some time with Miranda. I haven't seen her in so long."

"You just saw her a couple days ago."

"But we haven't had girl time yet."

He spread his hands, flexing them on the steering wheel. "What is so important that you have to be alone with her? We've gotta focus on our training. You know that. I thought you were more serious about winning gold?"

Her mouth dropped. She couldn't believe what she was hearing. How could he be so insensitive about her friendship with Miranda?

She slapped her knee and looked straight forward. "Miranda is my best friend."

"*If* she's your best friend, she'll understand. Training comes first."

Tanya's face felt hot.

He kept talking: "It's hard being an athlete. It takes a lot of sacrifice. You'll see her more once the Olympics are over." He nudged her with his knee. "And you'll be glad when you can show her your gold medal."

They parked at the hotel. In the elevator, Daniel took her hand, holding it all the way up to the ninth floor.

Heat shot through Tanya like a flame sparked by oil. She thought about what Daniel had said. Was he right? She knew as well as him that it took sacrifice to win a gold medal. The last few years after college, she'd worked hard. Really hard. Hours of doing the same movements, the same routine, the same thing over and over until she reached perfection. She danced and flipped in her sleep. She dreamed about falls that did happen and could happen. She nursed sore muscles and injuries back to health. She limited what she ate so that she'd stay trim and fit.

So, he couldn't ask her if she was serious about winning gold. And was she willing to sacrifice? Her life had been the *epitome* of sacrifice. She lived and breathed gymnastics. But did that mean she had to give up her friendships and the people in her life that had always been there for her? She owed her life to Miranda, and to Justine, for that matter. They were there for her when her parents weren't. Growing up, Tanya's parents had been so involved in their own abusive and dysfunctional marriage that they didn't care about Tanya or her two brothers. There were times when there wasn't food in the fridge because her mom had been beaten up by her dad and was too embarrassed to go grocery shopping.

Tanya would spend many nights at the Graafs' house for refuge. They were the ones who encouraged her gift in gymnastics, not her own parents. But she knew the Olympics were a different beast, and she had to give it her all. As much as she hated to admit it, maybe she had to focus more, and Daniel was right.

They watched a couple shows on TV and then went to bed. Daniel fell fast asleep. But Tanya laid awake most of the night, getting only a couple hours of sleep. She woke before Daniel and just wanted to get away from him to sort things out. Tanya slipped her gymnastics warmup suit on and pulled her hair back in a ponytail. She grabbed the keys off the TV stand and quietly snuck out the door. On her way out of the hotel, she plucked an apple from the dining area and noshed as she drove Miranda's truck onto I-80.

They'd been dating for a few months, and Tanya felt like she was falling for Daniel. Maybe she already had. She knew she cared for him more than anyone else she'd dated. And they wanted the same things. They were both athletes, and health and fitness were important to them. Being number one in their sport was at the top of their goal list. They enjoyed working out together at the gym, and Tanya even took up running, which she'd always hated, just to be with him, enjoying the same things he did.

After her twenty-minute drive, Tanya steered toward the Graafs and turned onto their long gravel driveway. She parked in front of Miranda's office and hopped out of the truck. Just then, Hank opened the door of the barn. Walking behind him was a guy clad in a brown cowboy hat and mud-covered boots, looking like the Marlboro man without the cigarette in his mouth. He had long legs that filled his black jeans. His broad shoulders and muscled arms formed curves along the blue jean shirt he wore.

Tanya's breath caught in her throat when the cowboy's arm muscles rippled as his rugged hand swiped dirt from across his tanned face. When he came closer, she smelled the fresh scent of leather and earth.

"Hey, Tanya," Hank said. He gestured to the sexy cowboy. "This is my buddy Nash from Wyoming."

Nash tipped his hat. "Nice to meet ya." His bass voice ran through her body like a gentle, warm breeze.

Tanya's mouth hung open for a moment before words finally fell out: "Likewise."

Nash's scruffy black beard and clear gray eyes sent a jolt throughout her body. She held out her hand. When they shook, she felt the warmth of his calloused palms. The smell of fresh air whirled around him. He seemed different than any guy she'd ever met. Grounded, humble, with a quiet presence.

Hank broke the trance Tanya was in. "Miranda's in her office. Go on in. She'd be glad to see you." The guys headed for Hank's truck. Before Hank got in the truck, he turned and said, "Where's Daniel?"

Tanya shrugged. "He didn't come." She wasn't sure if she wanted to talk about Daniel with Miranda, let alone discuss her love life with Hank. Her legs took her to the office, but she felt as though she'd left part of her body still standing where she'd met Nash, tingling from ponytail to sneaker. Tanya stopped before she put her hand on the doorknob, trying to shake loose the nonsense that had gotten into her. What was wrong with her? Why was this guy—Nash—affecting her so much? She felt more rattled than when she'd left the hotel. Miranda would know something was up. She was Tanya's best friend, after all. Tanya ran her hand over the sign next to the door: Miranda Graaf, DVM, taking a few moments to get her bearings.

If she told Miranda about the fight she'd had with Daniel, Miranda would warn her about how Daniel was like the other guys she'd dated. That he was controlling and possessive. That Tanya should dump him and move on.

A couple years before, Tanya had cautioned Miranda about Dylan, her previous fiancé, and how controlling he was. He had been caring at times, and yet, at other times, jealous and even violent. Like the time he got into a fight because he didn't trust Miranda or Hank. Pot calling the kettle black, that was. Dylan ended up being a liar and a cheat.

But Daniel was different. He could be jealous of Tanya's time with Miranda. He just didn't understand what it was like to have a close best friend. After all, he didn't have a best friend himself. She would help him understand how important Miranda had been in Tanya's life. Yep, her relationship with Daniel was different.

But there was no way she'd tell Miranda about the sudden attraction to Nash. Tanya rolled her eyes. She thought, *I've really lost it. Too many flips in the air. My brain has gone upside down one too many times.* Before Tanya went inside, she glanced back at the cowboy she'd just met, and her heart rate kicked up a notch. She closed her eyes, took a deep breath, and then exhaled, ridding herself of the distracting feelings that had just hijacked her body.

Tanya stepped into Miranda's office. She found her friend carving her hands through her hair, holding it back and then releasing it. A cat meowed in a nearby cage. Ben sat with his head on her knee, consoling her. What had happened in the three days since she'd last seen her? Miranda's eyes glazed over, and it was as if she didn't realize Tanya was in the room.

She took a few baby steps toward her. Voice barely audible, Tanya said, "What's wrong, Ran?"

Miranda shook her head slowly. "I just got off the phone. Susan, the receptionist from my doctor's office, called." She sniffled, grabbed a Kleenex, and wiped her eyes. "What am I going to do?"

Tanya grabbed a chair and dragged it next to Miranda. She perched on the edge and petted Ben's back. "What are you going to do about what?"

"You were right." Miranda's lower lip trembled when she made eye contact with Tanya. "I'm pregnant."

Tanya leaned over and gave Miranda a hug. She was excited for her friend but could see Miranda did not feel the same. She took her hand. "Ran, you'll figure it out." She studied Miranda's tear-laden eyes. "I take it you're not too happy about this."

Ben curled up next to Miranda's feet.

"I know I should be. I know that some women have a hard time getting pregnant, and I should feel blessed. But it's not the right time. I've never really had the strong yearning to have kids."

"You think Hank will be excited?"

Tears started to fall down Miranda's cheeks. "I don't want to tell him."

"Ran." Tanya squeezed the hand she'd been holding. "I think you should."

Miranda shook her head. "I know he'll be excited. He began talking about having kids as soon as I got back from Europe. But I just don't feel the same. And now … I. Am. *Pregnant.*"

"At least tell Justine."

"My mom and I aren't getting along right now." She forced a laugh. "I know she'd be thrilled." A storm passed over Miranda's face as she turned an eye on Tanya, and her eyebrows furrowed. "Don't tell anyone."

An overall weighted feeling spread throughout Tanya as she sympathized with her best friend's predicament. She pressed her hands upward in a prayer gesture. "I got it. What about at least telling Hank."

Miranda's lips pursed.

"He should know if he's having a baby." Tanya didn't want to be the only one in on this secret.

Miranda raised her voice, stabbing her own chest. "I'm the one who is pregnant."

"Why are you so secretive about this?" Tanya took Miranda's other hand, leaned in, and scanned Miranda's eyes. "It should be an exciting time for you both."

Miranda looked downward. In a low voice, she said, "I don't know if I want a baby."

Tanya wanted to be supportive of her best friend. But she didn't agree with leaving Hank out of this news. It was his baby too. Why was Miranda being so stubborn and keeping it all to herself? Would she even have told Tanya if she hadn't stopped by at that very moment? She knew Miranda was terrified, but she needed to let her family and friends rally around her and help. "What are you going to do?"

"I don't know yet." Miranda wiped her tears with the back of her hand. "I just have to wrap my head around this."

Tanya leaned back in her chair. Her thoughts drifted to earlier that morning when she'd left Daniel in the hotel room. Images pinged back and forth of the night before and how they had argued. She wished Miranda could leave her funk and talk to Tanya about her problems. But she knew it wasn't the right time for that. Being someone who couldn't sit for very long, she felt tension in her neck and shoulders, tapped her foot, and started fidgeting. She blurted, "I'm here for you. I'll follow your lead on this. Just tell me what I can do."

"Right now, nothing." Miranda grabbed another Kleenex off the desk and blew her nose. She threw the wadded-up tissue in the nearby waste basket. "Where's Daniel?"

Tanya ran her fingers through her ponytail and let it flip. "He's back at the hotel. We're taking a couple hours away from each other. Lover's quarrel." She shrugged. "You know how it is."

Tanya hoped Miranda would be so much into her own stuff that she wouldn't ask questions about their fight. The two of them knew each other so well they read each other's minds. Sometimes she thought it'd be easier to pretend and not talk about the heavy stuff. It'd be nice to just have fun and keep everything light. But that's not who they were. And she knew if not now, then soon, Miranda would come at her with questions that she couldn't fend off.

They both jerked their heads around when they heard yelling in the drive that led to Miranda and Hank's house.

"Isn't that Daniel?"

Tanya's face reddened. She nodded. She walked to the door that separated Miranda's clinic from the barn's interior. "If he comes here, tell him I'm not here."

"Tanya, what's going on? He seems pretty upset."

"He has a hard time being away from me."

"Tonny?" Miranda stood. "What aren't you telling me?"

Tanya slipped into the barn just when Daniel entered Miranda's office. His tall, athletic body filled the doorway. The puppy sleeping in a crate on a counter next to the wall started whining.

Daniel boomed, "Where's Tanya?"

Tanya heard Ben's nails scratch on the cement floor, sounding like he was quickly rising to his feet. He growled in a low rumble as if warning Daniel not to get too close.

"I'm not telling you until you calm down."

Tanya peeked through the crack in the barn door. Daniel stood there looking like he would explode any minute. He stroked his dark moustache and stood tall in his navy running suit. Her stomach rolled as guilt filled her belly. Miranda had a lot going on right then, and she'd left this mess for her friend to deal with. But she didn't want to talk to Daniel. She was confused as to how she felt about him. One minute, she was angry with how he got into her head and made her feel insecure, doubting herself and what she felt was important. And the next minute, her mind unloaded several aerial cartwheels when she thought about him.

Daniel lowered his voice. "When I woke up this morning, she was gone. Your truck was gone. She didn't leave a note. Nothing. Here I am in a strange town. I didn't even know your number to call you. What was I supposed to do? I was worried."

In a tight voice, Miranda said, "You made it here somehow."

"Luckily, there was a car rental place a couple blocks down from the hotel, so I rented a car."

"She went for a run."

At that moment, Daniel sounded like Tanya's loser boyfriends from the past. And they all turned out to be emotionally abusive and controlling. One guy even hit Tanya. And that was the end of that relationship. But Daniel just had to cool off and he'd come around. He always did. And then they'd get past his little outbursts, and they'd move forward. It'd be the same this time. Tanya just needed to give him a little time to himself. She scooted down the back of the wall and sat on the cement floor. She waited for Daniel to leave. But he didn't. She could hear them talking about her through the wall. She could barely make out what they said over the tractor puttering outside. She peeked out a window and saw the neighbor delivering hay to the Graafs' farm.

How, she asked herself, was Daniel different than the other guys she'd dated? What did she like about him? He was handsome. He was athletic. He had charisma. He was an overachiever. When he gathered his team members before a competition and pumped them up with his pep talk, she thought it was charming.

She didn't like his controlling attitude when it came to her, but she knew it was because he loved her. He had so much potential as her partner, and Tanya was determined to focus on the good things about him.

Finally, Tanya couldn't stand it any longer. She didn't need Miranda to do her bidding for her. She opened the barn door and walked into Miranda's office. "Hi, Daniel."

He stood. His face reddened, and his mouth opened.

Tanya held up a finger. "Before you say anything, let me explain. I wanted to get up and go running before you. You're so fast, and I feel inept when we run together. So, I came here to run with Miranda. She's been a runner for years, and I thought she could help me run faster."

Miranda shot Tanya a look.

"Besides, I wanted to let you rest. You were still asleep when I left, and I didn't want to wake you. You've worked so hard these past few weeks I thought you needed your rest."

Daniel's face softened a little. "You could have left me a note. It freaked me out when I woke up and you weren't there."

"I know. I know. I should have, but I didn't have anything to write with, and I didn't want to start opening drawers looking for a pen and paper, waking you."

Daniel sauntered toward Tanya. He had the well-developed upper body of a sprinter. Her eyes traveled the length of his long, lean, muscled legs that exuded extreme fitness. A slow smile came across Daniel's face as he noticed her ogling him. He put his arms around her and pulled her in, kissing her hard on the mouth. Warmth radiated throughout Tanya's body.

"I'm sorry about our fight last night."

Tanya leaned in. "I'm sorry too. I was irrational." She wrapped her arms around his waist and then lowered them to his glutes that filled his navy warm-up pants.

Daniel nodded. "I was stubborn."

They kissed again.

Miranda cleared her throat. "Get a room, you two."

They both looked at her, eyes blinking, as if they'd forgotten anyone else was in the room.

"There's an entire barn with lots of hay if you can't make it back to the hotel."

Tanya snickered. "Let's go."

He nodded. "We're leaving your truck, Miranda. Thanks for letting us use it."

Tanya reached into her pocket for the truck keys. "You gonna be ok?"

Miranda nodded. "I'll figure it out."

Tanya stood still for a moment, studying Miranda's face. She hated leaving her friend to solve this problem on her own. But Tanya thought if she was out of the picture, maybe Miranda would tell Hank. He needed to know his wife was pregnant. "Call me at the hotel later." Tanya tossed Miranda the key to the truck.

Daniel held Tanya's hand as they headed outside. When they reached the door, Tanya turned around. "Run again tomorrow, Ran?"

Miranda chuckled. "How 'bout you guys come for dinner tonight?"

Tanya looked at Daniel.

He nodded. "Can we bring anything?"

Maybe Daniel understood that it was up to Tanya how she lived her life and pursued her dream of going to the Olympics. He seemed different, somehow, more agreeable and open to spending time with her friends. Maybe she had been overreacting earlier. After all, he had been worried about her because he loved her.

"Just your appetites."

Tanya and Daniel walked out into the morning sunshine. The air was rich with the scent of freshly cut hay. She glanced over to see Hank and Nash lifting heavy bales off a truck bed onto a John Deere front-end loader. She couldn't help but notice the muscles on Nash's bare back glistening from the sweat of hard work as he filled the bucket on the front of the tractor.

CHAPTER 22

Later that evening, Tanya and Daniel arrived at Miranda and Hank's in time for dinner. They'd had a fun day at the gym, shopping in downtown Davenport, and relaxing at their hotel. Daniel encouraged Tanya while they worked out together, telling her she was beautiful and buff from all her hard work as a gymnast and that she was a sure thing for gold at the Olympics.

They had snuggled in bed while they watched a movie on the TV at the hotel, and Daniel gave her a back rub. Tanya thought maybe he had let go of the jealousy and controlling behavior from earlier that day. She felt embarrassed that Miranda had seen the temperamental side of her new boyfriend, acting out in such a demanding and angry way when he pounded on the door of her office that morning.

Hank met them at the front door with a white apron wrapped around his torso and a plate of raw hamburgers. "Come on in, you guys. I was just about to put these on the grill."

They continued into the living room. Tanya's nostrils flared. The smell of brownies and garlic potatoes made her mouth water.

"Help yourself to drinks in the fridge. And come on out to the back patio."

Tanya grabbed a Tab and Daniel, a water. They headed out the slider and ambled onto the deck. Miranda sat across from Nash at a patio table, having a friendly debate over the benefits of English versus Western riding.

Miranda rose from her seat, bent downward, giving Tanya a hug. "Hi, Tonny." She then reached over to hug Daniel. "Welcome." She gestured. "This is Hank's friend from Wyoming. Nash, this is Daniel, Tanya's boyfriend."

Tanya saw that Nash had cleaned up nicely. His blue Levis hugged his long legs, stretched out in front of him. Her eyes followed the length of his legs all the way to his bare feet crossed at the ankles. His crisp white, short-sleeved T-shirt showed off his tanned biceps. Heat flowed through her when she spotted them for the first time. He had a buzz cut, showing hints of black hair accenting those gorgeous clear gray eyes that sent jolts through her, just as they had when she first met him. What was she doing? Why was she lusting after this guy when Daniel was right beside her? She'd have to block these thoughts from taking hold of her body.

She forced herself to keep her eyes moving. She took in the panoramic view of the horses grazing in the fields, a white fence fifty feet from their lawn. A couple apple trees stood off to the left and a corn field beyond the trees. And to the right, large flat stones formed a walk leading to the side of the barn.

Hank stood at the barbecue, flipping burgers. Ben was stretched out on his side in the middle of the deck, his legs running against the floorboards as he dreamed about who knows what, chasing rabbits perhaps.

The men shook hands.

Daniel took hold of Tanya's hand and they scooted into chairs at the table, setting their drinks down.

Nash said, "Hi, Tanya."

She dry-swallowed and croaked, "Hello. Nice to see you again."

Daniel put his arm around Tanya.

"I hear you're headed for the Olympics," Nash said.

"We're working on it."

Tanya's eyes cascaded along the stubble shadowing Nash's jaw, imagining what it would be like to run her hands over his face.

Nash interrupted her thoughts. "That's impressive."

They all sat and chatted about the unusually warm weather for late September. Tanya wondered if Miranda had told Hank about her pregnancy and looked at Miranda, cocking her head slightly, throwing her a question mark with her eyes, their secret language of friendship.

Miranda moved her head from side to side in such a subtle way that only Tanya would notice.

Tanya felt her face warm. How could her friend omit telling her own husband that she was pregnant? Miranda should tell him. But it was up to her what she shared with Hank. There was nothing Tanya could do about her friend's decision.

Tanya took in the span of the farm, attempting to calm herself, and saw that there was beauty in the rows and rows of corn lining the fields on the left. Harvest season was soon approaching. A couple pheasants worked their way into the grass to roost. Their shiny, colorful feathers glistened in the late afternoon sunlight. And on the right, Mandy, Rocko, and Red grazed in the pasture. Their tails swished biting flies as they took small steps and yanked grass with their strong teeth.

Tanya scanned the patio and back of the house. She understood that Miranda was scared. But secretly, Tanya thought it wasn't fair to Hank for Miranda to keep her pregnancy from him. He was such a devoted, loyal husband. Miranda had found a prize when she married Hank. Why was she treating him that way?

The heat in Tanya boiled to the surface, and she couldn't help herself. "You guys have made this a beautiful home. So much space and charm." She snatched a carrot stick from the platter of vegetables in the center of the table. "There's one thing missing, though." She ran the carrot through the dip.

Hank and Miranda looked at Tanya at the same time.

"You guys need to fill this place up with children. Lots of kiddos running around."

The silence was deafening.

Daniel chipped in, oblivious to the temperament of the crowd: "Yeah, that'd be great. My sister has a couple kids. I think they're two and four. It's great being an uncle, all the fun. When they get too rowdy, I pass them off to Susy. Course, I haven't seen them in several months. Competing and all."

Tanya pressed his knee. He smiled at her and then took her hand. "It'd be fun having kids with you, babe."

She eye rolled and chuckled. "That'd be something, hoisting my pregnant belly over the vault."

The tension lightened with the joke, and they all laughed. Hank came to the table with a stack of hamburgers. "There's enough to get everyone started. I'll go get more patties."

Hank not knowing about Miranda gnawed on Tanya's brain. She wanted to support her bestie, but Hank was her friend too. And she thought Miranda was unfair, and Tanya wanted Hank to know that he was a father. She scanned the table. "I don't see any mustard. I'll go inside and get some."

Hank had a platter in one hand and reached for the slider with the other. "I can bring some on my way out."

Tanya rose from the table. "Looks like you could use some help."

Hank shrugged. "You can help me bring out the chips and pickles too."

Miranda cast a glance back and forth between them.

Nash stood. "I can help too." He scooted around the table. "I don't need to be waited on."

Tanya's shoulders lowered.

With Nash inside, she'd miss the opportunity to hint about Miranda's pregnancy. Tanya wouldn't have said outright that her friend was pregnant, but she could have given hints. It may have caused a disruption in the evening, but Tanya didn't like secrets. Her parents always kept secrets from each other, and growing up, she had always been in the middle. Hank couldn't be left in the dark. It was his baby too.

Daniel suddenly jumped up and took a couple wide steps, walking in front of Nash to catch up to Tanya. She clucked her tongue. "Daniel, I'm not going far." She gestured. "You can wait with Miranda." But his hand on her back nudged them over the threshold into the kitchen.

Just then Nash came through the door.

Miranda followed closely behind her guests. She glanced at everyone in the kitchen. "Looks like the party is in here now."

Tanya swallowed her disappointment. She gestured as her eyes danced back and forth between Miranda and Hank. "I'm sorry for putting you on the spot about having babies. It's none of my business, and you guys do what you want to do. Kids or no kids."

Miranda moved to Tanya's side and pressed her arm.

Hank's lips turned upward. "I'd love to have kids, lots of them. My grandma raised me, and I always felt like I missed out on having a normal family growing up."

"Enough talk about having children," Miranda said. "Let's get back to the party. Hank, are you cooking more of those burgers? I already ate mine and I'm starving." She took a handful of chips from a bag on the counter and stuffed them in her mouth.

"Quite a switch from the last few days, feeling nauseous and all." Hank shaped the last ball of meat into a patty and placed it on the plate, nudging it next to the other patties. "I'm glad you're feeling better, honey."

Miranda glanced away, mumbling, "Thanks, honey." She picked up the plate of burgers. "I'll take this out to the deck."

Hank followed close behind, carrying a bag of burger buns, with a puzzled look on his face.

Tanya blocked the slider to the deck with her body just as Nash grabbed the mustard and a bag of chips off the counter and headed for the deck. He stopped inches from Tanya. It felt like fingers of heat trailing all over her skin having him so close. She tried to steady the stutter in her voice. "I think we'd better stay in here, guys. They have stuff to talk about."

Nash backed away from Tanya. "What's up with them?" He leaned against the counter in the kitchen.

Standing within earshot, Tanya heard Miranda's voice raise. Tanya said to the guys, "It's not my place to say, but we need to give them space."

With a twinge of anger in his voice, Hank said, "Why don't you want to talk about having kids? Just because we talk about it doesn't mean we'll have kids. I just want to talk about it and clear the air about this."

Tanya sat in a chair at the dining room table closest to the slider so she could hear the conversation. "Have a seat, boys. It's about to get ugly."

"Eavesdropping?" Nash smirked. "I didn't think you'd be the kind of friend that would listen in on a conversation." He strode from the kitchen and through the living room. At the front door, he turned: "Tell Hank I'm in the barn taking care of the horses."

Daniel folded his arms. "What did Nash mean by 'he didn't think you'd be that kind of friend?' How do you know him?"

"What?" Tanya huffed. "Hank introduced us. I've only just met him out in the barn."

Daniel walked to the fridge, opened it, and grabbed a beer. "I don't trust that guy. I can tell by the way he looks at you he's got the hots for you."

"That's ridiculous. He's just a nice guy, is all."

"Let's go." He gestured toward the deck. "This feels weird, staying when they're arguing."

"I want to stay. I'm Miranda's best friend and she needs me. Or she will when they're done talking."

"When I'm done with this beer, let's just go."

"I'm staying here."

"Come on, Tanya, don't be stubborn. Just come back to the hotel."

"We came all this way so I could spend time with Miranda. I'm staying."

"Besides, we need to do another run and workout at the gym. You've gained a couple pounds from all the food you've been eating." He snickered. "Your coach isn't going to like it if you can't mount the balance beam when we get back from our vacation."

Tanya flinched at Daniel's harsh words. She had been eating a lot—pizza, ice cream, and now hamburgers and chips at Miranda's. The several months of diet restrictions so she could keep her lean figure for gymnastics competition had taken its toll. She loved to eat and sometimes she got cranky eating only veggies, chicken, and a bowl of granola every morning. Gymnastics was very competitive, and there were a lot of young women who had eating disorders and constantly thought about their weight. Just a few extra pounds could make the difference between winning the gold or striking out in a competition. She'd worked too hard to fail now.

As much as she hated to admit it, Daniel was right. She sighed. "Ok, babe. Let's go." She opened the slider and popped her head outside. "Ran, sorry to interrupt. We're going to get going. See you guys later." She stepped back inside before Miranda could object, sliding the door behind her. "Come on, babe."

Outside, they climbed into the rental, Daniel behind the wheel. Neither of them said a word on the drive back to the hotel.

CHAPTER 23

The next morning, Hank and Nash traveled west along the I-80 freeway. They were headed to a quarter horse farm fifty miles from Hank's house. Nash towed a trailer behind his truck.

Hank cast a glance out the window. "I miss riding in Wyoming. All the mountains and trails."

"There is that."

"Remember the time we had to spend the night on the side of the mountain."

"That was a close one. We saw those grizzly tracks right by our campsite."

"It's a wonder it didn't come after the horses."

They drove in silence for a while until Hank said, "I haven't told Miranda about the lawsuit."

Nash did a double take. "Why not?"

"She doesn't even know I have a felony. All she knows is that I worked in Wyoming as a farrier."

"Which is true … but you're leaving out a *whole* lotta story."

His muscled shoulders shrugged. "I don't know how to tell her."

A few of Nash's fingers lifted off the steering wheel. "Just tell her, man."

Hank thought about the argument he'd had with Miranda the night before after their guests left for the evening. It was the worst fight they'd ever had.

Miranda had stood, her back leaning against the kitchen counter, one arm grasping the other at the elbow. "We can't afford to have a baby right now. I just started my practice. All our savings have gone into building this house."

Hank's neck and shoulders had felt so tight a headache crept up the back of his head and into his eyes. "I'm working, and we can start saving for children." He leaned on the opposing counter with his arms folded, one hand cupping the tip of his chin. "Besides, I started adding money to our account when we finished the house."

She looked flush and her chin jutted. He'd never seen Miranda's body that rigid and set in her way of thinking. "You never told me you wanted kids before we got married."

Ben sat in the middle of the kitchen floor, his head bobbing back and forth.

"Like it's my fault we didn't talk about it." He exhaled audibly. "You could have brought up the subject too."

Her brow furrowed as if worries logjammed her mind. "There's a lot going on right now. We've been so much into building our house, me going to Europe, and planning for life when I got back." Her lips stutter-stepped over her teeth and she flicked her tongue around her mouth. "You just don't understand me."

His heart banged against his rib cage. He looked fixedly at Miranda for a few moments and then his voice rose. "I can't believe you haven't thought about having kids."

Ben yipped and stood. He went to Miranda, sat down, leaning against her leg.

His head lowered. "Have you even thought about it ever in your life?"

"Not really. I've always just had a dream of being a vet. I know lots of women dream about getting married and having children when they're little girls, but that was never me."

"Then why did you get married in the first place?" He regretted the words the moment they traveled out of his mouth and into the air.

Her mouth dropped. They stood and looked at each other for a few moments. In a hushed tone, she said, through tears, "Because I fell in love with you."

She started walking away from the kitchen and turned before she went into the bedroom. "And I still do." She slammed the door of the bedroom.

His stomach felt like he'd swallowed a load of bricks. He went to the bedroom and stood for a minute before knocking on the closed door. "I'll sleep out in the barn."

She didn't say anything in return, so he grabbed a blanket and pillow from the couch and headed outside. He didn't know what he'd tell Nash, but he couldn't stay in the house.

The next morning, he brushed off the straw from his restless night in a stall and went into the house. Miranda was at the kitchen table, drinking a cup of tea, looking straight ahead.

He sat opposite her and took her hand. "I'm going to Tipton with Nash to get some horses. I'll be home this afternoon."

She gave him a quick glance. In a monotone, she said, "Have a good trip."

When he stood from his chair he said, "I love you." He kissed her cheek and left a cavern of unsaid feelings between them.

✳

Hank regretted the fight and the things he had said. The exchange of harsh words between them left his gut twisted in painful knots.

As Hank rode shotgun, he wished he could tell Miranda everything about his legal issues, but he feared it would only make things even worse than they were already. He thought about Nash's comment "just tell her." Hank choked on a swallow. After a couple coughs, he said, "I wish it was that easy." He'd call the Wyoming courthouse and take care of it when they got home. Hank changed the subject. "What's the boss looking for at the place we're headed?" His gaze stuck on the fields of soybeans out the truck window.

"He wants a few more trail riding horses." Nash's thumbs drummed on the steering wheel. "Who's that woman we saw at your place before we left? Tanya, was it?"

Hank chuckled and thumped Nash's shoulder. "Why, do you want to know more about her?"

"Just curious. She seemed nice."

"Yeah, right. You thought she was cute."

The corner of Nash's mouth turned up slightly.

"She's Miranda's best friend. They've known each other a long time."

"What is it with that track dude?"

"You mean, Daniel?"

"He seems like a controlling kind of guy. Wouldn't let her out of his sight."

Hank chuckled. "Maybe it was the way your eyes glazed over when you looked at Tanya."

Nash put up one of his forearms. "Hey, I'm not going to overstep. No harm in looking."

"He does seem a little needy when it comes to Tanya."

Nash flicked his turn signal and exited the freeway. "Just a few miles and we'll be there."

They drove through the small town of Tipton. They passed a post office, a diner, and a gas station. On the corner was a hardware store and next to it, an A&W drive-in restaurant. They traveled by soybean fields on either side of the two-lane highway. After ten minutes, they turned, and the truck bounced over a rutted gravel road.

Hank pointed. "There it is."

Several horses grazed in a pasture beside a red barn and a white house. Hank had a lightness in his chest as he fixed his gaze on what could be not only Nash's find, but Hank's future as well. He hadn't told a soul, but Hank had been dreaming of raising horses for a long time, training them as foals for barrel racing or pleasure riding. He could picture their pasture full of purebreds; chestnuts, bays, and buckskins grazing in the fields of alfalfa or trotting as they played in the grass. Another thing he wanted to tell Miranda, but their conversation the previous night only made things harder to talk with her about his dream. It seemed lately their focus was on getting her vet practice going. If he told her about what he wanted, it would be too stressful, with Miranda's new practice, their new house, Justine's new boyfriend. He'd wait to tell her.

Nash steered the truck around to the side of the barn. Opposite the barn stood the large white farmhouse. They opened their doors, and two Border Collies ran barking to Nash's side.

"Whoa!" He backed up into his truck and shut the door. He rolled down the window part way. "Shoo. Go away."

"What's your problem?" Hank snickered. "You afraid of dogs?"

"Maybe."

Hank gave Nash an incredulous look. "You work on a ranch where there are dogs herding cattle and you're afraid?"

"Hey. I got bit once." He yelled at the dogs, still barking, "Get out of here. Shoo."

"I've been bit a few times, and you don't see me cowering." Hank got out of the truck and whistled. The dogs came running around to his side. He extended his fisted hand and lowered his voice. "Hey, buddies. You're just protecting your turf, aren't ya?" They began licking his hand and wagging their tails. He bent and petted their heads, rubbed behind their ears. He looked toward the inside of the truck. "They just have to know that you're not afraid and you're their friend."

Just then, a man wearing a CASE cap, jean jacket, faded jeans, and cowboy boots came out of the house eating a sandwich. "Just tell them boys to go away. They're harmless."

Nash grumbled from inside the truck, "Yeah, harmless until they bite your hand off." He got out and came around the truck's other side. When the dogs sniffed him, he crossed his arms.

The man took a bite of his sandwich. Food fell out of his mouth as he yelled, "Go on, get back to the house." The dogs ran toward the house.

Nash reached out to shake the man's hand. "I'm Nash Ryder. My boss sent me to look at your horses."

"From Wyoming?" The man noshed on his sandwich. With a full mouth, he said, "Jim." He wiped mustard on his jeans.

"This is my buddy, Hank. He's a farrier and has worked a lot with horses, so he's got a good eye."

Jim motioned toward the barn. "Most of the horses are out in the pasture, but we can start inside."

When they reached the barn, Jim slid the door open. "Most of our horses are quarter horses, as you probably know. We've got a couple paint and a stallion in the paddock."

Hank said, "Stallion for sale?"

Nash looked at Hank with wide eyes.

Jim said, "For the right price, maybe." He edged over to a stall, and a sorrel-colored horse popped its head out of the opening. "Hi, Penny." He brushed his hand over her velvety nose. "This is our best broodmare. She's a quarter horse and has foaled a few champion barrel racers. She's seven months along now. We're expecting great things." He nodded toward the outside. "That stallion out there is the father."

Hank bobbed his head toward Penny's stall. "How much for her?"

Jim shook his head. "Not for sale."

Nash said, "My boss doesn't want to deal with a foal, anyway."

"I wasn't thinking about your boss."

"For *you*?"

Hank shrugged. Hank could have told Nash about his dream, but he had wanted to tell Miranda first. His belly twisted as he thought about their argument and the cold shoulder Miranda gave him that morning.

"Is this trip for you or for my boss?"

Hank took a couple steps. "Let's look at what Jim has for sale."

After they viewed a few horses in the barn, Nash ran to the truck and grabbed a couple lead ropes, and Jim led them out to the pasture. The men kicked dirt, stirring up a cloud of dust as they walked until they reached the gate at the pasture. A group of horses grazing near the fence perked their heads when the men approached.

One of the horses, a long-legged paint, nuzzled up to Nash.

"This guy's a tall one, but he's friendly." Nash rubbed the horse's brown and white face and back. "He'd be good for a beginner rider." He continued examining the rest of the horses and settled on three chestnut quarter horses and the paint.

They led the horses into the barn.

While Nash was busy settling his business with Jim, Hank thought about the idea of having a pasture full of quarter horses. Would his dream of breeding horses fit in with the farm he had married into? Even though the deed listed him as part owner, it still felt like Miranda and Justine's farm. Would they understand and allow room for his dream?

Jim and Nash completed paperwork for the transfer of ownership, and Nash paid Jim.

Before they loaded the horses into the trailer, Hank handed Jim a wad of cash he'd been saving throughout the summer in a coffee tin kept in his sock drawer. "I want to buy Penny."

Jim gave the cash back to Hank and shook his head. "Like I said, she's not for sale."

"What if I bought both Penny and the stallion out in the paddock?"

Jim swung his head and eyed Hank. "What do you want with a stallion? It's a big chore keeping them away from the mares."

"I want to breed quarter horses." It felt odd saying it out loud.

Concern grew on Nash's face. "And how do you think we're going to transport a stallion with all those mares?"

"I can come back for him."

"Miranda knows about this?"

In a gruff voice, Hank said, "That's our business." It was their business, and he would tell her, but he deserved to live his dreams too. This was an opportunity he didn't want to miss.

Nash's mouth twisted into a smirk as he haltered one of the horses and began leading her to the trailer. Just then, the dogs came running up to Nash, barking and jumping on Nash's legs. He yelled and swatted for them to get away.

Hank's eyes cut to Nash running with the horse across the yard to the truck. Nash reached the trailer and tried to open the door with one hand while hanging onto the lead rope with the other. The dogs followed him, nipping at his ankles. Hank felt sorry for his friend, but it was such a funny sight, seeing him dance around, dodging the dogs' nips, that he bent over laughing. Jim snickered beside him.

Nash lost his grip on the lead rope. The horse perked his head and trotted back toward the barn, straight inside his stall. The dogs circled Nash, barking as he jumped up into the trailer and shut the door.

A smile creased Jim's face. "This is entertaining, but I think I'd better help the poor guy out." He patted his leg, and the dogs came to him. He opened an empty stall and gestured the dogs inside, and then he secured the latch.

Nash opened the trailer door and peeked out. He jumped down and hoofed it to the barn. Once inside, he shook his head. "Those damn dogs." He glanced at Hank and said, "I could sure use some help with the horses."

Hank grinned. "Looked like you had it all under control to me."

Nash glared at Hank. In a gravelly voice, he said, "Grab a halter from the tack room, will ya?"

After all the horses were loaded in the trailer, Hank turned toward Jim. "How much would it take to buy Penny?"

"Like I said, she's not for sale." He jerked a thumb toward the pasture. "I've got another mare I could sell ya."

Hank folded his arms and tapped his cowboy boot. "It could take a year before another mare could foal. But here's the thing. I want to get started soon. Besides, my wife's a vet, and we live next to her clinic. She'd be right there should Penny need help when she gives birth."

Jim rubbed his forehead and stared at the ground.

"You wouldn't have to worry about late nights keeping watch."

Jim's chin jutted as he gave Hank a silent look.

"I helped my wife before she finished vet school when a neighbor's mare was having a rough time giving birth. No one else was around, so she had to step in. Afterward, when the mare's vet finally came to the farm, he told her he couldn't have done any better." Hank smiled. "She's that good."

Jim crossed his arms, looked out over the field beside the barn, considering the offer. "My wife and I have wanted to take a vacation. We haven't been anywhere in years. Our farm help can only be here during the day." He glanced over at Hank. "It would free us up to go somewhere in case Penny surprised us during the night." He took a few moments to ponder as he gazed at the fields once again. "I reckon it's the last time I'll breed her. She's getting old. Just like me and my wife." His eyes darted toward Hank. "Maybe you're right. It'd be good to have someone young look after her."

Hank returned the money he'd given Jim earlier, and they shook hands.

Once they were on the road headed home, Nash looked over at Hank. "That was a bold move, committing your wife to be there for that broodmare. You sure she wants to take that on? Seems she's pretty busy as it is."

Hank stared straight ahead. His chest felt tight, and he had an upset stomach.

"She'll be thrilled."

Since they hadn't resolved the fight they'd had the night before, what would she think about this new development? Would she even want this new horse? It was a lot of responsibility to care for a pregnant horse. And it would be up to Miranda to make sure things went well during the birth. But he was up for the task. He wasn't sure how he'd break the news. Maybe it would smooth things over, and the broodmare could be a bridge to make things better and back to the way they were before their fight.

Because their conversations were normally about Miranda's dreams, not Hank's, he hadn't even told Miranda that he wanted to raise quarter horses. But he had hopes too. He would farrier some because it brought in money, but his real wish was to raise quality horses that people could use for barrel racing, trail riding, and shows. Though Hank didn't know anything about raising horses, he'd trained his horse from the time it was a foal. How hard could it be? He'd soon find out. But first things first. He had to tell Miranda about Penny and about his dream of raising horses. He knew he'd jumped in feet first before he'd even discussed it with his new wife. But she was open-minded. She'd be fine with it. Or would she?

CHAPTER 24

Nash coasted the large dually, pulling the loaded trailer down the Graaf's gravel driveway. The horses behind them snorted and thumped their hooves against the metal flooring.

"We'd better let the horses out in the pasture right away so they can burn off the nervous energy they worked up on the freeway," Hank said.

Nash nodded. "Got that right. They're making a lot of noise for sure." He parked the rig next to the barn.

Hank drew in a breath. "What the ..."

An ambulance occupied the backyard, next to the garden. Before the dually came to a full stop, Hank had jumped out of the truck. Miranda and Richard faced each other, yelling. Two EMTs attended to Justine on the ground.

He rushed over to Miranda. "What's going on?"

Miranda wrapped her arms around him. "I'm glad you're here. We found Mom passed out. Richard called the ambulance and so here we are."

Justine was talking and gesturing with her hands.

"Looks like she's come to. What happened?"

Miranda's voice thickened with emotion. "We're trying to figure that out. Richard seems to think he knows better than me what Mom needs. He keeps telling the ambulance driver what to do. And how to do their job."

Richard stood with his arms folded and his mouth in a straight line, glaring at Miranda as she talked. Did Richard really think he'd win this battle? When it came to Miranda and Justine, there was no getting between them. Miranda held strong when it concerned the welfare of her family. Hank recalled how she stood strong for her dad when he was ill with cancer. She was the rock that held the family together when Stanley died. Nope. Richard could bristle all he wanted, but he wasn't going to win.

Hank squeezed Miranda's hand. "I'll go ask the EMTs what's happening."

Nash tapped on Hank's shoulder. "You got this?"

Hank nodded.

"I'll take care of the horses."

"Thanks. Feel free to get them settled in the barn until you're ready to go back to Wyoming."

Nash headed to the horse trailer.

Miranda rested her hand on Hank's shoulder. "Good luck reasoning with the paramedics," Miranda said. "They made me step away."

Hank approached the guys crouched by Justine. She was stretched out on her back. He kneeled by her head. "How you doing, Mom?"

"I feel ridiculous." Justine folded her hands on her chest. "This is all so unnecessary. I just tripped on a rock in the garden."

Hank looked at her pale face and then glanced at one of the guys taking her blood pressure. The sound of horses' hooves thumping on metal caught Hank's attention as Nash led them out of the horse trailer. He watched briefly as Nash led them into the pasture one by one.

The other tech was putting pressure on Justine's leg with a large bandage. He glanced at Hank. "She's got a bad cut. I think we should take her to the hospital for some stitches."

"Why don't you let her daughter ride with you in the ambulance? She'll need to be with her."

The EMT said, "Her husband said he wants to go with her."

Hank shook his head. "That's not her husband. Her daughter gets first dibs."

The EMTs lifted Justine, placing her on a stretcher and carrying her into the back of the ambulance. Miranda and Richard ran to her side.

"I'm coming with you," Miranda said.

Richard stepped in front of Miranda, putting his hand on Justine's arm. "I'm coming with you, darling."

One of the EMTs said, "Only one person. Only family."

Miranda jumped in the back of the ambulance beside her mom. She glared at Richard as they closed the door.

"Richard, get in my truck," Hank hollered. "We'll follow them to the hospital."

He made a sour face. "I can take my car."

Hank shrugged. "Suit yourself." He backed his truck out of its spot near the barn and started to roll down the driveway when Richard came up to the truck, his hand up. Hank braked. A blast of dust floated into the cab as Richard got in. Hank jammed the truck in gear and gunned the engine as they caught up to the ambulance streaming down the gravel road.

They rode in silence for a couple miles. Then Richard started talking fast: "I went outside to call Justine in for dinner. I'd made some hamburgers on the grill. She was just lying there on the ground. I found my wife on the side of the road when she got in a car accident. She died in that accident. Drunk driver."

Hank glanced at Richard. "Sorry to hear that."

"I know Miranda hates me."

"She's protective of her mom. They went through a lot when Stanley died. It was a big loss for Miranda, losing her dad."

"I just want her to like me." Richard dabbed at his forehead with the white cloth handkerchief he grabbed from his shirt pocket.

"You want my advice?" Hank paused a moment. "You can't push her. She's a strong woman, and she can't be told what to do. Or how to feel about someone."

"Hard to do." Richard glanced over at Hank. "Keep this between you and me." He cleared his throat. "I'm going to ask Justine to marry me."

Hank looked straight ahead and didn't say anything. Trees whizzed past the windows as they sailed down the freeway toward the hospital.

His thoughts led him to the horse he had bought and how he'd approach Miranda. It was a rushed decision, and now that he'd done it, he wished he had talked to her first. But he had made other decisions without her input. Like when he built the house and designed her office. She seemed happy about that. But he knew this was different. It was the beginning of a whole new career for him. He hadn't told her anything about wanting to raise horses. As far as she knew, he was content with being a farrier.

But he hadn't been satisfied with his career for a long time. He'd done that kind of work for a few years, and he felt bored with it. Plus, it was a dangerous job. The chance of getting kicked in the head was high, and he knew guys that had brain damage because of it. But mostly, he wanted a change. He hadn't told Miranda about his dream because there was a lot going on with her internship and starting her veterinary practice. It never seemed like the right time. He'd kept one thing from her already. His criminal background. And now this. He didn't want to start out their marriage with secrets. Yet he already had. And now things were compounded by their fight from the previous night.

Miranda was standing at the entrance to the emergency room when Hank pulled his truck into a parking space. Hank rushed toward Miranda. Richard followed close behind.

Miranda shot daggers at Richard. "Mom hit her head when she fell, and I think she has a concussion. She's back in x-ray right now to see if she broke any bones in her leg."

Just then a couple headed toward them. The man was holding a crying baby, and the woman beside him rubbed the baby's back. The adults' faces looked ashen as they rushed through the emergency room doors and up to the reception area.

Miranda shivered as she remembered again that she was pregnant. Would that be their life? Always afraid that something could happen to their child. And terrified when something did happen?

Hank kissed Miranda on the cheek. "Let's go wait in the waiting area." He took her hand and led her to a chair.

Richard went up to the reception desk.

Hank knew they needed to talk about their argument from that morning, but now wasn't the time. Miranda needed him to be supportive and he had to put his feelings aside.

"I'm glad you're here, babe. Thanks for talking to the EMT earlier." Miranda lowered her voice. "I thought I was going to punch Richard. He was so bossy, trying to tell me and the EMTs what to do." She shook her head. "He acts like he's mom's husband."

Hank recalled Richard's announcement in the truck about marrying Justine. He looked straight ahead and remained quiet.

She pressed her hands along her thighs and angled a glance toward Hank. "What aren't you telling me?"

Richard walked toward Miranda and Hank. A nurse approached. "They're wheeling Justine into exam room number 5." She looked over all three of them. "You can join her if you'd like. The rooms are small, so only two of you."

Miranda grabbed Hank's arm. "You come with me." Over her shoulder, she muttered, "Richard, we'll let you know how she's doing."

As they walked away, Richard sat so hard the chair scraped along the gray and white checkered linoleum floor.

The small, ten by ten-foot room had an odor of antiseptic. A container of cotton balls, rubbing alcohol, and a small tray of instruments were displayed on the white counter. Beside the counter, a small sink with a paper towel canister squatted above it in the corner. Justine sat on the examining table with her legs stretched out, leaning against a pillow.

Miranda went to her mother's side. "How're you feeling, Mom?"

Hank positioned himself in a chair against the wall.

Justine winced. "I feel so silly." Her head slowly drifted from side to side. "I can't believe I tripped on a rock. I was gathering lettuce and tomatoes to make a salad for dinner."

Miranda laid her hand on Justine's arm.

"I just want to go home."

A doctor in a long white coat with a stethoscope around his neck stepped into the room. 'Dr. Johnson' was monogrammed on his pocket. The tall man with short, speckled gray and black hair glanced between Hank and Miranda and then settled his eyes on Hank. "Justine has a mild concussion."

Hank gestured. "You'll want to talk to Miranda, her daughter, Dr. Graaf."

Miranda threw Hank a quick smile. The doctor was being chauvinistic, and she loved her husband even more for sticking up for her.

Dr. Johnson hesitated and then turned an eye on Miranda. "You're a doctor?"

"I'm a veterinarian, yes."

"Wake her every couple hours tonight to make sure things aren't getting worse." The doctor glanced at a nurse coming into the small room.

The nurse went to the medicine cupboard, pulling out a kit for stitching up wounds. "Justine, I'm going to give you a shot to numb the area around the wound so we can stitch it up." She placed her hand on Justine's arm. "Then you can go home."

After Justine's cut was stitched and bandaged, they helped her into a wheelchair and wheeled her toward the waiting area. Richard crouched in a chair, eyes on his loafers. He scooted over to Justine and hugged her. "You alright? I was so worried." He shot Miranda a look. "They wouldn't let me come in." He took hold of the back of the wheelchair and headed for the door. "Let's take you home."

Miranda's lips pressed into a white slash. She grabbed Hank's hand and followed. When they reached Hank's truck, Miranda's eyes bounced back and forth between Justine, Hank, and Richard. Her gaze then stuck on Richard. "Looks like there's only room for three of us in the truck. You mind taking a taxi?"

Richard scowled. "I'll ride in the back." He pulled himself over the tailgate, grunted, and sat down. Richard thumped his hand on the side of the truck. "Let's go."

Miranda shrugged. She helped Justine into the cab, and after her mother was settled in the middle, she got in and buckled them both. Hank returned the wheelchair to the emergency room, and then Hank ran around to the driver's side and hopped in.

"I'm sorry for all this fuss." Justine put a hand on each of their thighs. "My silly accident has interrupted your day."

"Mom, we love you. I'm glad it wasn't more serious."

After thirty minutes, they pulled into the driveway. Miranda helped Justine out of the truck.

Richard had climbed out of the truck bed and stood beside Justine. He wrapped an arm around her shoulders. "Let's get you inside, darling."

Miranda stepped to the other side of her mom. "I think it would be better if she stayed with us for the night." She pursed her lips and took hold of Justine's elbow.

"Really, you two," Justine said, "I'm not an invalid. I can still take care of myself. I want to sleep in my own bed. I'll be fine." She took a few steps toward the house and swayed slightly. Richard jumped to her side and took an arm. They turned their heads when they heard barking. Ben ran up to them, nuzzling Justine's leg.

"Where'd you come from?" She rubbed his ear.

Miranda chuckled. "Ok, buddy, let's get Mom into the house."

Hank came up beside Miranda and whispered in her ear, "Let's give your mom some space and let Richard take her in."

She grimaced.

"She'll be fine," Hank said in a low voice. "He'll let us know if something's up."

Miranda folded her arms across her chest and watched her mom and Richard head to the house where a man she barely knew would take care of her mom. A shiver ran down her spine as she thought of Stanley getting weak before he died.

Hank took her hand in his and led her toward the back of the property. He stopped midway and turned to face her. "I know we need to talk about last night."

She dipped her head.

"I'm sorry for the things I said."

She looked upward toward the sky. "I'm sorry too."

He cupped her face with his hand, looking deeply into her eyes. "What I said was mean. I'm really sorry."

"I'm not completely against kids. It's just a lot to take in right now."

He bent and kissed her with a passion that took away all the hurt and painful words. His kiss poured out of him, replacing the hurt with deep love.

Tears slipped from the corner of her eyes. "I hate it when we fight."

They embraced, wrapping their arms around each other tightly. In a raspy voice, as his heart swelled, he said, "I hate it too."

Hank let go and took both of Miranda's hands in his. "There's something I want to talk to you about."

A shadow came over her face. "That sounds ominous."

"It's about what I did on our trip to the horse farm."

"What … did you … do?"

"It'd be better to show you." They held hands as they walked to the barn.

CHAPTER 25

The sweet smell of timothy hay met them as Miranda and Hank stepped inside the barn. They heard the clatter of grain spilling into a trough and the *crunch, crunch* of horses chewing. They headed for the stalls.

Nash met them as he was scooping grain to feed the horses. He nodded. "Miranda." He went back to filling the bucket.

"Hi Nash. Hank says he has something to show me." Hank's stomach clenched as Miranda asked, "You know anything about this?"

Nash twisted the grain scoop around in his hand a few times and then gave a quick shrug. "I got stuff to do outside." He dropped the scoop in the bucket and turned and trudged toward the open barn door.

She narrowed her eyes. "Now I'm curious, Hank. What is going on?"

"Before you get too excited ..." He investigated the stalls until he stopped and said, "Come here, Miranda."

The horses' munching filled the silence between Miranda and Hank.

Miranda popped her head into the opening of the stall. There stood a chestnut horse: her belly big and round, munching on some hay. She stroked the horse's muzzle and examined the broodmare with her eyes. "This one of the horses Nash bought?

She looks pregnant. I'm surprised his boss would want to raise and train a foal. That's a lot of work."

"I bought the mare," Hank said, his voice barely audible.

"You *what*?"

"I bought her today after Nash chose the horses for his boss."

"Without talking to me?" Miranda took another look at the horse. "This mare looks like a purebred. She must have cost a fortune." She thumped the edge of the stall door. "Two more horses to feed and care for. We're just breaking even as it is. She looks like she's ready to give birth anytime. I can't believe you did this." She threw her hands in the air, turned, and headed for the door.

"Miranda …"

She marched out of the barn.

Hank dropped his shoulders and leaned his head on the stall doorframe.

Nash returned to the barn. "That went well. Miranda looked like a windstorm blowing through a dusty field."

"Don't start. I know I screwed up."

Nash gave him a crooked smile. "Good luck, man." He poured more grain into another feed bucket. "I'll stay the night in the barn and head out in the morning."

As he was leaving the barn, Hank said, "We'll make up the couch for the night. You don't have to stay out here."

Nash shook his head. "I'd rather sleep where it's quiet. I know better than to be in the middle of you two right now."

A chill ran over Hank's shoulders and down his body. With a vinegary sound, he said, "Thanks for the support, bud."

Hank went to the barn phone and pulled the letter from the inside of his jean jacket. He could at least lighten the stress load a little.

"Cheyenne County District Court," a woman answered on the other end of the phone line.

"This is Hank Driskill. I'm calling about a letter I received."

"What's the case number, please?"

"Number 43967047."

She transferred him to a case worker. A gruff voice answered: "Rodgers."

"This is Hank Driskill. I'm calling about a letter I received."

"Case number?"

"43967047."

"Four, three, nine … Oh, yeah, here we are." He barked, "We've had a hard time tracking you down. Apparently, you left Wyoming. You had community service to finish, my friend. And probation for a year."

"I thought it was all set at the hearing before I left."

"Nope."

"What do I have to do to clear this mess up?"

Rogers guffawed and then started hacking a smoker's cough. "You best get back here and finish what you started. That is, probation and community service. And now, since you bolted, we've added a year to your probation and more hours of community service. The sooner you get here, the better."

"I can't go to Wyoming. I have a job here in Iowa."

"You're screwed, my friend, screwed."

Hank was never told by the judge at the court hearing before he left Wyoming two years prior that he had anything else to do other than pay a large fine. "I'll fight this, then."

"Do what you gotta do. My advice is to get here ASAP."

Hank hung up the phone, slamming the receiver on the cradle. Blood rushed through his ears. He marched between the stalls until he reached the end of the cement and then he punched the bales of straw again and again, gritting his teeth until his jaw ached. He stood on shaky legs and let out a guttural sigh.

In the house, Miranda was on the couch, flipping through a magazine. She whipped each page over one by one as her eyes bore acrid heat into the photos.

Hank scuffed over to her, spent from his outburst in the barn. "I'm sorry. I know I should have talked to you first."

She looked up, tears in her eyes. "I thought we'd be honest about money and tell each other everything."

"We are. I'm sorry. I screwed up. What can I do to make it up to you?"

"How much was the horse?"

"It was money I had saved up. It wasn't out of our savings."

"How much?"

Hank hesitated.

"How much, Hank?"

The words slid from his mouth: "Fifteen hundred."

Her mouth opened and then she closed it, lips tightened together. She went into the kitchen and started washing dishes, setting a glass down hard in the strainer on the counter.

He followed. "I know you're mad but give me a chance to explain."

Miranda continued cleaning the kitchen, ignoring his plea. She wiped the breadcrumbs from the sandwich she'd made earlier in the day off the white Corion.

He wasn't getting anywhere with this conversation if she was going to ignore him. He clenched his teeth, twitching his jaw muscles. He'd run an errand, then, and calm down.

"We're out of milk. I'm going into town for supplies." Hank spun and slammed the door behind him as he headed to his truck.

CHAPTER 26

At the Hy-Vee grocery store in Davenport, Hank pushed a cart down the dairy aisle. He stopped in front of the milk cooler and stared at the selection in front of him, eyes glazing over. Whole, skim, two percent. And even chocolate. He rubbed his forehead where a headache had formed during his drive.

He knew he'd screwed up. But Miranda could at least have listened to him as to why he bought the horse. True, he hadn't given her a heads up or told her about his dream of being a horse trainer, but at least she could hear him out. Why was she so temperamental? She seemed so moody the last month. Maybe when he returned home, she'd have cooled off and they could talk. They had cleared the air about their fight from last night. But now they were in another argument. How much more could they take?

As he reached into the cooler to grab a gallon of two percent milk, a voice behind him said, "Well, hello, Hank. Congratulations."

He whirled and spotted Susan, the receptionist from their doctor's office. She brushed the primped curls on her forehead from her short brown bouffant. "It'll be a big change for you and Miranda." She patted his arm. "You'll make a great dad. I can sense these things."

Hank's eyes widened, and his skin prickled. "What are you talking about?"

"Oh." Susan clasped a hand over her mouth. "Me and my big mouth. Miranda hasn't told you yet, has she?"

"What exactly are we talking about, Susan?"

"I'll let her tell you. You two haven't talked about it, and I don't want to ruin the surprise," she rambled on, her face reddened. "Which I think I already have. I can see by the look on your face. Sorry, Hank. Give Miranda my best." She turned and hurried down the aisle, a shopping basket on her arm filled with grape jelly, Ritz crackers, and bananas.

Hank shifted the weight of his body forward as he leaned on his shopping cart. His stomach churned and he thought he was going to be sick. Miranda's doctor's appointment had been a couple days ago. Why didn't she say anything to him? How could she keep this news from him? He hooked his hand around the milk jug handle, shoving it back on the cooler shelf and then pushed his cart to the front of the store. He rammed it into the rest of the stacked carts.

On one hand, he was elated. He was going to be a father. He had looked forward to this moment since the day they got married. But the low burn in his belly reflected the hurt he felt from Miranda not sharing this wonderful news with him first thing. He knew she wasn't sure about being a mother. She had told him so a month ago. But why would she keep it from him? Being married meant talking about the good and difficult times.

Hank jammed the truck into gear and sped out of the Hy-Vee parking lot. He careened down the freeway, not knowing where to go. It's like they had had a triple fight within the last couple days, and Miranda didn't even know about the third one yet. They'd fought the night before about having kids, and Miranda was mad at him for buying the broodmare without telling her. Now he'd learned that she had kept her pregnancy from him. What was happening to them? Why were they keeping so many secrets from each other? They had only been married a few months, and they were already treading on thin ice. Feelings of anger, hurt, and joy swept through Hank like cattle stampeding, rattling the walls of his mind.

When he arrived at their driveway, he pushed on the gas. In front of his house, he stamped on the brake. He didn't know how he'd approach Miranda with what he wanted to say. He knew he needed to be careful. A slight heaviness came over him. *Tread lightly*, he kept telling himself, *tread lightly*. He jumped out of the truck and ran inside, hoping Miranda would be there as it was near dinnertime and he assumed she'd be cooking. He looked around the living room and kitchen and then went into the bedroom. She was not in the house. His heart pounded. He bounded out to the barn, and still, he couldn't find her.

After opening the door to her office and seeing she wasn't there, Hank stormed up to the main house, hoping Justine could tell him where Miranda had gone.

He banged on the door of the old farmhouse.

A minute later, Richard opened the door wrapped in a navy velour bathrobe. "Hi, Hank. What can I help you with?"

He boomed, "Have you seen Miranda?"

Richard backed up. "She's inside, talking to Justine."

Hank clapped his shoulder, stepped around Richard, and stomped into the kitchen. Miranda sat at the table, shucking corn. Hank glared at her. "I've been looking everywhere for you."

She shoved corn husks into a large metal bowl. "Just seeing how Mom is."

He briefly addressed Justine. "Hi, Mom."

"Hi, Hank. Take Miranda with you, will you please?" She smiled and gestured toward the door. "She's hovering."

Miranda stood and stepped around him. "Fine. Let's go then." She turned before she got to the door. "I'm coming back later to check on you, Mom. Whether you like it or not." She looked at Richard. "Call me if you need me."

Hank followed Miranda outside. As they walked down the pathway to their house, Hank said, "I know you're mad at me, but could you wait up a minute?"

"Yes. I am still mad at you."

He jogged to her side. "We need to talk."

"I know, but I don't know if this is such a good time. Maybe tomorrow. I'm so mad I can't even talk about it. You kept something important from me. I thought we had a marriage where we don't keep secrets."

Hank reminded himself to be careful with what he said next. They reached the front door of their house, and Hank put his hand on her shoulder. His voice cracked. "I know what that's like."

"What do you mean?"

Tread lightly, Hank. Tread lightly. His thoughts jumped to Susan at the grocery store, congratulating him. It pained him that this exciting news of Miranda's pregnancy knocked him over like a boulder rolling down a mountain in Wyoming. Why couldn't his own wife tell him about their baby? Why did he have to hear it from someone he hardly knew?

"Hank? ... Honey?"

His brain was shutting down, and he was unable to think. He glanced down at her.

"What is it? What aren't you telling me?"

He launched into an internal berating. *Come on, you big chicken. Ya jerk. Tell her what you know.* But instead, he hesitated. And words just fell out of his mouth: "How's Mom really doing? She can put on a good front."

"She'll be fine," Miranda barked. "But what is it, really?"

He felt as though his world was spinning. Like on a carnival ride, going faster and faster, the world a blur, and he couldn't get off until someone other than himself stopped the ride. He reached down in his belly, found some strength, and focused on a piece of loose wood on the doorframe, hanging on by a splinter, thinking he'd need to fix it. Finally, he blurted, "Is there anything you want to tell me?"

"Other than still being mad at you?" She shook her head, pursing her lips. "No."

He studied her face.

Miranda's eyes diverted from his gaze quickly. And then she opened the door, greeting Ben at the threshold. Her voice rose an octave. "Hey, Buddy. You need to go on a walk, I bet."

Ben circled Miranda, panting and whining in excitement to see them.

Her gaze bounced back and forth between Ben and Hank. "Walk with me?"

He nodded slowly.

"I'll get our jackets. It's getting cool this afternoon." She scurried to the closet and pulled out two Carhartt's, one camel, one black.

He took the black one when she handed it to him.

They both donned their jackets and went outside.

CHAPTER 27

In silence, Miranda and Hank hiked along a path that edged stalks of corn. She thought about the secret that was brewing, rolling around in the air between them. How could she tell him that she was pregnant when it was hard to accept the news herself? She knew that he'd be excited. He so much as said so when they last argued about having children. He wanted kids, and she was confused about the situation. What was wrong with her? What woman wouldn't be thrilled upon hearing this news? And if her mom found out, she'd be over the moon. But Miranda wasn't there. She felt numb. Having a baby would change their whole life. It wouldn't be just the two of them anymore. There'd be another little person to direct their focus on and someone to love that would take away time and energy from them. They hadn't had enough time as a married couple yet.

Growing up, she had a great role model for motherhood. Her mom was the best. But did she inherit that gene? And what about her vet practice? How could she do all of it? It was a lot. Miranda took in a deep breath, sighing audibly as she exhaled.

"What is it?" Hank reached over and held her hand as they walked. "I'm sorry about buying that horse. It was selfish of me, a dumb move. I can sell her back. The guy had a hard time giving her up, anyway."

The autumn wind blew a bit of dirt into the air, creating a mini tornado. It careened down the path in front of them.

"I'm sorry for reacting like I did. It made me crazy hearing about you doing something without my input."

"I know. And I'm sorry." Hank squeezed her hand. "From now on, no more secrets."

Miranda kept quiet.

"Ok? Honey?"

"Yeah. You're right. No more secrets."

She knew she should tell him she was pregnant, but she just couldn't formulate the words.

"Honey?"

Miranda suddenly felt a little lightheaded, and it wasn't from being pregnant. What she was about to tell Hank would change their lives forever. She scraped her hand through her hair and then announced, "There's something I need to share."

He stopped walking. Turning toward her, he looked into her eyes.

"I just don't know how to say it ..."

Just then, Ben ran toward them full speed with a rabbit in his mouth, its hind legs drooped on one side and its head bobbing along on the other side of Ben's mouth.

"Ben," Miranda said, "Drop it!"

Ben sat in front of Miranda, looking at her with doting eyes, the rabbit sagging toward the ground, struggling to get free from Ben's mouth.

Miranda gently put one hand around the rabbit's feet and the other around the dog's head. "Ben, let go. Drop it."

Ben wagged his tail but wouldn't let go of the pathetic bunny fighting for its life.

Miranda slowly squeezed her fingers around Ben's nose, causing him to drop the rabbit to the ground. The bunny was in freeze mode, breathing rapidly and staring into space. It couldn't move.

Hank quickly took hold of Ben's collar and pulled him away from the rabbit.

Miranda scooped up the rabbit and headed back toward their house. "I'm going to take this poor creature to my clinic and see if I can save him."

"I'll handle Ben." Hank thumped his thigh. "Come on, Ben. Let's burn off some of that energy."

They moved in the opposite direction of her. Hank threw a stick, Ben racing ahead to fetch it. Miranda pivoted and strode toward her clinic, stunned rabbit in her arms.

As she walked, Miranda turned her secret over and over in her mind. It was like she was living in their future and Hank was still living in their past. They were on two different sides of the same fence.

Inside the clinic she gently placed the injured rabbit on the metal examination table, grabbed a stethoscope, listened to its heart and lungs, and conducted an examination.

Miranda filled a syringe with an antibiotic and gave the rabbit a shot. It had two bite wounds from Ben's mouth, and she wanted to prevent an infection. She dabbed the cuts with an antimicrobial wound gel and gently placed the rabbit into a cage, allowing it to calm and settle. She knew she'd need to keep an eye on it for the day, making sure it was alright before letting it loose. It was a wild animal where it was survival of the fittest. Why was she going to this much trouble for this animal that would naturally die in the wild?

Because she was a helper by nature. And because she couldn't stand to see any creature suffer, especially at the mouth of her dog. So, she healed and helped where she could. She just wanted to give this little guy a fighting chance.

CHAPTER 28

That night, Miranda and Hank went to bed early. Nothing was said to clear the air from all the swirling thoughts trapped inside their heads. So, they drifted off to sleep. In the morning, Hank had an early appointment at a farm and Miranda got to work in her clinic.

Miranda picked up a stool from the lab and placed it in front of the rabbit they'd saved the previous day. She looked into the cage and talked in a soothing, low voice, trying to comfort the trembling animal.

Just then, Nash swung open the door to her office and said, "Miranda, excuse me for interrupting, but one of my boss's mares is having a hard time." A pained look marred his face. "She's groaning and looking back at her belly and scraping the floor of the stall with her hoof."

Miranda looked up from the rabbit's cage. "I'll be right out." She grabbed her medical bag and carried it to the barn.

She went into the stall of the small sorrel. Miranda listened to the horse's abdomen with the stethoscope, and her gut sounded still, as if it were blocked. The mare nipped at her belly. "I think she may have colic. Get the lead rope and halter. Take her for a slow walk outside. It's best to get things moving, and walking can sometimes cure the problem."

Nash quickly left the stall and came back with the tack Miranda requested. "Poor thing. She looks miserable." He put the halter on the mare. He then snapped the lead rope to the halter and guided her through the stall.

"Keep walking her. I'll come out and check her in a few minutes."

"Thanks, Miranda." Nash led the mare outside along the edge of the barn in the grass. The horse tried to lay down and roll on the ground, but Nash pulled gently on the lead rope and tried to move her forward.

"Looks like you could use another pair of hands."

He looked up and it was Tanya. A light flush swept over his face as she smiled at him.

Tanya thought it was cute that Nash was shy around her, and yet he seemed so sure of himself at the same time. His forearms rippled as he gently held the lead rope, keeping the mare from lying down. Tanya moved to the other side of the horse. She stroked the mare's reddish withers. "It's ok, baby. You'll be ok. You're in good hands."

"How do you know that?" He walked a couple steps, and the mare moved forward. "I could be terrible with horses."

"Most cowboys are good with horses."

"Oh. Yeah. You know a lot of cowboys?"

"I know Hank."

Nash smiled. "He *is* good with horses."

They continued walking, Nash on one side, Tanya on the other. She gave the horse long strokes on her neck.

"Where's your Olympian?"

"Daniel?"

They continued toward the field on the side of the yard.

"At the gym, lifting weights."

"You're not training today?"

"Seems we do better when we work out separately. I woke up early and went to the gym. I'm here to steal Miranda for lunch. I'm taking her for a girl's afternoon. She doesn't know it yet."

A few minutes later, Miranda approached. "Tonny. What are you doing here? Not working out with Daniel?"

Tanya threw a hand up in the air. "Geez, everyone thinks I should be joined at the hip with him."

Miranda's ran a hand down the mare's belly. "He does seem to have a hard time without you by his side."

Tanya flipped her ponytail between her fingers and swept her hand through the air. "Miranda. Get your jacket. I'm taking you out for a girl's afternoon. Lunch. The salon. The whole kit and caboodle." She giggled. "We can get our nails done."

"When have you ever known me to get my nails done?"

"Never." Tanya shrugged. "But there's a first time for everything."

Miranda spread her fingers and presented her hands to Tanya and Nash. "These are my tools. I don't want anyone messing with them."

"Fine." Tanya rolled her eyes. "You can just get a hand massage."

"I can't leave this horse while she's in pain and suffering anyway."

The group walked through the pasture for another half hour until the mare eased up on trying to lie down and roll. She started passing manure and tried to eat grass. When Miranda examined the mare, the horse nuzzled her hand.

"I think she's getting better." Miranda let out a sigh. "What a relief. You never know which way colic will go. Sometimes it can get bad. But it looks like we're out of the woods."

She looked at Nash. "Could you keep walking her for a bit? Try to see if she'll drink some water. Keep a close eye on her."

"Will do." They returned to the barn with Nash and the horse.

Tanya said, "It looks like you can go for our girl's time after all."

Miranda's eyes diverted to the horse, and she studied her for a few minutes, hesitating to answer Tanya. Then she said, "I guess so. I hate to leave when an animal is in trouble. Let's go while the getting is good."

Tanya let out a little whoop and threw her hands in the air.

Miranda asked Nash, "You ok with this?"

"Go. Get outta here. We'll be fine." As the women walked to the barn door, he said, "You ladies have fun."

CHAPTER 29

Tanya drove her Buick LeSabre rental down the driveway and peeled onto the main road. In the passenger seat, Miranda rode beside her. Dust flew behind them as Tanya sped toward the freeway.

"Slow down, Tonnie. What's your hurry?"

"I want to get to the spa before anything else happens." She took a quick glance toward Miranda. Her friend looked pale and worn, like she hadn't had much sleep. "Or you change your mind."

Miranda tapped her fingers on the door's armrest. "I left the farm, didn't I?"

"Once we're inside getting our nails done, sorry ..." Her eyelashes fluttered. "... Hand massage, no one can bother us."

"It's not like anyone can get a hold of us now."

She giggled. "I can picture Nash careening down the highway, trying to get our attention." Tanya's hand flicked upward away from the steering wheel. "Another animal emergency."

"This is what I do, ya know."

"I know. I know. I just want some time with my best friend. We haven't had that in a while. Lately, there's always been someone interfering with our girl time."

"True. True."

Outside the car windows, a spattering of maples looked like clumps of red rubies in the fields.

"Speaking of which," Tanya said. "Have you told Hank?"

Miranda leaned toward the passenger door and folded her arms. "That's it. Get right to it, Tonny."

"I don't think it's fair he doesn't know." Tanya tried to keep her cool with Miranda. "I know I said I would back you up. I want to be your supportive best friend, but I'm starting to sway toward team Hank on this one." She slapped the steering wheel. "I'm having a hard time keeping quiet." Her parents kept secrets from each other all the time, and they were so unhappy. She didn't want that to happen to Miranda and Hank.

"I noticed." Miranda's hands clenched into fists and released again. "The other night. At our party," she exhaled, "you made it clear to me with all your eye gestures and wanting to help Hank out with the condiments. Really, Tanya? You don't think I could see beyond that and what you were up to? I knew how you felt the minute I told you I was pregnant." Her lips formed a sneer. "Maybe someday, if you ever get pregnant, you'll know how it feels to have a human growing inside of you." She stared out the window. Her voice turned sour. "I've heard some gymnasts can't even get pregnant because their periods are all messed up, with all the dieting and extreme exercise." She spat out the words. "So maybe you'll never have to worry about it."

Miranda's words cut through Tanya like sharp glass. She'd heard the same thing regarding the recent studies conducted on extreme female athletes like marathon runners, skaters, and gymnasts. Women who made a career of competing in their sport. But why did Miranda have to be so mean and point out Tanya's dread about her maternal future? Tanya spewed sharp and jagged words that fell from her tongue: "You're right. I don't know what it feels like to be pregnant. You don't know what it's like to have the pressure of being an elite gymnast, traveling all over the world competing. You went to England. Big deal. A farm girl coming back home to live your narrow, perfect little life."

Tanya felt like she'd dived into the deep end of a pool, and the sound of her heartbeat echoed within the pool's walls. After what seemed like a long dive, swimming underwater from one end of the pool to the other, Tanya came up for air. She swallowed the dry lump that was caught in her throat. Her voice cracked when she said, "What are you so afraid of?"

Miranda shrugged and bent her head forward. She shoved her fisted hands against her closed eyes, trying to stop the silent tears that leaked onto her cheeks and cascaded down her neck.

Tanya planted a callused palm, rough from swinging around and around on the uneven bars, on Miranda's upper back. Her voice softened to a whisper, "Hank loves you. He'll understand and be there for you no matter what happens."

Miranda sniffled and wiped her face with her T-shirt. "I know. It's just that he wants children so bad." Her reddened eyes looked up at Tanya. "I'm just not in the same space."

"You've got to tell him, Ran. He's the father."

"I tried last night, but then we had a thing with a rabbit and Ben. The conversation just didn't happen."

"Don't be like my parents. They always kept secrets from each other. And look where they are now."

Tanya's two older brothers moved out the day after they graduated from high school. Tanya was left to pick up the pieces. And she was the only one in the family that talked to her parents, barely. Her mother was weak and submissive. It sickened Tanya, observing her mother from the sidelines all these years. She had lost respect for her parents a long time ago. No man was going to dominate Tanya and tell her what to do like her father controlled her mother.

One of the reasons she had spent most of her time at the Graaf's house was because Justine and Stanley showed Tanya what a healthy marriage could be like. They were equals, and Justine was a strong, independent woman. Stanley never tried to control Justine or tell her what to do. They worked as a team, and that's what Tanya wanted for her life. She wanted someone she could share her life with and someone she could count on. But mostly, she wanted a relationship with complete honesty. Watching Miranda keep information from Hank was the same as lying as far as she was concerned. She hated seeing her best friend's marriage going in the wrong direction.

"It's not the same thing."

Tanya flicked on the turn signal.

Miranda sniffled. "I'm just processing all this."

"Wouldn't you rather process with Hank? He's your partner." The bile rose in Tanya's belly. She couldn't let this go. It was a baby's life. "Why keep it from him?"

"I'm just not ready yet."

Tanya groaned. This conversation was as futile as carrying water across a parking lot with a fork. "You're so stubborn. You don't have to do this alone."

Miranda gave Tanya the evil eye.

"I thought you were going to be there for me and back me up. That's what you told me the other day."

Tanya exited toward Bettendorf. The car came to an abrupt stop at the end of the exit ramp as Tanya jammed on the brakes. "I *am* here for you." She looked both ways and turned right, headed to Bettendorf. "As your best friend, I'm telling you I think you're making a big mistake not telling Hank."

They passed a Shell station, Taco Bell, and an Eagle grocery store.

"*You're* giving me relationship advice? You keep ditching Daniel at the hotel. And, besides, you've never been married. It's different when you're married."

Tanya knew she would regret what she said next. But she just couldn't help herself. "Since when is keeping secrets a way to nurture a marriage?"

Tanya steered the car into the spa parking lot. Pictures of women relaxing on massage tables, women getting pedicures, their feet soaking in foot baths, and women getting blissful facials decorated the windows at the front entrance.

In a surly voice, Tanya said, "We're here. Let's just get this over with."

Miranda got out of the car and marched toward the front door. Over her shoulder, the sarcasm so thick you could cut it with a butcher knife, she said, "Can't wait to sit beside you in the pedicure chair." She batted her eyes. "Giggling and talking about the men in our lives and the latest color in nail polish."

Tanya followed, three steps behind, as they headed into the spa. She only hoped she could tolerate what was supposed to be a bonding experience with her best friend. Since she'd come to Dewitt to visit Miranda, it had been one drama after another. From her struggles with Daniel and keeping him happy to Miranda's moodiness from pregnancy, Tanya suddenly wanted to head back to Colorado and focus on the Olympics. Eight-hour days of exhaustive training and bumps, bruises, and demands from her coach seemed like doing a couple cartwheels compared to dealing with her best friend's and boyfriend's temperaments.

After they had massages, facials, and manicures in silence, Miranda and Tanya left the spa and returned to the farm. Their spa was anything but relaxing. The deathlike quiet between them screamed louder than a blow horn. Tanya wished they hadn't stayed. Instead of a fun bonding time between friends, it had been torturous. She couldn't wait to drop Miranda off at her house. She felt farther away from her best friend than when she was in Colorado training. Because of the fight on the way to the spa, it felt like they were in different countries with an ocean in the middle.

Tanya and Miranda rarely fought and were always there to have each other's backs. But this time, both said harsh and mean things. Tanya didn't know if they'd ever get past this. She just needed time away from Miranda to think things over.

The LeSabre skidded on the gravel driveway, flinging up stones as Tanya sped toward Miranda and Hank's house. She mashed the brakes to the floor.

Miranda shoved the door open with her foot. She slammed it behind her.

Tanya watched Miranda march to the barn. Before she reached the barn door, Tanya reversed and careened down the driveway. A cloud of dust followed behind the car. She clenched the steering wheel, her nostrils flared, eyes glaring at the road ahead. Miranda had been in Tanya's life since they were in elementary school. Sadness bubbled up, overflowing into tears that soaked her face, clouding the smooth brightness from the facial she'd received at the spa.

CHAPTER 30

At the hotel, Tanya parked and wiped her face with her sleeve. She wanted to run to Daniel and bury her head in his chest and cry. He would surely comfort her, understanding the pain she felt at the potential loss of her best friend.

Tanya burst into the hotel room. Daniel wore his running shorts. He flipped a T-shirt soaked with sweat over his head and flung it in the bathroom sink. "Hey, babe. Just got done with a five-mile run."

She took a quick moment to notice the athletic and chiseled body in front of her. She hiccupped a tear. "Hi."

"What's wrong?"

Tanya flung herself onto him and wrapped her arms tightly around his wet chest, muscles rippling beneath her skin.

Daniel held her for a couple minutes. He then lifted her chin and looked into her eyes. "What's got you so upset? I don't think I've ever seen you this way before."

Her breath hitched. "Miranda and I got into a fight."

He wiped her red eyes. "What about?"

She shook her head. "She'd kill me if I told you."

Daniel sat on the edge of the bed and took his socks and shoes off. "I won't tell. It's not like I know anyone in the Quad Cities anyway."

Tanya dragged her hands over her eyes. She burst the news aloud into the room: "Miranda's pregnant."

"That's what you argued about?"

She knew it was going against the friend code to reveal secrets. But were they even friends anymore? Tanya had to tell someone.

"Wait a minute. Are you jealous because she's having a kid?" He tilted his head slightly. "That's a long way off for you. Right?"

"It's not about that."

"Whew. That was a close one." He threw his running shoes to the edge of the room, and they thumped when they hit the corner of the wall. "We're not ready for that now. We haven't even talked about it. Plus, how could you get a pregnant belly onto the beam?"

"It's not about us. Or you, for that matter."

He took a step toward her. "Then what?"

"She's not telling Hank she's pregnant."

"That's wrong." He shook his head. "He's the father; he should know." He lifted an eyebrow. "He is the father, right?"

She tapped his arm lightly, and her eyes rolled. "Of course, he's the father."

Daniel extended one leg out into a runner's stretch and then the other leg. After a few moments, he said, "Ya know, maybe it's for the best, the two of you not being friends anymore."

Tanya frowned.

"Since we came here and I met Miranda, it's been nothing but trouble for you. For us. We've had a couple arguments, and you've just had a fight with her. She didn't seem to be getting along with Hank too well at the barbecue the other night. Maybe you're better off with her *not* in your life."

Tanya rubbed her forehead, ran a hand over her hair, and flipped her ponytail. She sat on the edge of the bed. "I don't know what to do."

Daniel flopped beside her. He took her hand in his. "I know this is hard. But I think it's for the best. Let's go back to Colorado. We can focus on training and get back to our goals of making the Olympic teams."

"But she's been my best friend my whole life." Tanya put her head in her hands and wept. "I can't see my life without her. We've always been there for each other."

Daniel rubbed her back. "Things change. Sometimes, it's best to cut your losses and move on. You've been miserable since we got here. Your friendship with Miranda is not worth getting upset about. You need to get on with your life." He put his arm around Tanya. "Come on. I'll help you pack."

Tanya looked at Daniel through tear-filled eyes. "I want to call her at least and tell her I'm leaving."

"I think you're asking for more heartache if you do that. You can call her when we get back to Colorado. Or send a letter. But I think we need to just go."

She stared at her feet, taking stock of the bruise on her big toe and the callouses on the others. One of the hazards of being a gymnast. It wrecked your body. "Maybe you're right. I don't know what I'd say at this point. Things are such a mess between us." Tanya stood and picked up her suitcase.

Daniel called the airlines from their hotel room and booked a flight back to Colorado for that day. When they finished packing, they returned the rental car and left for Colorado.

CHAPTER 31

After Tanya had dropped Miranda at the farm with fresh skin and waxed eyebrows, Miranda marched to the door of her clinic. She slammed the door behind her. The animals in the cages stirred, meowing and a couple yips from the dogs. She plunked on her office chair and put her head in her hands. She and Tanya had never argued like that before. Tanya had been so mad at her for not telling Hank about the pregnancy. She slowly lifted her head and looked at her polished fuchsia nails. They looked beautiful. Miranda didn't know why she'd gotten her nails done. They'd get chipped and wrecked as soon as she treated any pets or worked in the barn. She ran her fingers over the smoothness of her face. Miranda hadn't taken care of herself in a long time, if ever. Her shoulders drooped, and her stomach felt queasy, different from the pregnancy nausea she'd experienced. This was a pit-in-her-stomach-feeling as she recalled the harsh words they'd said to each other. Tanya usually had Miranda's back. But today, she felt like Tanya was against her. Maybe Tanya had been right, and she should have told Hank, but her friend could have at least been on her side. Miranda didn't know if they'd ever recover their friendship after their fight that day. She sighed and decided to groom Mandy. Brushing horses always soothed her, so she got up from her chair and headed for the barn.

CHAPTER 32

A week passed, and on a warm Saturday October afternoon, Justine took her kitchen scissors and cut one of the butternut squashes from the vine in the garden. She planned on making squash soup that evening for dinner. Humming as she worked, Justine noticed some parsley and chives hidden under the shelter of dried tomato plants. She plunked the squash in her basket, carrying it in the crook of her elbow, and stepped over two rows of pumpkins. She snipped the remaining herbs and continued humming "Top of the World" by the Carpenters as she headed for the house. She enjoyed making meals from her garden and was excited to try the new soup recipe that she'd clipped from *Country Woman* magazine. She really was a salt-of-the-earth woman, after all. And she loved this time of year when she could enjoy the fruits of her labor, melting butter and pouring cream from their cows into a large Dutch oven. Her mouth watered as she imagined the nutty, buttery taste of her favorite soup.

Once inside, Justine placed her bounty on the kitchen table. She washed the produce in the sink. She turned on the radio, and "Girls Just Want to Have Fun" by Cindi Lauper was playing. Justine giggled and danced to the beat of the music as she chopped the squash into small chunks. She finished filling a bowl with squash and started in on the chives, dicing them into tiny pieces, their oniony aroma filling the air.

Hearing a car pull into the driveway, she parted the curtain on the kitchen window and peeked outside. She smiled as she saw Richard getting out of his Cadillac and heading for the door, a large bouquet of yellow roses in hand.

Justine held the door open for Richard as he came up the steps. He offered her the roses. "For you, dear."

She nestled her nose into the long-stemmed flowers and inhaled. "These smell so good; such a lovely fragrance. Even better than last week's bouquet."

He kissed her cheek. "Only the best for you, dear. Only the best."

"You spoil me." Justine reentered the kitchen to find a vase. Richard followed close behind. She struggled as she reached for the top shelf to grab a white vase. Richard wrapped one arm around her and, with his other hand, plucked the vase off the shelf and handed it to her.

She put the vase on the counter next to the roses.

A smile crept across Richard's lips, and he pulled her in close, kissing her once, twice, and a third time in a long, tender kiss that sent a wave of heat throughout Justine's body.

"I enjoy giving you the finest." Richard kissed her again and wiggled his eyebrows. "And giving you experiences like you've never had before."

Justine drew one eyebrow upward. "Like taking me to the opera and fancy restaurants in Chicago?"

"Which reminds me." He released his embrace and held her hands. "I just got great tickets for *Cats* at the Auditorium Theatre in Chicago. Practically front row."

"I love that theatre. When we went to see *Les Misérables* this summer, I just stared at the beautiful decor on the ceiling and walls. It was amazing." She glanced up at the popcorn ceiling of her kitchen. "And the acoustics." Looking at him, she said, "I'm not a music person, but I not only heard the orchestra playing the music, I felt it through my bones." She smiled. "It was glorious."

She filled the vase with water and began arranging the roses into a bouquet. "What day is the show?"

"Tonight."

She whirled. Her breath sank in her chest. "Tonight?"

"I know it's last minute. But I wanted to surprise you."

Her fingernails did a drumroll on the table. "I was planning on making dinner using squash from the garden."

He raked bent fingers through his crew cut. "You can do that anytime. These are great seats."

She studied Richard. She knew he'd gone out of his way to make this night special for her, and she didn't want to disappoint him. But she'd planned on doing something nice for him too. She could put the things from the garden into the fridge and make soup another day. Her belly fluttered from excitement and then flopped from side to side in disappointment as Justine wrapped Saran Wrap over the filled bowls of chopped vegetables. She deposited the containers into the fridge. Tomorrow. She'd make soup tomorrow.

Justine turned to Richard. "What time is our reservation?"

"Dinner at 6:30 at the seafood place next door. The show is at 8:30."

She glanced at her watch, and her eyes bugged. "That leaves an hour to get ready."

"Pack your bags, darling; I want you to stay the weekend at my place."

Justine felt a wave of irritation roll over her. She'd planned to stay at home and take care of the garden. Get it ready for winter. She also wanted to work on her lesson plans for the following week. And the soup. The soup she wanted to make. Just a little thing, but it was big to her. It was what she loved doing. Putzing around the house and yard. Stanley never pressured her to do anything other than what she wanted to do. She turned back to the roses on the counter and continued arranging them.

Richard came up behind her and placed his hands on her shoulders. "Justine. You don't seem very excited about going to Chicago."

"It's just that I had plans for the weekend. I wanted to stay here." She finished arranging the bouquet and turned. "You do so many nice things for me. We've been going to Chicago a lot lately."

Richard tilted his head downward slightly, sucking his lip as he tried to hide his disappointment. "I can cancel if you want. We don't have to go." He looked at her. "If you want to stay here, we can."

She studied his face. Richard was so good to her; how could she disappoint him? She could put her small-sighted weekend aside for another time. He was being thoughtful, and she was being selfish. She smiled slightly. "Let's go. I'd love to see *Cats*. I've read in the newspaper it is supposed to be a good show." She turned on her heel. "I'll get ready now."

In her bedroom, Justine looked at her closet. Her stomach contracted into a tight ball. She flicked through her dresses. She ran her hand over the sequins on a sleeveless sapphire dress that Richard had given her a month ago. He had bought her two black dresses, a red one, and an emerald-green dress for formal occasions. Who was this person who owned five cocktail dresses? She had never owned clothing like that when Stanley was alive. Justine and Stanley had lived a simple life. She had dresses for church and work. But nothing with sequins.

Justine pulled out a black cocktail dress with shoulder pads and slipped the black glittery dress over her head. She tugged it over her hips and legs. The lacey bottom fell to her ankles. She closed the side zipper, went to the mirror on the wall beside the closet, and twirled, proud of the slim figure she'd kept even in her mid-fifties.

What would Stanley think of her now? Going to fancy restaurants and shows in ornate theatres? She felt a thickness in her throat. Would he have wanted her to enjoy the company of another man? Richard was so different from Stanley. She couldn't think of any similarities. She had loved Stanley with all her heart. She *still* loved him.

What was it about Richard that she liked? Why was she attracted to him? He doted on her and made her feel special. He took her places and bought her gifts. He said all the right things. Dating was different being with Richard. He swept her off her feet. Stanley was so grounded. She felt safe and loved by Stanley. She had everything she needed with him. They were two unique men. Why *wouldn't* she feel different with Richard?

Yet, there was something she couldn't put her finger on about Richard. He wowed and dazzled her. The attention he gave her left her lightheaded and giddy. But something didn't feel quite right. Maybe her thoughts ping-ponged too much between Richard and Stanley. She needed to enjoy Richard's attention and quit comparing the two men.

Justine scoffed out loud, plucked an evening purse from her drawer, and plopped it on her bed. After slipping on pantyhose and sparkly black high heels, she went to her bathroom and applied makeup, finishing with a dab of red lipstick. She styled her blond bob. She looked at herself, glad she'd had her hair done and colored a couple days before. She hurried back into her bedroom, grabbed her purse, and, as a last-minute thought, packed a small overnight bag with toiletries and a few clothes. She tottered down the stairs, carrying her suitcase, careful not to fall on her high heels.

When she reached the bottom of the stairs, she found Richard waiting for her, reading a newspaper at the kitchen table. He looked up and whistled. "Woowee. You look beautiful."

She blushed. "Stop. You're making me uncomfortable."

Richard rose from his chair, came to her and kissed her passionately. She hugged him, thinking, *I could get used to this. What was I so confused about before?*

Minutes later, Richard closed the passenger side of his Cadillac after Justine got in the car. He rounded the back of the car, got in on the driver's side, and they took off down the gravel driveway, dust trailing as they sped onto the freeway toward Chicago.

CHAPTER 33

Nash had stayed at the Graaf farm for a couple days to settle the horses and get to know them before he headed back to Wyoming. It was a cool November morning, and he wore a black Carhartt jacket, black cowboy hat, and dusty black cowboy boots. His leather gloves held the long lunge rope as he worked one of the chestnuts, trotting the gelding in a large circle.

Meanwhile, Hank and Miranda worked side by side in the barn, vaccinating horses. Miranda peeled off her jean jacket and tossed it on a peg outside Rocko's stall. She wiped the sweat off her brow with the collar of her gray T-shirt.

Hank followed Miranda inside the stall and handed her a syringe. He stroked the horse's powerful neck while Miranda injected the vaccine. They continued to the next stall and moved in tandem like a pilot and co-pilot on a commercial airline.

But Hank's belly felt like it was rolling around like a Tilt a Whirl on a carnival ride.

Miranda and Hank worked silently, careful not to get in each other's way. They hadn't said much since their near make-up moment a few nights before when Ben caught the rabbit. Neither one knew how to approach the other with what was on their mind. They had gone day to day without resolving anything, and now here they were, again, not talking.

Hank's belly went back and forth between the nauseous carnival ride and simmering coals the whole morning. He had a hurt in his heart that Miranda hadn't told him what he already knew. She was pregnant. The dark cloud in his chest grew bigger and bigger the longer they went without sharing this wonderful news. He could tell she wasn't happy about it. Otherwise, she'd come to him with the news. When they'd gotten married in the spring, he'd hoped she could tell him anything. But he knew he was a hypocrite since he wasn't being straight with her either.

Miranda had an ache in the back of her throat, and her chest felt weighted when she thought about finishing the conversation with Hank they'd started. She couldn't imagine a positive outcome, and scenarios of escaping the talk they needed to have floated across her mind. A call from her mom needing her, someone bringing a wounded dog to her clinic, or she could fake a sprained ankle. She knew he needed to know about her pregnancy. Tanya had been right. Hank was the father, and he should know. She felt like she was holding her breath, gulping air to stay quiet.

They approached Penny's stall. She had become a favorite for anyone who took the time to get to know her. Miranda fell in love with her instantly. Penny was gentle, nuzzling barn cats when they approached her and nickering when people either pat her or called out her name. She had a calm nature, and the other horses gravitated to her in the pasture.

But today, Penny seemed restless. She pawed at the cement floor with her hoof, and her back legs danced back and forth in the stall as her weight shifted. Her tail swished, and she looked at her abdomen.

Hank stroked her withers. "What's wrong, Penny?"

Miranda's pulse quickened, and the thoughts she had earlier took up space in the back of her mind, packed away. Miranda examined Penny with her eyes, observing the mare's muscle tremors. She stroked her back, and her hand was wet with sweat. "I wonder if she's in labor?"

Penny bent her front legs, and her hind quarters leaned to one side as they flopped onto the straw on the stall floor. She groaned as she lay on her side and rocked, and within a few moments, two tiny hooves appeared outside of the birth canal. Within minutes, a tiny head followed and then the rest of the foal slid out onto the floor quickly.

"Well, that was fast," Miranda gasped.

Hank stood beside Miranda and put his arm around her. His eyes filled. "That never gets old, seeing a foal being born."

A couple other horses in the barn whinnied as if to welcome the new member to their equine family.

Hank glanced at Miranda as she pressed a hand to her chest. Her face looked like it was glowing with a light of pure wonderment. "Remember when we helped the neighbor's mare?" he asked.

Miranda continued to watch the mare and foal, tilting her head to the side.

It had been over a year ago when the Brown's horse was in distress. Doc was out of town, and Miranda didn't even have her vet's license then. Hank thought it was a turning point that evening and bonded them to more than just farm help and farm owner. The seeds of their feelings for each other came out of dormancy and began to germinate and grow.

Miranda rested her head on Hank's shoulder. "That was something, wasn't it? The way we worked so well together."

He felt the featheriness of her hair on his chin and breathed in the familiar rainwater scent, feeling like he'd arrived home.

She said softly, barely audible, "I knew at that moment that I loved you. I tried to convince myself that Dylan was the man for me." She turned to look at him, her voice thick with emotion. "But deep down, I knew it was you."

He took her hand and squeezed it. His chest felt like it might explode with emotion as all the love and care for

Miranda surfaced, and the anger, hurt, and distrust from the past few days disintegrated into the atmosphere.

Miranda pointed with slender fingers. "Look at Penny cleaning off her baby and nuzzling up to her. You can tell she's done this many times before." Turning to face Hank, she said, "There's something I need to tell you."

Every hair on his body stood at attention, every synapse in his brain wide open, waiting to hear the message Miranda was about to give him. He knew what she was about to tell him would change their world forever. He held her gaze for a moment as he held both her hands. "Tell me."

"I'm pregnant."

His breath caught, and he froze. Even though he knew this was what he had waited to hear from her, his mouth went bone dry. He couldn't connect the words in his brain that he wanted to say to the words he had just heard. His eyebrows scrunched in worry. Fear jammed in his throat, leaving him speechless. What did she feel about this? Did she want to have a baby? It wasn't up to him. It was her body. His voice croaked out the question that held him hostage. "How do you feel about that?"

Miranda motioned to the horses on the stall floor. The mare nuzzled and licked her new baby. The foal whinnied a tiny soft tune as he looked for his mother's milk. "Seeing them here now made me realize how beautiful new life is. I was terrified when I first found out. But right here in this moment …" She put her hand on her belly. "I feel so much love for our baby."

The sound of her voice seeped through his veins like the healing balm he'd wanted and needed. He let out a sigh from the breath he'd been holding the past couple of weeks. Tears welled up behind his eyelids. Even though he'd known about their baby, he hadn't known how Miranda felt. Until now.

She winced. "How do you feel about it?"

He wrapped his arms around her. "I am over the moon." He then picked her up and twirled her around in the air. When he put her down, his face beamed.

"I have known for a while," Miranda said. "I'm sorry I didn't tell you sooner. I was so scared when I found out. It rocked my world. I see now that it was selfish of me not to involve you in my news."

"I've known about it too."

Her breath hitched. "How?"

"Susan from the doctor's office told me in the milk aisle at the store."

Miranda opened her mouth and kept it open, and then said, "She's not supposed to tell you that. That's private information."

"She thought I knew."

"I'm sorry. I should have told you. It was wrong of me." Miranda took his hands in hers. "Will you forgive me, babe?"

"Of course, I will." Hank cupped her face. "I understand now that you were scared and needed to know how you felt first." He hugged her. "I'm glad that you're happy about being pregnant now." He lifted her chin. "You are happy, right?"

She radiated joy. "I'm over the moon."

They held each other as they watched the momma and baby bonding. The foal wiggled his way up to standing on wobbly legs. He partially fell and then stood again. The mare nickered as she looked at her baby. She stood and then the foal wobbled his way over to nurse on his momma.

Miranda whispered between tears. "What a beautiful picture they make." She snuggled up to Hank and rested her head on his shoulder. "I can't wait to meet our little one."

"We're so blessed. We've got a lot to look forward to."

Her lips ignited into a smile. "The dream of having a family is a dream I never knew I wanted, but it's the best dream I could ever hope for."

CHAPTER 34

That evening, Richard drove his Cadillac east on I-80, the freeway headed for Chicago. Only three hours apart, the cities were extremely different.

Dewitt was all country: farmhouses, barns, and pastures scattered between fields of corn and soybeans, generations of families working hard in the soil to provide food for others. The sounds of cattle braying, chickens cackling, and the hum of tractors planting or gathering crops. The smells of raw earth and the welcoming aroma of home-cooked meals gave this small city its essence.

Chicago was mostly urban, a big city full of energy and culture: aromas of pizza, baked bread, grilled meats, and Mexican, Chinese, and Greek spices, to name a few, mixed with smells of car exhaust and water from Lake Michigan. The sight of skyscrapers, museums, and crowded sidewalks met with sounds of honking cars, brakes squealing, and the whoosh of city buses passing, contrasting with the calmer atmosphere of Dewitt.

When they finally arrived, Richard pulled into the valet line in front of La Vie, the finest French restaurant in Chicago. Gardens of red roses lined each side of the front entrance at the elegant restaurant. Lanterns lit up large picture windows and the sidewalk leading to the door.

Justine's stomach fluttered. "Why aren't we going to the seafood place by the theatre?"

Richard shrugged and then his face lit up. "I thought we might enjoy this place more." He stepped out of the car and gave his keys to the valet. Scooting to Justine's side of the car, he offered his hand. "This way, my dear."

Justine tucked her black, beaded clutch under her arm and then, with her other arm, reached out, took his hand, and got out of the car. Questions swirled. Richard didn't usually surprise her with a change of plans. She was puzzled he hadn't told her of this restaurant on their way.

Inside, Justine felt like she'd stepped into the city of Paris. The low hum of people conversing at tables and the air rich with the scents of garlic and butter flowed through the restaurant. Antique and vintage art, such as Claude Monet and Paul Cezanne paintings, adorned the walls. Baskets of croissants and whipped butter occupied the center of white linen tablecloths. Several waiters milled about carrying trays of Bouillabaisse, boeuf bourguignon, and first-course salads and soups.

The maître d', dressed in a black tux, recognized Richard and said, "This way, Mr. Baker."

Justine was glad she'd worn her black evening dress. This was an upscale restaurant, and most everyone wore semi-formal attire. At their table, the maître d' pulled out a chair for Justine. She thanked him and sat. After Richard and Justine ordered, they relaxed at the table and made small talk about the lack of rain and the traffic congestion on the freeway to Chicago.

When Stanley was alive, they always had something to talk about when they shared meals. Even if they talked about the weather, it meant something because it was an important topic for farmers. Their livelihood depended on good meteorological conditions.

Conversation was more formal with Richard. Justine hoped in time she'd quit comparing the two men. But for now, she'd appreciate their time together and enjoy the fancy French meal.

A few minutes later, the waiter served them escargot and filled their wine glasses. For the next course, they were served French onion soup and warm French bread. After that, boeuf bourguignon. Each bite of sweet, salty, and savory food created a choreography of flavors on Justine's tongue.

When it came time for dessert, Justine knew something was up with Richard when he whispered in the waiter's ear.

Richard fidgeted with the cloth napkin and cleared his throat a few times. Several minutes later, the waiter set crème brulee in front of Justine and then Richard.

Richard studied Justine as she took her first bite. She did a double take at him. "Why are you watching me eat? And why aren't you eating *your* dessert?"

His eyes sparkled. "I just like watching the most beautiful woman in the restaurant eat her crème brulee."

She took another spoonful and bit on something hard, hurting her tooth. "Ow!" She plucked the object from her mouth and looked at her hand. "*Oh.*" Her eyes bulged. In her hand was a gorgeous two-carat diamond, bigger than she'd ever seen. It sparkled in the light reflecting off the candle on their table.

Just then, Richard stood from the table and glanced around the room, clearing his throat. He lowered onto one knee.

Her eyes bounced back and forth between him and the diamond, knowing what was about to happen. Her torso quivered with anticipation, and her brain buzzed with excitement. Both feelings collided in her heartbeat as it tripled in speed.

The low hum of conversations at the tables surrounding them suddenly hushed. All eyes were on them.

"Justine Graaf. Will you …" His voice caught in mid-sentence.

For such a polished man, Justine had never seen Richard so undone. His leg trembled slightly as he tried to keep kneeling steadily. His eyes filled. Her love for Richard was different than her love for Stanley. Stanley was her first love. That's always different than the next love. If you are lucky enough to have a next love after your husband dies. She was lucky to have Richard in her life.

He brushed away his tears. "Will you do me the honor and marry me?"

Justine laid her hand on her chest. For a few moments, she couldn't speak. The air was filled with scents of warm buttered bread, grapes from the wine, herbs de Provence, and roasted chicken. Adrenaline surged through her veins as she froze. It felt like everyone in the restaurant was waiting for her. Waiting for her to decide what the next step would be for her life. And for Richard's life. And to the conclusion of the story in front of them.

"Justine?" Richard continued to lean on one knee as he waited for her answer.

Thoughts rolled through her mind as she pondered her answer. She was lucky, but this would change her whole future. She missed Stanley terribly, but he wouldn't want her to be alone for the rest of her life. She was only fifty-four. Since Richard came into her life, she wasn't lonely. He wasn't Stanley for sure, but Richard was nice to her and treated her like a queen. But did she love him in the way a wife should love her husband? She loved him, but was it enough?

Tears sprouted. It was time to make that move into the next chapter in her life. She squeezed her eyes shut. And then opened them again. Her gaze stuck on Richard. "Yes. Yes, I will marry you."

He reached for her, and they kissed. People nearby cheered and yelled. And then, in an instant, the diners resumed eating at their tables.

Richard perched on the edge of his seat. "Try on your ring."

Justine's cheeks burned hot as she slipped the giant rock on her finger. "It fits perfectly. How did you …?"

"I took one of your rings to the jeweler. He got the size, and then the same day, I slipped the ring back into your box."

"Clever man." Justine spread her fingers and looked at the ring on her hand. It was beautiful and much larger than her first engagement ring. In fact, it was ten times bigger. When she married thirty years ago, that was all Stanley could afford, and it was fine for her then. In fact, this ring was a little too flashy. But it was beautiful. She hadn't known she could like extravagant jewelry like this. And the finer things in life, like fancy restaurants and nice cars. Richard spoiled her for sure, bought her clothing and jewelry and had a beautiful house in the suburbs where they often stayed. It was five times bigger than her farmhouse. She just needed to appreciate the finer things in life. She could do that. She deserved to be happy. Justine's brain flooded with memories from the past and new memories she'd created with Richard, and her heart swelled with gratitude for her full life.

They spent the night in Chicago at Richard's house, the five-bedroom, four-bath white colonial with black shutters. He had a three-car garage and a gardener who kept the lawn nicely manicured. He had a maid who cleaned his house weekly. There was a pool in the backyard and someone who maintained it. When they visited his house, it felt like a fairy tale.

The next morning, Richard brought her breakfast in bed. There were muffins from the local bakery and steaming coffee in a silver coffee pot on a teak tray. Beside the coffee posed a pitcher of cream and tiny sugar cubes in silver serving dishes.

"Morning, wife-to-be," Richard said as he placed the tray on the California king.

Justine scooted upright and leaned against the giant pillows on the bed. Richard wore a crisp white shirt, tie, and slacks. He set the tray on the bed. Yep. A fairy tale. She'd never had anyone ever bring her breakfast in bed. Making sure everyone she loved was fed had always been her turf, her way of showing she cared. But to have Richard wait on her was like she was a princess or maybe a queen. Leaning back and stretching her arms out wide, Justine felt light and airy. A slow smile spread over her face. "I could get used to this." She started humming as she poured coffee into the flowery teacup on the tray.

Richard kissed her cheek. "Enjoy. I'm going to make a few calls in my study." He handed her the remote. "Watch the morning news if you'd like." Before he left the room, Richard said, "Why don't you take a cab to Oak Street near Michigan Avenue and go shopping at Chanel? I have an account there."

She ran a hand through her hair, primping the back of her blond bob.

He smiled. "I'll call them and tell them you're coming." He blew her a kiss. "Buy whatever you want. My treat."

She watched as Richard left the room. How different her life had become in the last couple years. When Stanley died, she thought she'd be living alone and on the family farm the rest of her life. She was starting to get used to working outside their home, teaching her kindergarteners and tending to the garden and animals on the farm, yet now, with Richard …

Who knew what the next couple years would bring?

CHAPTER 35

Later that morning, after Justine showered, she sorted through her overnight bag. She pulled out everything and laid it on the bed to view before deciding what to wear. With hands on her hips, she tilted her head to the side, looking at her clothes. The high-waisted blue jeans and printed blouses looked too dowdy compared to what she'd worn last night. She looked around the bedroom. The fancy breakfast tray she'd enjoyed earlier before her shower still sat on the king-sized bed. She picked up the flowery teacup and ran her fingers over the smooth curves of its shape, studying the forget-me-not design. Back home, she drank from chip-proof white Corelle cups.

As she looked at the dainty cup and held it in her hand, Justine thought about one wrong move in the kitchen: if she bumped it on the farmhouse sink or a plate accidentally, this formal dishware would break in half. But what woman wouldn't want the finest and prettiest in her kitchen? It was all so new to her. She'd been comfortable for all these years in her home and loved cooking and baking and never thought twice about the dishes and cookware she had to work with.

Justine gently placed the teacup on the teak tray, and as it settled in a saucer, a flash of light sparkled on the outside of the silver coffee pot. She was startled. Spreading the fingers on her left hand, she held it in the air and stared. A jolt of adrenaline shot from her feet all the way to the top of her head. What would Miranda say? She had been in such a daze and dream of getting engaged that she hadn't thought about how her daughter would feel.

She had to tell her but …

"Aaagh!" Justine said aloud. Miranda was not going to be happy. Maybe they could just elope and not tell her daughter or anyone else. They could go back and forth between Chicago and Dewitt, Iowa. Carry on with life as it had been the last few months. No one would be the wiser. Richard would agree to that idea, right? Yeah, that wouldn't work.

Justine's eyes followed the light in her diamond as her hand waltzed in the air. It *was* a gorgeous ring. Richard did well selecting it. She was lucky to have him in her life. Her life would change, and Miranda would just have to get used to it.

Justine removed her makeup bag from her suitcase and scurried into the bathroom. She plucked out the Covergirl makeup and started spreading it on her face, getting ready for the day. She would take Richard's advice and go shopping for new clothes.

CHAPTER 36

Justine and Richard spent another night in Chicago, and the next day, in the late afternoon, they drove back to the farm in Dewitt. Along their journey they talked about how they would announce their engagement.

Justine said, "We could have dinner at my house tomorrow and invite Miranda and Hank, announcing it then." Her eyes lowered to gaze at the new diamond on her hand, shifting the ring in the sunlight that shone through the passenger window.

Richard added, "Let's have a barbecue and invite a bunch of people."

"I want to tell Miranda first." Justine glanced at him. "Plus, it's November. It's not exactly barbecue weather."

"We could have it in the barn. Or an open house in Chicago at my house." He reached for her hand, and the flicker of a smile passed his lips. "Soon to be our place."

While Richard said *our* place and talked about their future life together, it was as if a bucket full of thoughts were poured into Justine's head and swirled about in her brain like sediment in a pond, flowing slowly through her skull and eventually landing at the bottom. Did he think she wanted to give up her house and live in Chicago? They hadn't talked about where they would live when they got married.

She rubbed her forehead.

Richard glanced at her, his eyes doing a double take. "What's wrong, Justine? You feel alright?"

A throbbing sensation had started at the base of her neck and shot from the back of her head all the way over her skull, landing right between her eyes. "Just getting a headache is all." She pawed through her purse. "I think I have an aspirin in here somewhere."

He pointed to the glove compartment. "There should be one in the first aid kit."

She plucked a small bottle of Bayer out of her purse. "Found it." She plopped an aspirin in her mouth and swallowed it down with a sip from a bottle of Coke. Justine smoothed the front of the navy cashmere pea coat she'd bought that weekend. They rode for a few more miles in silence.

As they pulled into the long driveway leading up to Justine's house, she saw Miranda and Hank heading toward them at a trot. Their faces beamed.

Richard stopped the car in front of the garage and turned off the ignition. "Feeling better?"

Justine glanced at him. "Mm-hmm. I'll be fine." She turned her focus back to Miranda. "They look happy. I wonder what's going on?" As she opened the car door and got out, Miranda grabbed her in a hug.

Justine hugged her daughter and then leaned backwards, still holding on to Miranda's arms, studying her. "It's nice to see you too."

Richard came from around the driver's side of the car. "Hello Miranda," he said, with a salesman's grin. He nodded. "Hank."

Miranda jumped up and down a couple inches off the ground and her whole body seemed to wiggle. "We've …" She gave a quick look toward Hank. "Got something to tell you."

Richard began taking the bags out of the Cadillac's trunk. As he set both suitcases on the ground, Miranda said, "Mom."

A sparkling brilliance swirled around her. She glowed. "I'm pregnant."

Justine let out a whoop, then grabbed Miranda close to her chest.

Miranda chirped. "I thought you'd be happy."

Richard extended his arm toward Hank. "Congratulations, Dad." They shook hands.

When Richard leaned in to give Miranda a hug, Justine slipped the engagement ring off her finger and tucked it into the pocket of her coat. Tears dotted the corners of her eyes. "Come inside and chat a while."

"We'd like to, Mom, but we both have lots to do. I couldn't wait to tell you the news."

Justine wiped her eyes. "How're you feeling?"

"I had it pretty bad with morning sickness earlier. I thought it was food poisoning until I found out."

After more congratulations and hugs, Hank and Miranda turned and went toward the barn to continue their work for the day.

Justine watched them leave. She sing-songed, "I'm going to be a grandma." Her thoughts jumped to missing Stanley and wishing he could be there to enjoy his first grandchild.

"They haven't been married a year, have they? Seems a little rushed." Richard carried the suitcases up to the house and went inside, leaving Justine standing in thought.

Miranda was pregnant. Her daughter was going to have a baby. Justine felt like doing a backflip. She'd seen Tanya do one many times on their lawn. In fact, several backflips in a row. This news was thrilling. She was going to be a grandma. She couldn't wait to meet this new baby girl or boy. Pictures of rocking a newborn and reading to a toddler and then a little four-year-old helping Justine plant a garden danced in her mind.

At the same time, in addition to the handsprings in her chest, she suddenly felt the pit in her stomach aching for Stanley.

She wished he were there sharing this milestone in Miranda's life. He would have loved to be a grandpa, grandchild riding on the tractor or helping him feed the animals.

Justine inhaled deeply, breathing in fresh country air, and shoved her hands in her pockets. She gasped. She felt a sharp pain. The prongs on the large rock of the engagement ring she'd shoved inside her pocket earlier scraped the back of her pinky finger. She'd forgotten all about it. She rushed toward the house and went inside.

Richard was in the kitchen. He had brewed coffee and was pouring cream in a mug. He looked up, his face sour and his voice prickly. "You want some coffee?"

Justine took one look at Richard's negative attitude and crossed her arms in a protective stance. Her facial muscles tightened, causing discomfort. She wasn't going to let his bad mood spoil Miranda's good news. Why couldn't he be happy for her? A twinge of anger laced her voice. "Thank you, Richard. Coffee would be lovely." She took off her coat and looped the collar around a hook in the entryway. With slight sarcasm, she said, "Could you please put cream and sugar in mine? I'm going to the bathroom to freshen up after our trip from Chicago." She bolted from the room.

A few minutes later, she'd changed from the new Chanel sweater she'd bought in Chicago the day prior into a cotton sweatshirt with pheasants roosting in a cornfield on the front. "There. That's more comfortable." She sat at the kitchen table, picked up the mug, and took a sip. Her gaze went to the window and out into the backyard, barren cornfields in sight.

He sat across from her and glared.

She glanced back at him. "What's wrong?"

He cocked his head and sighed. "You didn't mention our engagement." He nudged the sugar bowl a few inches and then folded his hands in front of him. "You totally disregarded me and *my* feelings. I'm hurt that you forgot about us." His lips went in a straight line.

Justine's heart sank. She had omitted telling Miranda about their news. "I'm sorry, honey." She put her hand on top of his.

He quickly jerked it away from her gesture. "How could you forget?" He went over to the coffee pot, filled his mug, and leaned against the counter.

"I didn't want to steal Miranda and Hank's thunder. This is big news for them." Her hand pressed on her chest. "For me too."

"Don't you think getting engaged is big news too?"

"Of course, it is."

He sighted her bare hand. A crimson curtain veiled his face. "*Where* is your diamond ring?"

Justine's face drained. "I took it off. Like I said, I didn't want to take away their thunder."

"Are you even going to tell them?"

She rose to her feet. "Of course, I will. I'll tell Miranda when the time is right." She went over to Richard, put her hands around his waist, and kissed him on the cheek. "As soon as their news has had time to sink in."

He didn't return the kiss and jammed his hands in his front pockets. "I have to think about all of this. I don't think you're taking my proposal seriously. You seemed so happy when we were in Chicago. Coming back here has changed your mind."

"This has nothing to do with coming back to my house."

The lines between his brow came together as if forming a net around his thoughts. "I can't deal with this right now." Richard stepped around her and went into the other room.

Justine pressed her fingers to her mouth. When he reappeared in the kitchen, he had his suitcase in hand.

"You're *leaving*?" Her eyes followed him as he carried his large black suitcase to the door.

At the door, Richard turned his head. "I'm going home. I'll call you later. Think about what you want, Justine." He headed outside, and the door slammed behind him.

Justine went to the window and watched him throw the suitcase in the trunk, get into his Cadillac, and speed down the driveway, dust clouds and pebbles flying behind him.

Justine crept to a chair in the kitchen and sat, dragging her fingers down the front of her neck, taking a deep breath as she put her head back, dazed by what Richard had just done. In all her marriage to Stanley, he'd never been so dramatic about anything. He had been cool-headed. They rarely fought. They'd had serious discussions, for sure, but never once walked out on the other. They always talked things through and reached the other side of the disagreement, coming to a solution that they both liked. They always worked together.

Justine felt more alone than ever. Maybe Richard was right. She had to think about what she wanted. Did she want to get married? Did she want someone in her life who would react with such selfishness?

She chewed on the side of her cheek while tapping her fingers on the table, staring out the kitchen window. Maybe *she* was selfish, putting her daughter's happiness in front of Richard's and pushing the announcement of their engagement to a rear seat. Was it really because she thought of Miranda and didn't want to water down their pregnancy news? Or was it really because she hadn't wanted to tell Miranda, knowing her daughter would react to the news and her reaction would not be happy? Maybe Justine was chicken.

She and Richard deserved to be happy and celebrate too, right? Her stomach fluttered, and her chest tightened as she sorted through the confusion of the last half hour. She went to the cupboard and gathered flour, baking soda, baking powder, salt, chocolate chips, and a large bowl. Gazing at her pantry, she decided to try something different and added a package of vanilla pudding mix to her bowl. She shrugged. Why not? It couldn't get much worse. Being creative always made her feel better. As she sifted and blended the dry ingredients for cookies, she reflected on the last couple days.

She opened the fridge and picked out a couple eggs and some butter. She measured and plopped the wet ingredients into the mixing bowl and blended them on low speed. Gradually, she added the dry ingredients and pondered what she wanted in her life. Did she want to be married to Richard? Was he the right man for her? Did she love him? All these questions and feelings trampled over the beautiful weekend in Chicago and trudged through the terrain of her future as she tried to sort it all out. What would she do? The pushing and pulling of the thoughts in her brain made her stomach churn. She decided to go to bed early, and when she woke, she hoped she'd know what to do. Justine covered the cookie dough with Saran Wrap and placed it on a shelf in the fridge. She plodded upstairs to her bedroom.

CHAPTER 37

The next morning, Justine crawled out of bed from a restless night of tossing and turning. She peeked outside and clouds hovered in the sky. Richard had not called her yet like he said he would. Her stomach started churning again. Was he done with her? Would he break off their engagement?

The special moments she and Richard had shared over the last few months came to the forefront of her mind. Richard brought her flowers and jewelry. He lavished her with expensive clothing and took her out to nice restaurants and the theater. He treated her like a queen. They'd had a lot of fun together. She had been happier in the last few months since Stanley died. It had been a gut-wrenching couple of years full of grief and loneliness. Richard had been a beacon of light, lifting her from the depths of grief. Justine deserved to be happy. She pulled back her shoulders, lifted her head, and smoothed her hair.

Justine would go see her daughter; that's what she'd do. If Justine wanted to make things right with Richard and show him that their engagement was important, she'd go tell Miranda. Right then. Well, as soon as she finished what she'd started the previous night.

The tantalizing aroma of cookies baking in the oven wafted throughout Justine's house. Usually, she'd wait impatiently for them to be done, eager to take that first bite, the chocolate chips melting in her mouth. But when she removed the first batch from the oven, she scraped them off the cookie sheet with a spatula and placed them on the cooling rack, not even tempted to take a tiny taste. Her stomach had clenched into a ball, and the thought of eating anything made her queasy.

Once the cookies had cooled off slightly, Justine placed them in Tupperware, closing the lid with a pop. She grabbed her jacket and tucked the cookies under her arm as she put on her coat and went outside. It was chilly, and she put one of her hands in her pocket and brushed against the diamond ring at the bottom. Should she just wear the ring and let Miranda notice it? That would be the easy way out. She kept the ring tucked away in her pocket. Justine continued up the trail toward Miranda's office.

When she arrived, Justine knocked on the clinic door.

She heard Miranda inside. "Come in."

Miranda glanced up while she was examining a tabby Maine Coon on her exam table. His feet slid around on the metal as she tried looking in his eyes. "You know you don't have to knock, Mom. You can just come in." She chuckled. "Like it says on the door."

Justine waved her hand through the air. "I know. I just don't want to interrupt anything."

Miranda smiled. "What you got there?"

"Your favorite." She lifted the container a few inches. "I thought since you were eating for two now, you'd enjoy a treat." She moved a couple steps closer to Miranda. "I'm so excited, dear."

Miranda beamed. "I am too." The cat looked like an ice skater trying on his skates for the first time. "You think you could help me by holding this little guy?"

"Little?" She guffawed. "He's huge. I remember that big black cat you had in here a couple months ago. He was big too. Where do you get these big patients of yours?"

"You mean Lantis? He's a Maine Coon just like Leo here."

Justine put the Tupperware on a counter off to the side of the room. She stepped up to the table and took Leo in her arms. "Come here, you sweet beauty." She began stroking his fur, and he purred loudly. "What a sweety."

"They're both owned by Anna Shaw. She and her husband just bought the small farm a few miles down the road. She's raising Maine Coons. She owns four of them, so we may see them all at some point. They're gentle giants, for sure. Leo and Lantis are brothers. Leo has an eye infection, and I'm trying to get some antibiotic drops in his eyes." Miranda shook her head. "He's just not having it." Leo stretched out his long leg and plopped his paw on Miranda's shoulder as if to keep her away.

Justine laughed. "I've never seen a cat do that before."

"He's really expressive. He's been talking to me ever since he came in. He has different meows, and it's as if he's telling me he doesn't want me messing with his eyes every time I try to put some drops in." Miranda smiled. "He's never once tried to bite me or scratch. He just tells me how he feels."

Justine wrapped her arm around Leo's chest with all his legs tucked underneath him. "Try it now, honey."

Miranda quickly squeezed the tiny bottle of antibiotics, and a couple drops fell in each of Leo's eyes. Then she stroked his head. "There you are, big guy. All done. Your eyes should feel better soon." She lifted the cat from Justine's arms. "Thanks, Mom. You were a big help. I'm glad you came in." She put the cat inside a cage and then went to the sink and washed her hands. "Is there something you needed, Mom?"

Justine fingered the diamond inside her coat pocket. "Um … Just that …" She scooped the ring inside her palm. And then let it go. It fell to the bottom of the pocket. "I'm so excited about you having a baby."

Miranda gave her a quizzical look, cocking her head as she dried her hands with a paper towel. "You said that already. Is there something else?"

Justine went to the counter and grabbed the cookies. She opened the lid. "Chocolate chip."

Miranda plucked one from the container and took a bite. "Mmm. These are still warm. The chocolate chips are melty." She chewed and eyed her mom. "So moist. There's something different about these. Mmm. So good." She took another.

"Well, I'll leave you to it." Justine hugged Miranda and turned to leave.

Miranda licked her lips. "Mom? What is it?"

"Nothing really. Another time." Justine left, Miranda staring at her as she went outside. On her walk back to the house, she knew Miranda could tell she had something on her mind. But Justine couldn't go there. She had choked. She couldn't tell her daughter she was engaged to Richard. It just seemed so weird to tell her own daughter that she would marry someone other than her father, Stanley.

What was holding her back? Did she feel disloyal to Stanley? It had been a little over two years since he died. And yet, what was that dull ache in her chest from time to time? And why did her eyes prickle with tears when she smelled dust in the air, reminding her of when Stanley would come inside after working on the farm all day, his shirt sweaty and dirty from hard work? She'd hug him and breathe in his earthiness. There was no timeframe for grief, and she would always love Stanley.

Richard knew what it was like to lose a spouse. He'd lost his wife in a car accident, but it had been longer for him. The only time Justine had met his children, they seemed to be supportive of him, encouraging him to move on with his life.

But Justine had a different relationship with Miranda. They were close and a tight-knit family when Stanley was alive. When she told Miranda that she was engaged, she'd have to tread lightly.

CHAPTER 38

In December, during gymnastics practice, Tanya finished her routine on the balance beam with an aerial cartwheel and roundoff back summersault, landing on the mat below. She wiped her forehead with a towel. She'd worked hard this whole month getting ready for Nationals. She slipped on her warmup jacket and headed for the locker room.

Daniel would be picking her up in an hour for dinner. They had both been busy. He with track practice and her with gymnastics, and they hadn't seen each other at all that week. She was looking forward to their date and reconnecting with him.

It had been a long flight from Iowa back to Colorado after the fight Tanya had with Miranda in October. Daniel was understanding and caring when the plane took off, and Tanya cried much of the trip. He gave her his sweatshirt to wipe her face after the napkins the flight attendant gave them, along with their snacks, became soaked with her tears. He held her hand and rubbed her knee, telling her it would be alright. "Just give it time," he had said. "Things will work out. You'll see." When they landed and drove to their apartment, he drew her a hot bath. He grilled fish and made a large salad for dinner. They watched her favorite program, *Magnum PI*, a show that Daniel didn't like. But he turned through the channels and found Tom Selleck playing a detective in Hawaii, and they snuggled on the couch.

In the locker room, Tanya finished showering. As she blew her hair dry and got ready for the date with Daniel, she thought about the changes in her life. She hadn't talked to Miranda in over a month. The last time they'd gone that long without talking was when Miranda was in Europe. Phone calls were expensive, and she'd missed her best friend when she'd been out of the country.

But this was different. They parted ways in a fight and hadn't resolved things. Tanya didn't know if they could ever pick up the pieces after what they'd said to each other. She didn't know what she'd do if Daniel hadn't stepped in and cared for her, soothing her sadness. Miranda had always been her go-to person, her rock, her bestie forever. Ever since she was a little girl, when things had gone sour with her parents, and Tanya's mom cowered as her dad got controlling and even physically abusive at times, Tanya would run to the Graaf's and find safety and comfort in their home. The Graaf's, her second family, had not only given her reprieve, but they'd also saved her life. Miranda had not only been her bestie but her sister. They had always been so close. They shared everything and told each other their deepest secrets, from the boys they had crushes on to their feelings that came with losses and fears about living their dreams. When gymnastics got too hard and Tanya wanted to quit, like the time she broke her ankle, Miranda had always been there for her, encouraging her to dream.

How could Tanya just write off the past and move forward without Miranda in her corner? Tanya was the one there for Miranda when her dad got sick and died. She was Miranda's cheerleader when she broke up with Dylan and chose Hank as her husband.

But Tanya didn't know if she could forgive the things Miranda had said. It was as if she just put up a wall and wouldn't let Tanya in. She'd never known Miranda to be that way.

Tanya finished blowing her hair into a high bouffant, Farah Fawcett style, and slipped on her tight-fitting acid-washed jeans, white turtleneck, and down jacket with the Danskin logo on the sleeve. Danskin had sponsored her and paid for her living expenses ever since she began training for the Olympics. For a final touch, she dabbed her lips with bright red lipstick and put on big, looped earrings. She grabbed her gym bag, also with a Danskin logo, and her purse, and headed for the door. As she had been the last one in the gym that evening, she flicked off the lights in the locker room and eagerly trotted out to the parking lot to meet Daniel.

Tanya spotted Daniel at the curb, waiting in his red Camero. He smiled and she waved, and then she scurried to his car. She slid the seatbelt over her belly. Daniel's eyes washed over her body, and he took a couple extra minutes to look at her waist.

Tanya ran her hand over her belly. Any extra pounds always showed up in her stomach area first. But she'd been extra careful about what she'd eaten since they arrived in Colorado.

Any misgivings about her weight dissolved when he bent and kissed her. "Hey, beautiful. I've missed you this last week."

She smiled. "Even though we live in the same apartment, it feels like we're roommates."

He drove onto the main road. After a few minutes, Daniel asked, "Ok if we go to that new Chinese restaurant that opened close to our place? We can eat vegetables and low-calorie food rather than our usual Italian place. There's too much bread there." He sighed. "The life of an Olympian. Fat is our enemy."

Golden aspens flashed past the window as they rode in silence. In the distance, clouds hovered above the snowy tips of Pike's Peak. Tanya sensed something going on with Daniel.

He seemed quieter than usual, almost sullen. "How'd practice go this week?"

He grumbled. "Don't want to talk about it."

At a corner table in the back of the restaurant, the lights were low, and dark red adorned the seats, walls, and carpeting. The environment fit her mood. She shook her head slightly as if shaking off the moodiness about Miranda that had surfaced while at the gym. She was on a date now with the man that she loved. Time to put her life in Iowa aside and not let the past pull her down.

She scanned the menu. "Ooh, the deep-fried shrimp and rice looks good."

Daniel fixed his eyes on his menu. "That's too fattening. We came here to eat lean and have vegetables." He glared at Tanya. "You know that."

A bullet went through Tanya's gut, and she stared straight ahead at the menu. What had gotten into Daniel? He had been so sweet and caring when they first got back to training camp.

She put her hand on his. "Is everything alright? You don't seem yourself."

"I've had a bad week at practice. My coach kept hounding me. I can't seem to get the speed I had before our trip to Iowa. I shouldn't have gone."

"We were on break. Our coaches wanted us to let up on training."

"Maybe." Silence enveloped them and hung in the air like a cumulus cloud threatening to disrupt a meet at the track.

"Are you saying you wish you hadn't gone and met my friends?"

He cocked his head and looked at Tanya, his voice hurling cuts through the air. "Look how good that turned out. Your supposed best friend let you down. And it took a month for you to get back into shape."

A flush of heat went through her body, and her face flushed. She couldn't believe he was being so mean. Especially when a few weeks ago, he told her it would be ok. Things would work out. How could he be so insensitive?

The waiter came to the table, interrupting their disagreement. Daniel ordered steamed vegetables and brown rice for them both. The waiter glanced back and forth at them and quickly poured tea into small cups. He left the teapot on the table and scurried away.

Tanya and Daniel drank in silence and watched other people in the restaurant as they came and went.

Soon, their meal arrived. Tanya's appetite had left her, so she picked at the broccoli and pea pods.

"You don't like your dinner?"

"Just not that hungry is all."

"You have to eat something to keep up your strength for practice."

She dropped her fork on her plate and looked at him. "First, you tell me I need to watch my weight, and now you're telling me I need to eat."

"I said we need to eat lean, is all."

"I saw you looking at my body in the car. Eyeing me to see if I'd gained weight since the last time you saw me."

He threw his chin up in defiance. "You know I think you're hot."

Her eyes narrowed. "I'm not imagining it. You're constantly thinking I need to lose weight."

He shook his head. "You don't know what's in my head. You're just being paranoid." He stuffed a forkful of vegetables in his mouth.

"I'm not imagining things. You're always on me about my weight." She threw her napkin on the table. "Gymnasts have muscley bodies. We're not the skinny lean type like runners."

Tanya stood and vaulted toward the door. She was not going to let him get to her. She had felt self-conscious about her weight the entire time they'd been dating. Had she felt this way before? She didn't think so. But it was always on her mind these days, questioning everything that went into her mouth.

Weight was a big thing with all gymnasts; she knew that, but she wasn't going to become anorexic like a few of her teammates. She noticed a couple of the girls vomiting in the stalls of the bathroom at practice after lunch. She knew it was to keep their weight down. But it wasn't healthy. They worked hard eight hours a day. And they had to fuel themselves. Yes, they had to be fit, but this was ridiculous. She'd find a way to get enough to eat and be healthy without gaining weight.

Tanya pushed the door open and stepped onto the sidewalk beside the restaurant. She leaned against the passenger door of Daniel's car.

Tanya's mother came to mind. She cringed, remembering her dad getting on her mom about spending too much money on food. One time, in their country kitchen, her dad yelled about buying Campbell's canned soup instead of a store brand. Her mother was weak and submissive, and Tanya hated her for it. She hated her dad for being the controlling, bossy man that he was and was beginning to see the same thing in her relationship with Daniel. She didn't want to be like her parents. It made her stomach churn.

A couple of ten-year-olds flew past her on their bikes, and as Tanya watched them ride away down the road, she hoped they wouldn't grow up to be like her dad and treat women badly.

Tanya folded her arms and looked upward into the dusky sky. She reflected on the last few months and the troubles that had been in her life since she'd begun dating Daniel. Not only the issues with her weight that she never had before. She had always liked to eat. She loved food. But she never doubted herself before. And now … she did.

But also her struggles with Miranda. They never had fights before. If they disagreed, they always talked it out and got past it. Tanya realized that Daniel had instigated and fed the disagreements they'd had in Iowa. He encouraged Tanya to move forward without resolving things with Miranda. He hadn't liked it when Tanya wanted to spend time with her best friend. She thought he was jealous and possessive of her time, and he hadn't wanted her to spend time with anyone but him.

Just like her dad and mother. Her dad hadn't wanted Tanya's mother to do anything outside the home. He hadn't wanted her to have a job, friends, or talk to her extended family. And Tanya's mother became like a weak animal, caged in their house. That was a big reason Tanya spent so much time at the Graafs. Justine was a strong woman and a good role model for Tanya. She learned how to be an independent woman from her, not her own mother. And she learned how to relate to people in a healthy way from the Graaf family. Justine encouraged her to follow her dream of being a gymnast. Without Justine's mentoring, she never would have gone as far as she did with the gift she was born with. And mostly, she wouldn't have come this far if Miranda hadn't been there for her. Always.

Tanya's back stiffened. Heat radiated from the back of her ears, streaming down her neck and shoulders, across her midline, and into her legs. The rude awakening Tanya felt brought her whole body to attention. A strength she hadn't felt in a long time rose in her belly and core.

Tanya had to make it right with Miranda. She had to go home and call her and do whatever she had to do to resolve their issues and become friends once again. This had gone on too long.

She felt a tap on her shoulder. She turned and Daniel was standing there, concern on his face. "Come back and eat your dinner."

Tanya shook her head. Her voice radiated confidence and power. She growled, "Take me home."

"Don't overreact. This whole conversation is stupid. I think you're beautiful. You know that. I won't say anything about your weight again. I promise. I just want you to win a gold is all." He put his hand on her shoulder, pulling her toward the restaurant.

She shrugged away from him. "You don't get it."

He huffed. "Don't be difficult. Come back inside."

"I want to go back home." She pulled on the door handle. "Could you unlock the door so I can get in?"

Daniel stood with his arms crossed in front of him.

"If you don't drive me home, I'll get a taxi."

His resolve softened. His voice said one thing, but the energy backing it sounded like a little boy. "You're acting like a child." He turned to go back into the restaurant. Over his shoulder he said, "I'll go pay the bill and then drive you home."

CHAPTER 39

Meanwhile, on the farm, Justine carried on after Richard left for Chicago in a huff. After delivering cookies to Miranda in her clinic that Monday morning, Justine stuffed her feelings deep in the cavern of her belly and left for school. She focused her attention on teaching her morning kindergarteners.

After arriving home at noon, her head hung as she pouted, moving about her kitchen like a lost puppy looking for her water dish. She was thirsty for a resolution and wanted so badly for Richard to call her and tell her what he was thinking. Justine hadn't even wanted to putter in her garden, her favorite hobby, which she often did after work. She had resorted to cleaning and sorting through the pantry, throwing out expired spices and baking supplies. A pile of garbage filled her kitchen trash container. She twisted a binder around the opening of the garbage bag and heard the gravel crackle in the driveway. She glanced out the window. It was Richard in his Cadillac.

Her heart froze. What would she say to him? Was he here to take his ring back? He trudged on the path leading to the house. His face looked serious, his expression hard to determine.

She clutched her hand to her throat as Richard approached the door. She opened it before he could knock.

He ran a hand through his short salt and pepper hair. "Ok if I come in?"

"Of course." She stepped aside.

He gave her a brief kiss on the cheek before entering the house.

"Do you want anything to drink?"

He shook his head and then they both sat at the kitchen table.

Richard hung his head. "I think I made a big mistake." The words lingered in the air like confetti falling from a three-story window.

Justine's chest got heavy. Was he breaking up with her?

"I was too quick with my actions. I should have thought before I spoke. And it's not fair to you to give you the wrong impression." He took her hand in his, and sadness hung in his eyes.

He was breaking up with her. She just knew it. How could he reject her after just one fight? Couples fight. It's what they do. It wouldn't be realistic otherwise. And that's how couples work through things.

"What are you saying ..."

He let go of her hand and said, "Let me finish. Let me say what I need to say." His lips dragged over his teeth, and he licked them, trying to moisten his dry mouth. "I've been thinking a lot about us since I went back home to Chicago. Getting engaged and how that all happened so soon. We haven't known each other that long."

Her stomach fell to the floor. She hadn't thought she was this attached to Richard, but she was. The thought of them not getting married made her sad. Really sad. She willed the tears pressuring her eye sockets to dry up.

"Please forgive me for not understanding your desire to keep our engagement quiet right now. I know it can be tricky with Miranda. She just lost her dad a couple years ago. I need to be patient."

Justine studied his eyes. "Does this mean you still want to get married?"

"Of course. Why would you think I didn't want to marry you?"

"The way you said things … I just thought you were breaking up with me."

He came over to her side and knelt on one knee. "Justine. I love you. I want you to be my wife."

She smiled. Then she slapped him playfully on his thigh. "Don't ever do that again. You didn't talk to me for a couple of days. I thought we were done."

"I promise." He kissed her. "I was a jerk."

She nodded, then exhaled as the insides of her gut settled from two days of riding on a speed boat in a lake of waves. "Mothers and daughters can be complicated. You must know I need to think about Miranda too. Not just us."

"I'll do my best." He took both Justine's hands and pulled her upright. "Let's invite Miranda and Hank out to dinner to celebrate the baby."

She hugged him. "That's a great idea." She wrapped her fingers around his shoulders and looked into his eyes. "Thank you, Richard. That is so thoughtful. I'll call Miranda right now and make plans."

After a few minutes, Justine found Richard reading the paper on the couch, and she sat on his lap. "It's settled then. We're having dinner at the new steakhouse in Bettendorf."

That evening, Richard spent the night, and Justine felt like all was right with the world.

CHAPTER 40

The next morning, Justine woke and quietly left her room, letting Richard sleep in. She made coffee and padded out to the back porch with a mug and sat in a chair. Her vision brightened as she scanned the farm and felt a warmth come over her body. She was truly happy. She was going to be a grandma, and she was engaged to a great guy. She took in the panoramic view of the pink, yellow, and orange stripes in the sky. The beautiful colors cast a sprinkle of joy on her lengthy two years of grief and struggle. As a family, they had come a long way.

Suddenly, she realized she hadn't put her engagement ring back on since she'd stuffed it in her pocket that day Miranda had announced her pregnancy. Justine scrambled to the coats in the entryway. She jammed her hand in the pocket of her coat and searched inside. The ring wasn't there! She checked the pocket on the other side of her coat. The ring was gone.

Her heart pounded like a summer storm filling the air with thunder as she checked the floor around her coat and the pockets in other jackets, even though she knew it wouldn't be there either. What would she do? Richard would be upset, mad, hurt; he'd feel like she didn't care about their engagement, especially after the special evening they'd had reconnecting and planning their future. She sighed heavily, sat again on a porch chair, and put her head in her hands. This couldn't be happening. She had to find her ring. *Think*, she told herself. *Think*. Did she put it somewhere else? Maybe in her jewelry box? Or maybe in one of her drawers upstairs in her bedroom? That had to be it. She had just forgotten where she put it for safekeeping. She stared at the horizon as she thought about where her ring could be.

She jumped in her chair when Richard said, "Here you are, darling." And rubbed her shoulders. "Didn't mean to startle you. What are you thinking about? It seemed like you were far away."

Justine forced a smile. "Oh. Nothing. Just daydreaming and looking at the sunrise. Get yourself a cup of coffee and join me."

"Don't mind if I do." He went into the kitchen and came out with a mug, steam swirling above it. He nestled into a chair next to Justine and took her hand. "It is beautiful. I must admit you don't see this in Chicago. The sunrises are blocked by skyscrapers and even smog sometimes."

As he held her left hand, Justine hoped he wouldn't notice the missing ring on her finger.

Richard stayed the rest of the week, letting his team at the bank know where he'd be if they needed his input. He didn't mention the ring.

They enjoyed each other's company, preparing the garden for winter: gathering the last of the squashes and kale, removing fallen leaves and debris, and covering plants with straw mulch. Justine taught Richard about growing flowers and vegetables. He even helped her cook. They made pumpkin soup and baked muffins and bread. Justine kept looking for her two-carat diamond without avail. Richard helped her can tomatoes. Justine admitted that they did things that Stanley wouldn't even participate in, like cooking and canning.

That was a wife's work on a farm. It was just a given and part of being married to a farmer. But since Richard hadn't lived on a farm, he hadn't "learned" the rules. It was a fun week, although Justine kept thinking that Richard would say something about her bare finger.

CHAPTER 41

Later that week, on a Friday evening, Justine, Richard, Miranda, and Hank all headed for dinner in Richard's Cadillac. Miranda sat behind Justine, and Hank sat behind Richard. Miranda eyeballed Richard. It was the first time she'd been able to observe the man who had supposedly stolen Justine's heart. The way his arm stretched out, rubbing Justine's left shoulder as if marking his turf, along with the woody scent of Richard's Aramis, made Miranda feel queasy. She cracked a window.

Hank reached over and held Miranda's hand, giving it a quick squeeze.

Her heart radiated with warmth from the gesture of support her husband had given her. She quirked her lips, blowing Hank a kiss.

Secretly, Miranda wished something would happen to Richard, or he'd do something Justine couldn't accept and they'd break up. Miranda felt a hot buzzing between her eyebrows.

After a twenty-minute ride, they arrived at Steven's Steakhouse in Bettendorf. As soon as Richard parked the car, Miranda flung the door open and hopped out. She breathed in fresh air as Hank scooted around the car and took her hand. Richard and Justine followed close behind as they headed inside the dimly lit room where their reservations awaited.

The aroma of grilled meat flowed through the entryway, and Justine breathed in the succulent smell. She was a country girl through and through and liked a good steak.

Burgandy and gold wallpaper adorned the walls. The hostess took their coats and hung them in a large closet, then led the group through a deafening room of diners talking and laughing. They trailed the hostess until they arrived at an intimate table for four in the corner. Richard had made reservations, and Justine breathed a sigh of relief. Otherwise, they'd have to talk above the noise. The volume lowered to a murmur of conversations at the tables nearby.

Once they were seated, Justine pulled out a card from her handbag. She had a lightness in her chest as she handed it to Miranda. "This is a little something for your baby and his/her future."

Miranda opened the envelope and gasped. A check fell out of the card. "Mom. This is amazing." Miranda showed the gift to Hank. "Thanks, Mom. That's so generous of you."

Richard smiled at Justine. "Your mom is excited about her grandbaby."

"One of the bonds matured that your dad and I had invested in years ago. It was time to cash it in. He would have wanted me to give it to you."

Richard's smile turned into a straight line as he crossed his arms in front of his chest. Justine glanced at him, noticing his reaction. The lightness she'd felt a moment earlier in her chest tightened.

The waiter approached their table, and Justine shoved aside the feeling that she'd done something wrong by bringing up Stanley. This evening was all about Miranda, Hank, and their baby. She'd try to focus on that and have a good time.

They ordered juicy steaks and large baked potatoes. Richard ordered a bottle of expensive champagne to celebrate the new baby, and everyone except for Miranda toasted with a glass of bubbly. Justine glanced around the table at everyone laughing and having a good time. She clasped her hand to her chest, and a smile quirked her lips. Her own baby seemed so happy. Miranda was married to a man she loved, and in a few months, she would have a baby of her own, knowing what it was like to have the incredible experience of raising a child with all the ups and downs. Her life would never be the same again.

When they had finished their meals, Richard stood, went across the room, leaned in toward the waiter, and said something. A few minutes later, the waiter brought over a large cake with white frosting. And another bottle of champagne.

Miranda said, "Wow, Richard, you're really going all out about our new baby."

"It's a night of celebrations." Richard stood again, then bent on one knee in front of Justine.

Miranda looked at her mom and gasped.

Justine put her hands on either side of her face. Her stomach seemed to roll from one side to the other. "Richard? What …?"

He took out a ring box and then opened it.

Justine's jaw hung open. No wonder he hadn't said anything. She felt an angry bubble in her throat. He had deceived her and let her think she had lost the ring all week— she'd been frantic and in a panic. He'd had it the whole time! Not only that, but he was taking away the thunder of Miranda and Hank's news and making it about Richard and Justine.

Richard presented the ring. "Justine, will you marry me and make me a happy man?"

Justine didn't want to embarrass him. But she really wanted to yell at him for what he'd put her through. And she wanted to yell at him for taking the spotlight from what was supposed to be all about Miranda and Hank.

But instead, she fawned a big smile and said, "Yes. Yes. I'll marry you."

He put the ring on her finger and winked at her.

Miranda's face paled. She looked at Hank, and he shrugged. They both got up from their chairs. Miranda hugged Justine and then gave Richard a brief side hug, her arms like sticks.

Miranda croaked, "Congratulations, you two," her words shaky and clipped, and then she sat down.

Justine would have a talk with Miranda later and smooth things over with her.

They ate cake and once again toasted with champagne for the second celebration of the night.

The heavy air in the car loomed like overcast skies on a muggy night in August, choking out oxygen and making it hard to breathe on the drive home from the restaurant. Hank and Miranda hunkered in the back seat, holding hands. Hank glanced at Miranda and her chin was jutted and firm. He couldn't believe Richard was thoughtless enough to propose to Justine in front of Miranda. He'd warned him to be careful a few weeks back on their way to the hospital after Justine fell in the garden. Hank was much younger than Richard but felt all the wiser because he knew that you needed to treat the Graaf women with respect and care. Their love for people they cherished went deep, and he knew better than to cross the strong bond that both women had with Stanley. It would always remain that way. Yep. Richard made a huge error in judgment about how to handle his upcoming marriage with Justine. You cross her daughter, you cross Justine.

Hank sat behind Justine in the car, but he noticed the same firm jaw as her daughter when she fixed her stare out the window. She was not happy. He wouldn't want to be Richard right then. Hank wondered how the ole' guy was going to patch this up with Justine.

They arrived at the farm, and Richard parked the Cadillac. Hank raced to the other side of the car. He opened Miranda's door and offered his hand. She took his hand and got out of the car, looked at her mom, and said, her voice terse, "Congratulations, Mom." She glanced toward Richard. "Richard."

Hank gave Justine a hug. "Thanks for dinner, you guys. Miranda gets tired a lot lately. We're going home." He put his arm around Miranda, and they traipsed toward their house, hunkering against the icy snow that stung their faces.

Once inside the main house, Justine, not saying a word, emptied the dishwasher. The silverware clanged loudly in the drawer as she put the utensils away.

Justine grabbed a glass and started to put it in the cupboard when Richard cupped her hand and held it. "Come here, darling. Sit down a minute before something gets broken."

She glared at him and plopped down at the table, setting the glass down. Hard.

"Why did you do that? You knew I wanted to tell Miranda myself about our engagement. She was shocked when you proposed," Justine snapped. "Again."

The December wind howled outside, and a puff of snow swept by the kitchen window. "Did you really need to do that?" She turned the ring on her finger. "Take all the attention away from them and put the focus on us?" Her eyes widened. "You just don't get it, do you?"

"I get it. I do." He raised his hands. "I keep making a mess of things when it comes to trying to marry you." As he palmed her knee, he said in a weak voice, "What can I do to make it up to you?"

She thrust herself from the table. "You can quit interfering when it comes to Miranda and me." She stomped out of the kitchen and headed upstairs.

Justine heard Richard's footsteps as he followed her upstairs. She didn't look at him but sensed that he stood in the doorway of her bedroom. As she took off her earrings, the silence in the air hung like rain clouds and crept throughout the walls of the room until it found its way outside. The wind whistled, and heavy, wet snow pattered on the bedroom window.

Justine wasn't going to say anything, so it was up to Richard to take their conversation further if he chose.

"Justine?"

She didn't answer and looked upward. Snow came down hard and circled in the gale, making it difficult to see past the white curtain of flakes outside.

"You know I'm an idiot, right?"

She glanced quickly at him. A slight smile spread across her lips. "Go on."

"I know I screwed up. Again. It's hard for me. Hard for me to compete with Stanley. I know if he were alive, I wouldn't have a chance with you. I know that."

Justine gathered the earrings in the palm of her hand.

"It's not a competition." Her eyes darted around the room. "The two of you are just different, that's all."

He tucked his hands in his pockets and looked down. "But he was your first love. It's hard to compete with that."

Her lips pressed together, flattening. She plopped the earrings in her jewelry box, and said, "We were together a long time."

"I was married to my wife a long time, and there is no comparison between my marriage and the marriage you had with Stanley. I can tell by the way you talk about him."

She did not know what to say. Her marriage to Stanley was special. They had been very much in love. She was devastated when he died. Could she love Richard like that? You couldn't compare the two men. They were different individuals and led different lives.

"Do you still want to get married? I keep messing up since I asked you to marry me the first time."

Justine took a few steps toward him and grasped his hand. "Of course, I do." She lifted his chin with her other hand. "We have the future to look forward to, you and me."

He smiled. "I'm sorry about tonight. I'll try to do better."

She raised her hand and looked at her diamond glistening in the overhead light. "It is beautiful. Just don't scare me like you did. I thought I'd lost it."

"I know. Again, I'm sorry." He held her hand and then pulled her to him. They stood for a few moments, hugging, allowing all the emotions of the night to sink into them and melt away.

She pressed her hands to his chest and kissed him softly on the lips. "Let's go to bed."

CHAPTER 42

The next day, Saturday, Justine rose early. It had always been hard for her to sleep in because living on a farm meant there were things to get done. "Early bird gets the worm," Stanley used to say. Besides, Justine liked the feeling of the morning before anyone was awake. The quiet and cool mornings in the summer and the peaceful and cozy warmth in the winter.

Richard sleepily looked at her getting dressed into jeans and a sweatshirt. She noticed he was awake and said, "I'm going out to gather a basket of goodies for Miranda. Try and make things right with her. She'll be up early, tending to the animals in her clinic."

He groggily said, "You want me to help?"

"Thanks. But no. You've done enough helping for a while."

He sat up in bed, a blank look on his face. "It's December. There's still stuff in the garden?"

"There are still potatoes, carrots, and rutabagas. Underneath the ground." She smiled. "I cover the ground with a tarp." She kissed his cheek. "And Brussels sprouts."

Richard pulled the covers over him as he stretched out on the bed. "Have fun, Darling."

Justine dug carrots and potatoes from the garden and put them in a basket. The heavy snow from the previous night made it challenging to get to the vegetables, yet she felt more comfort with all things farm versus her feelings of newness in the fancy Chicago stores. Trailing in her boots through the garden, lifting tarps as she went, seeking produce from the last of the season, she spotted Brussels sprouts clinging to their stalks and plucked them, tossing them onto the mound of fresh produce. She hooked her arm under the handle and carried the bounty of vegetables toward the barn.

The barn door opened, and Ben snuck out. He loped easily to Justine, and she bent over as he licked her hand. "Hi, buddy." She stroked his smooth black and tan head.

Miranda approached. The expression on her face was tight, and her voice flat. "We've been feeding the horses."

Justine stopped petting Ben and straightened. "Miranda. We need to talk about last night."

"Ya think? That was a bombshell Richard dropped on us."

She raised her hand. "I know. I know." She studied Miranda. "Are you at least a little bit happy for us?"

Miranda didn't say anything for a few moments. She stared at her mom, one of her hands fisted on her hip. Finally, she said, "If you're happy, I'm happy."

"You don't seem very happy."

"Mom, you already know what I'm going to say."

Justine felt a heaviness in her limbs and muscles. "No. I don't. Tell me, please. I want to know what you really think."

"Ok." She bent, petting Ben. "But don't get mad at me."

Justine nodded, and her muscles stiffened as she braced herself, waiting for the barrage of negativity. She suddenly felt very tired.

Miranda's face reddened as she rattled off a long list of complaints: "I think you're rushing into marrying someone after Dad. I think you should take more time before even dating someone. Let alone marrying someone you've only known a few months. Who knows what this guy is all about?" A fitful wind swirled icy snow particles across the yard.

"Losing Dad is still fresh in my mind. I would think it would be the same for you." With both fists on her hips, she said, "I think you're making a huge mistake. But it's your life. Just don't expect me to be the doting stepdaughter." She stepped around Justine and headed for her house.

"Miranda." Justine's voice turned harsh. "Wait."

Miranda halted but didn't look back at her mom.

"One. Stanley is on my mind every day. I miss him all the time. Two. I don't expect you to be chummy with Richard. Just respectful and courteous. And three.

I'm surprised you could be that selfish, thinking only of yourself. Because … It is my life we're talking about, here. Not yours." She set the basket of produce on the ground and pivoted, eager to crawl back into bed and feel the warmth of Richard's body, sharing the bed with someone who cared about her after two years of sleeping alone.

Miranda scrambled and went inside, slamming the door. She plopped on the couch, covered her face with her hands, and rested her elbows on her knees. Miranda needed someone to talk to about this. She needed her best friend. But they had parted ways. And now she was at odds with her mom. She loved talking to Hank. He was such a good listener. And he had good advice. But he wasn't a girl. She needed to talk to a girl. How had she gotten into arguments with the two women closest to her at the same time?

It must be her. What was she not seeing? Was she that hard to get along with? Maybe this was how it was when you were pregnant. She knew her hormones were sailing all over the place and affecting her moods. Maybe she wasn't willing to see other's points of view as much as she should. She needed to listen more.

Miranda dialed Tanya's number. Three rings and Tanya picked up. Miranda couldn't believe it. She thought for sure Tanya would be at practice. She didn't say anything at first.

"Hello … hello. Who's there?"

A wave of fear careened throughout Miranda's body. What if Tanya didn't want to talk to her? What if she wouldn't forgive her? She took a deep breath and went for it. She needed her best friend.

In a soft, barely audible voice, she said, "Tonny?"

Silence on the other end. Then she heard a sniffle.

"Tonny? Are you there?"

"Ran?" In a nasal voice, she said, "I'm so glad you called. I've missed you."

Miranda pressed a hand to her heart. "I've missed you more. I'm such a jerk. Will you forgive the things I said?"

"I'm a bigger jerk. Will you forgive *me*?"

"Do you have a cold? Your nose is stuffy."

"Ya goof. I'm crying happy tears."

Miranda swiped tears from her face. "Me too."

"You called just at the right time."

"What's wrong?"

"Daniel and I had a big fight."

"My mom and I had a fight too. I needed my besty. I've missed talking to you."

They spent the next hour catching each other up on what had been happening in their lives. Miranda felt her shoulders lower and her breath deepen as the anxiety she'd felt the last month melted from her body. She stretched out on the couch and crossed her ankles. She tucked the phone under her chin as she rubbed Ben's ears.

Finally, Tanya said, "I'd better get to practice. You know I'm here for you."

Hearing Tanya's words felt like a warm blanket wrapped around her shoulders.

"I know it's hard seeing your mom with someone else. She loved your dad a lot. Give it time, Ran. You two will make up."

"And I know it's not fair for her to be alone the rest of her life. It's just weird."

"It's got to be."

"Tonny, I support your decision whatever you want to do with Daniel. Whether you want to stay or leave, I'm there for you."

"Thanks, Ran. I love you."

"Love you too."

After they hung up, Miranda sat for a minute, staring at the living room wall. She would forgive Justine for getting engaged. She might not like the idea of her mom living with someone other than Stanley, but she would let go of her resentment. She would wish Justine the best for her future with Richard.

CHAPTER 44

The hardships of life on a farm in winter passed, and spring finally arrived. The crocuses and daffodils showed their brilliance in the farm's yard. Snow melted from the ground. One bright Saturday morning, Justine was tilling the earth in her garden, getting ready to plant seeds for vegetables and flowers. In her mind, she mulled over busy wedding plans.

Miranda and she were courteous to one another. But there was a strain in their relationship that lingered since their argument over Justine's engagement with Richard a few months back. She figured, in time, Miranda would get used to the idea of Justine living with someone other than Stanley. Justine wasn't going to let her daughter's feelings dictate how she lived her own life.

When Justine first found out about Miranda's pregnancy, she was over the moon with thoughts of being a grandma. Her life was full. But something was missing. Deep in her heart, Justine wanted to be a part of Miranda's life, sharing in Miranda's first pregnancy, giving her daughter advice, and deepening their bond as mother and daughter. Instead, their relationship had drifted apart. What could have been a wonderful, joyous time for all of them had grown into a time of separation for the two families.

Hank and Miranda had their family, and Justine had Richard. Justine missed checking in with Miranda daily to see how she was feeling. And they only lived across the yard from each other. She missed shopping together for the baby and telling Miranda stories about when she was pregnant with her. Justine wished she could share her wisdom with her daughter about becoming a mother. An emotional numbness filled the void in her life every day.

As Justine loosened the hard soil with a hoe, she felt a gray murkiness settle in her chest as she realized their tiff had gotten in the way of sharing a special time they could never get back. Tears speckled her cheeks as she continued tearing the earth apart. The thought of where she went wrong hammered inside Justine's skull.

CHAPTER 45

Hank and Miranda were decorating the extra bedroom in their house as a nursery. Tanya and Daniel had gone back to Colorado for their training regime for the Olympics. Nash went back to Wyoming with the horses he'd bought. Everything was going smoothly for Miranda and her practice on the farm as far as Justine knew. They didn't talk much anymore, but as far as she could tell, Miranda had gained a few more animals as her patients and was happy about her future as a mother. She was about seven months along in her pregnancy, and she no longer had the morning sickness or tiredness that she felt in the first two trimesters and felt pretty good. Miranda remembered hearing Justine talk to a pregnant friend at church a couple of years ago about how the third trimester was the best.

She wished she could talk to Justine more. But whenever they spoke, words came out carefully, like handling a souffle fresh out of the oven, not wanting to disturb the hot air trapped inside so it would not come crashing down.

CHAPTER 46

One cold, blustery morning at the end of April, Miranda went out to feed the horses and tend to Penny's new foal, Dusty. Dusty stayed close to his momma. But when Miranda came to the edge of the pasture, he whinnied and trotted to her and the gate. Miranda rubbed the little horse's face. "You are such a sweety, yes you are. Look how beautiful you're becoming."

Penny sauntered over to her baby, and Miranda held out her hand with a chunk of apple. Penny gathered the apple with her lips and munched on the piece of fruit.

Miranda opened the gate, slipped a halter on Penny, and latched a lead rope onto the tie ring. She led Penny toward the barn, and the foal trotted close beside his mother. They glided along the icy ground, passing dried weeds and tall grass at the edge of the fence. Penny hit a batch of ice from the rainy day before. She slid, her hooves grasping for solid ground and her large belly bumping Miranda. Miranda tried to grab the nearby fence but missed and tumbled to the ground. Penny fell on top of her, squashing Miranda's belly. She shoved against the big horse as they both struggled to stand. Once they did, Miranda felt a pain in her abdomen. She hurried the horses into the barn, latching the door to the stall behind them. Once they were secured, she immediately sat on the cement outside the stall. She wrapped her arms around her torso and breathed deeply, trying to ease the cramping in her belly.

Even though she had years of training to be a doctor, her mind went blank, and panic took over, thinking that the baby had been hurt by the fall. A single tear streamed down her face as she prayed. "Please, let my baby be ok. Please let him or her be ok. Please." A nearby calico barn cat trotted up and rubbed his head against Miranda's shins. She reached out and petted his back and took deep, slow breaths.

She tried to get to her feet to get to the phone on the wall several feet away, but the cramping got worse. She sat back down, and the cat curled in her lap and purred. It was as if he knew something was wrong. Miranda stroked his fur and decided to stay anchored to the ground, hoping someone would find her there and help. After a few minutes, the cramping stopped. She gently pushed the cat off her lap and tried to stand, and once again, the cramping started. She sat back down, and the cat came up to her again, curled in her lap, and purred. Miranda looked at the brown and gray blotches on his white fur. "You're my good luck charm, I guess." She rested her head on the door of the stall and closed her eyes.

"Honey, honey, what's wrong."

Miranda felt a hand on her shoulder, nudging her.

She looked up with blurry eyes. Hank kneeled in front of her. How long had she been asleep? She glanced down and the cat was gone. She mumbled, "I fell when I went to get Penny." Miranda shifted her hips on the cement. "We slipped on a piece of ice." She placed her hand over Hank's. "I'm so tired."

His eyes widened. "Let's get you to the doctor."

Shaking her head, she said, "I'll be fine. Just help me to the house."

As Hank wrapped his arm around Miranda and lifted her up, the cramping began again. A vice grip crushed her and felt like an ice pick shredding the inside of her belly. She doubled over. Hank reached around her legs with one hand and her back with the other and scooped her up. He carried her to the truck and laid her down on the front seat. Hank closed the door and ran around to the driver's side. Once he jumped in, he took her head and rested it on a flannel shirt he had in the truck. He boomed, "I'm taking you to the emergency room."

She murmured, "That's probably a good idea." Miranda held her belly as Hank drove at top speed down the driveway, spinning gravel onto the main road. Every time they hit a bump, Miranda groaned.

"Hold on, babe."

Miranda spotted fear on Hank's pale face as he glanced at her. His voice grew shrill. "We'll be there soon."

Her legs and knees felt weak. "I'm so scared. I hope our baby's ok."

Hank's hollow reassurance comforted her even though she knew he was as scared as her. "It's going to be ok." He rested a hand on her shoulder. "We'll be ok, babe."

Miranda focused on the tops of budded trees and puffy clouds drifting in the sky as they sailed down the freeway.

Once they arrived at the emergency room, Hank parked the truck and scurried around to the passenger side, opened the door, and carried Miranda to the entryway. A nurse in the reception area looked up as they came inside the ER.

Hank shouted. "My wife is pregnant, and she's had an accident."

The nurse took out a clipboard and began asking questions.

He shook his head. "No time for that. She. Is. In. Pain. And she's kind of passing out." He shifted Miranda in his arms. He growled, "Help her. Now."

The nurse pursed her lips. She turned from the desk area and quickly returned with a wheelchair. "Get in, dear."

Hank settled Miranda into the chair. Once again, she bent forward, grabbing her torso.

The nurse grimaced. "Come this way." Hank pushed the chair, following the nurse as she darted down the hall to the elevator and jammed the button with two fingers. Miranda continued to hold her belly and groaned. The door of the elevator finally opened, and the nurse pushed her inside. The doors shut, and they went up three flights to the maternity floor. Then the nurse wheeled Miranda down the hall and into a room. "Wait here. I'll get a doctor."

Hank knelt beside Miranda and took her hand. "It's going to be ok. The doctor will tell us what's going on and then we'll know what to do."

Miranda's face tensed and she nodded. Hank scooted a chair near her, sat, and continued to hold her hand. Gradually, bit by bit, her cramps subsided as she noticed charts in pastel colors of pregnancy months and trimesters lining the walls and a photo of a mother cuddling her newborn. She felt exhausted from all the pain she'd experienced in the last couple of hours. She felt so sleepy.

A few minutes later, a doctor in a white coat with a stethoscope around his neck came into the room. The doctor was in his fifties and had short, dark brown hair and concerned eyes. "I'm doctor Goodrich. I'm the OB on call. The nurse tells me you've got some cramping going on." He studied the chart in his hand. "How far along are you, Miranda?"

She grimaced as she adjusted her seating. "Seven months."

"Let's get you on the table so I can examine you."

Hank hooked an arm around Miranda and helped her onto the treatment bed, where she stretched on her back. Dr. Goodrich went to the side of the room and wrote some notes in a file.

A minute later, a nurse came in and helped Miranda get into a gown. Dr. Goodrich finished his notes, and then palpated Miranda's abdomen, listening with a stethoscope.

He conducted a pelvic exam, and words flowed out of the doctor's mouth, somber as his brown-eyed gaze. "It looks like you're in premature labor."

Miranda's heart sped into high gear. What did that mean? Was she having her baby now? She suddenly felt hot all over.

Dr. Goodrich put his hand on her arm and gave it a light squeeze. "We'll give you some medicine to stop the labor. We'll see if we can get this under control."

The nurse put gel on an ultrasound scope. "This will be cold." She handed the probe to Dr. Goodrich, and he rubbed the instrument over Miranda's belly. The group turned an eye to the gray, fuzzy fetus moving on the screen. The doctor pointed to the baby, and with a slight smile, he said, "Do you want to hear the heartbeat?"

Hank held Miranda's hand, and they both nodded.

The nurse turned up the volume, and a steady "thump, thump" sounded in the room.

Tears pooled in Miranda's lower lids. "Is our baby ok?"

The doctor moved the scope around her middle. "It looks like you have what's called placenta previa. It's a condition when the placenta covers the cervix. It can correct itself. The best thing you can do right now is bed rest." He glanced back at Miranda. "Perhaps if you take it easy for a few weeks, things will return to normal, and you can return to normal activity." He looked back at the screen. "Have the cramps subsided?"

She nodded. "I feel better now."

"Good. Just stay off your feet." He gave a hard look at Miranda and then Hank. "Avoid any stress." He glanced back at the screen as he continued sliding the scope over Miranda's abdomen. "Do you want to know the sex of your baby?"

Miranda and Hank looked at each other, nodding at the same time.

Hank squeezed her hand. "Yes. We do."

"You're going to have a girl."

They beamed.

Hank gave Miranda a quick kiss.

Dr. Goodrich turned an eye on them. "Just make sure you don't extend yourself. And stay off your feet except to go to the bathroom. If things start acting up again or if there's any bleeding, come straight back." He turned to the nurse and said, "Right instructions down for them, please."

The doctor patted Miranda's knee. "Schedule an appointment with your obstetrician and he can see how things are then." He shot Hank with a stern look. "Make sure she rests." And then he left the room.

Hank put his arm around Miranda, looking her straight in the eye. "Hear that, babe. No work."

She exhaled. Although Miranda was in the medical field and conducted examinations all the time, she hated being a patient herself. She got so nervous, especially when it involved another person. Her baby. She just wanted things to go well. Parenting was hard even before she had her baby—her daughter. She wedged her hands behind her hips and pushed herself up. "I know. It's going to be tricky. My practice. How am I going to do it?"

Suddenly, she felt extreme appreciation for Justine. Kids didn't know or realize all that a mother went through until they had a child of their own. It was a hard job, full of worry and stress.

Great. She was stressed now, and the doctor told her not to get stressed. She'd have to find a way to calm down and make it through the next couple of months.

Hank cocked his head. "I think you're going to have to accept help for a while." Miranda held his hand as he helped her into the nearby wheelchair. As Hank pushed her down the hallway to the elevator, both remained quiet, deep in thought.

Hank knew that despite the riff between Miranda and her mom, they needed Justine, so after getting Miranda settled at home on the couch, he said, "I'm calling your mom."

Miranda shook her head. "I don't want her to know."

Hank stood and crossed his arms. "This isn't the time to be stubborn. We need her help."

She rolled her eyes and let out a long sigh. "Fine."

Hank picked up the phone and called his mother-in-law.

Within minutes of talking to Hank, Justine ran across the yard and burst into their house, rushing to Miranda, who was stretched out on the couch. They both broke down in tears and hugged.

"I'm so sorry, Mom. I was so stupid to shut you out."

Justine sat facing Miranda. "I was being stubborn. I'm sorry too."

"I'm scared." Miranda wiped her tears with the back of her hand.

Justine took Miranda's hands in hers. "It's going to be ok. We are all here for you. We'll get through this."

And in that instant, the brick wall that had divided Miranda and Justine the past few months came tumbling down, melding into powdered dust as their mother and daughter bond grew stronger than ever.

CHAPTER 47

Three weeks of bedrest eventually passed. Miranda stretched out on the couch most days with a cup of chamomile tea. Since she left the hospital, she'd taken her medicine daily to stop the contractions, and it seemed to work. She'd stayed off her feet and followed the doctor's orders. But a twitchy feeling on the inside of her limbs got bigger and bigger as time passed. Miranda was such an active person, and it was hard being sedentary. She constantly reminded herself this was for her baby. She read and reread every veterinary journal she had, watched reruns on television, and talked on the phone with Tanya.

Miranda stretched her legs, pointing and flexing her toes. She circled her ankles a couple inches off the couch. She flicked off a *Runner's World* magazine from the coffee table nearby. Hank had bought her every magazine on the shelf at the grocery store. She thought if she couldn't be active, she'd at least read about it. She didn't know how much more she could stand of this inactive lifestyle and took in a big breath and exhaled a sigh.

Her heart felt full as she thought about how everyone took up the slack for her while she convalesced. Hank fed the animals, mucked out the stalls, cleaned the house, and did laundry. On top of that, he had a full-time practice as a farrier, traveling from farm to farm, caring for cows' and horses' hooves. Justine helped when she could and brought food every day for them to eat. She felt blessed to have a wonderful family. Miranda even had a veterinarian, John McCurry, in the neighboring town of Clinton, taking care of her patients for the time-being. Her mentor, Doc Tanner, had recommended him.

Her thoughts shifted to what it would be like caring for a baby and caring for animals. Would she be able to handle both? Her head leaned against a throw pillow. As she closed her eyes and fell asleep, she pictured holding a gurgling baby in one arm and in the other, a cute little puppy squirming to get away as she tried to give it an immunization.

CHAPTER 48

In April, during the weeks of Miranda's bed rest, Hank got behind in his farrier business that kept him busy on the slowest days. He did farm chores before he left for work and household tasks when he returned. Exhaustion loomed throughout his body. Miranda voiced her concern about Hank taking on the work of three men. He knew it was temporary, and he was the happiest he'd ever been. He had a beautiful wife he loved, and a baby was on the way. But he knew he couldn't keep up with it all. Finally, he called Nash to help with the animals. He also called Tanya, and she offered to come home and help Miranda with household chores and answering the veterinary practice phone. Tanya was on a break from training and would be arriving in a few days.

The day Hank called Tanya, while Miranda was convalescing on the couch, the phone rang. She answered, and it was Tanya.

"Hey, Tonny. What's up?"

"Guess what? I get to see you soon. Your wonderful husband just called, and I get to come help you guys during my break from training."

"He shouldn't have done that." She rubbed her thigh. "We're doing ok."

"It sounds like he could use some help, Ran. He sounded exhausted."

Miranda twisted the cord around her finger. "Really? He puts on such a good front for me when he gets home. I know he's tired, but I didn't realize it was getting to him." She tsked. "I should have known. I've been so into myself."

"You and the baby. You're taking care of two now."

Miranda could hear the thumps of gymnasts landing on the vault and dismounting in the gymnasium Tanya used for training. "You're right. I need to keep remembering I'm doing this for both of us. It makes it easier somehow to keep that in mind while I'm going crazy sitting here."

"I'll see you in a few days."

"I'm so excited to see you."

"And Ran?"

"Yeah."

"You're going to be a great mom."

"Thanks, Tonny."

One spring morning, until help arrived, Hank awoke earlier than usual and went to the barn. After he led the horses one after the other out into the pasture, he grabbed a pitchfork leaning against the wall. The thud of droppings hitting the bottom of the wheelbarrow echoed as he mucked Mandy's stall. Then he shuffled to Rocko's and, one by one, cleaned out each of the horse's stalls.

Once he finished, Hank trudged to the house. He went inside and sat on the edge of the couch and looked at his wife flipping through a magazine. Miranda smiled, and he kissed her.

He took her hand, "You going to be ok?"

"You say that every time you leave. I'll be ... fine. Don't worry so much."

"Here's the number for the farm I'll be working at," Hank said and handed her the piece of paper. "Here's the phone." He laid it on the coffee table. "I'll just be a couple miles away."

Before he left, Hank glanced at Miranda turning pages, eyeing the new running shoes for the 1988 season. She needed a new pair of shoes, and he knew that it took all the patience she had to remain still on the couch, but she couldn't run then. It might be a few months until she could go outside and hit the pavement. She had to focus on keeping her body healthy and safe for their baby. His chest expanded as he felt love for the sacrifice Miranda endured for their baby.

They were both making sacrifices. They only had a few weeks to go, and they'd be parents. Anxiety churned in his belly when he thought about being a father but despite his fear, he gave a quick prayer to the universe, and a zap of excitement ran throughout his body. He shut the door behind him and headed for his truck, ready to make his rounds.

He reached for his truck handle and glanced over at the barn. His lips turned up into a smile. Petey trotted across the field toward their farm, his big ears bobbing from side to side. Ben was inside with Miranda. They'd have to wait until the end of the day to have their playdate.

Hank shook his head and hopped into his truck, muttering, "Stupid donkey, lovestruck over a German Shepherd."

CHAPTER 49

After Hank left for the day, Miranda marveled at the way her mind had done a U-turn since she first found out she was pregnant a few months ago. It was such a shock, and she wasn't ready to be a mom then. But after the moment she shared with Hank at the birth of their colt and all the trauma at the hospital forcing her to realize she could lose her baby, being a mom was all she could think about. She was excited as she pictured their daughter and the things she could teach her. How to ride horses. And all about animals. She'd teach her how to grow vegetables in the garden. She'd tell her about her grandpa and how Stanley encouraged her to be a veterinarian, especially when there were few women vets. Miranda knew that Hank would be a good dad too.

"Miranda, honey." Justine opened the front door and peeked her head inside. "I've brought some breakfast and made you and Hank dinner for tonight."

She flashed a smile. "Thanks, Mom."

Justine went into the kitchen and started the kettle on the stove. She put a casserole dish with lasagna wrapped in tin foil inside the fridge. Moving about the kitchen, Justine reached into a paper bag, took out a bowl with a plastic lid, and placed that beside the other dish. She shut the door and turned toward Miranda. "If you want me to come back, I can put that in the oven for you, so it will be nice and hot when Hank comes home from work."

When the kettle started to whistle, Justine added a tea bag into green John Deere mugs and poured hot water in each. She brought them to the coffee table, where Miranda rested on the couch.

Miranda sighed. "You're such a big help. I feel so spoiled. Everyone doting on me."

Justine clicked her tongue. "We want that baby of ours to come when she's supposed to, not a minute early. Whatever it takes."

"I know. I just feel so lazy, doing nothing." She placed her empty water glass on the coffee table and wrapped her hand around the hot mug of tea her mom had just made. "Thanks for the lasagna. I've had such a craving for tomatoes the last month. I thought you're supposed to crave pickles and ice cream when you're expecting." She shrugged. "Weird."

"I craved carrots when I was pregnant with you. I ate a lot of them. Cooked. Shredded on salads. And carrot sticks. I thought I was going to turn orange. And then," She clapped. "Suddenly, the craving stopped."

"The body knows what it wants."

Justine pressed her hand on Miranda's leg. "How are you feeling, otherwise?"

"A little tired. Probably from the stress of it all. Thank goodness the cramping stopped."

Ben padded in from the bedroom and stretched. He yawned and then plopped down beside Miranda on the floor. She scratched his ears, and he licked her hand.

They both turned when they heard a knock on the door.

Miranda said, "Come in."

Richard popped inside. He had on a white polo shirt tucked into a pair of khakis. The strong scent of his woody cologne filled the living room. "Are you ready to go?"

Justine bit her lip.

Miranda noticed her mom's new look, different than her typical jeans and sweatshirt. A black blazer with shoulder pads and a pink turtleneck underneath. She had on black slacks to match.

"In a minute. I want to make sure that Miranda is all set."

"Mom. Go ahead." Her eyes were soft, filled with an inner glow. "Hank will be home soon."

Justine gestured to the telephone on the small table beside the couch. "Can you reach the phone?"

"I'll be fine, Mom."

Justine stayed seated, studying Miranda.

Richard glanced at his watch, and his gaze bounced back and forth between the door and Justine. "Come on, Justine. You're fussing over Miranda. She's a big girl."

"He's right, Mom. I'm fine. You guys go to your appointment."

"We can try wedding cake anytime."

Richard's eyes darted from Justine to Miranda and then back again. "But …"

"Go, Mom. Have fun. Bring back a piece for me." She giggled. "Chocolate, of course."

Justine bent to kiss her daughter on the cheek. "Take care of that baby while we're gone."

"Mom." She rolled her eyes. "You'll only be gone a couple hours."

Justine waved as she headed for the door. "Bye, honey."

As soon as they left, Miranda sighed. It was difficult reassuring everybody when she wasn't so sure how this pregnancy and bedrest were going herself. She felt terrified that it could all go south, literally, and she'd have the baby early. She was determined to go the full term. But … try as she might, the thought kept creeping in. The doctor told her to relax, not get anxious, and avoid all stress. Ha! Like that could happen when you had a human being growing inside you, preparing to come into the world. Everyone in her life was supporting her and keeping things as stress-free as possible. No surprises. Nothing was expected of her other than growing a human.

Miranda would just have to do her best, thinking good and calming thoughts. She'd think about bunnies and kittens. Kittens! She hoped Mrs. VanBuren had found a vet to care for her cat after he cut his paw. On the answering machine, Miranda recorded a message saying that she'd be away from her practice on maternity leave and all calls were to go to Dr. McCurry in Clinton, the next town over.

Yet Mrs. VanBuren knew Miranda's home number; she had called yesterday wanting her to care for her cat, their family's special pet. Miranda had recommended Dr. McCurry, but Mrs. VanBuren seemed unimpressed.

Miranda's stomach knotted as she pondered the situation. She didn't want the cat to suffer. If Miranda were to drive to the VanBuren's, she could find out for herself if the cat needed care. After all, she would be sitting in her truck. It would be the same as sitting on her couch. Wouldn't it?

She rose from the couch, slipped into her loafers, grabbed the keys from the counter, and threw on her jean jacket. If she hurried, she could be back before anyone knew about her excursion.

Luckily her vet bag was in the truck from her last home visit. As she drove down her driveway, she rolled down the window, breathed in the fresh air, and patted her belly. "Don't tell, little one, your momma is being naughty. I know you understand. You'll probably be a brain surgeon or something. Duty calls." She looked both ways before driving onto the road. Across the field on the edge of the woods, she spotted the same coyote they saw at the pond last August. A shiver ran through her. She shrugged it off, hoping the animal would keep its distance.

Within five minutes, she parked in the VanBuren's barnyard. Mr. VanBuren was on a tractor headed for his soybean field. He looked up, and Miranda waved.

He climbed down from his tractor and plodded over to her truck. "Morning, neighbor. What brings you by?"

"I'm checking on Boots."

"Thought you were laid up?"

"Your wife left a message."

He grumbled as he walked away. "That nuisance of a cat should be outside with the rest of the barn cats." He reached the back door of their house and popped his head inside. He boomed, "Mother, you get Boots' paw fixed?"

Miranda chuckled, hearing Mr. VanBuren calling his wife "mother." It was strange how many older farmers called their spouses mother or dad.

He pivoted and headed toward the truck. "Looks like she went to Clinton yesterday." He shook his head. "The cat's resting inside."

"Thanks, Mr. VanBuren."

"You bet." He waved. "Take care."

Miranda backed her truck around and headed home. She sighed. Losing her prospective patients a couple months after she had started her veterinary practice loomed in her mind every time she referred elsewhere. She would have to put her veterinarian practice on hold until she could get back on her feet. Just when things were going well, and she was getting more and more patients, she had to close it down. She felt a heaviness in her body. All that schooling, training, and work setting up her business and getting the word out that she was open put to a halt. She was the only vet within a ten-mile radius. Hopefully, she'd be able to start again soon.

Miranda hurried her truck home and snuck into the house. She stretched out on the couch and flipped through a *Good Housekeeping* magazine, suddenly remembering an owner was supposed to pick up a prescription for an antibiotic that she had forgotten. Dr. McCurry had called Miranda to ask if she had this type of eye antibiotic in her clinic because he had run out. One of his patients, a collie, had an infection and must start the medication right away lest he lose his eyesight. Miranda had to find out. She could call Hank but didn't want to bother him. If he had a horse hoof in his hands, it would be inconvenient to stop working.

Miranda decided it wouldn't hurt if she quickly went out to her clinic to see if the prescription was available. Ben followed her as she slipped on her loafers once again and stepped outside. She headed for the clinic in the barn. At the medicine cabinet, she found the antibiotic. She wrote a note for the dog's owner and bagged the medicine tube, intending to hang it on the clinic's doorknob to be picked up. She'd call the vet once she returned to the house.

Suddenly, the cramps she'd felt weeks before returned, and she doubled over, holding her belly. Oh, no. Not again. What was she thinking going on her excursions? Stupid girl. She sat on her office chair and took some slow, deep breaths. The number for the farm where Hank was working was in the house. What was she going to do? Nobody was there to help her. She closed her eyes and said a silent prayer: "Daddy, help us. Our baby can't come yet. It's too soon." Ben nuzzled her legs and leaned in. Miranda imagined her dad's arms wrapped around them, radiating a calming peacefulness.

Slowly, her body settled, and the cramps went away. But she wasn't confident about going back to the house by herself. She decided to stay in the clinic and wait for someone to come. In the interim, she removed a veterinarian journal from her desk and flipped through the pages, looking at an article about worming horses.

An hour later, Hank came through the door. "What are you doing out here? I called to check in, and there was no answer."

"I came out to check if there was an eye antibiotic for that collie I told you about."

He ran a hand through his hair. "Honey, you're supposed to be off your feet. What if something happened?"

"I know. You're right." She hesitated.

"What?"

"I got cramps again." She plopped her face in her hands. "It was foolish of me to come out here." Miranda didn't tell Hank about the trip to the Van Burens. He'd be furious. If something happened to their baby, Miranda wouldn't be able to forgive herself.

"Tanya's flying in tomorrow, and Nash is coming the day after that. Help is on the way. We're all here to help you." Hank crouched on his haunches and looked at her. "This is for our baby, Miranda."

"I know. I'm sorry."

Hank scooped her up and carried her to the house. After showering and settling in to watch TV, Miranda kissed Hank, thanked him, and he left for the barn to attend to chores.

CHAPTER 50

The next afternoon, Tanya arrived by taxi. She carried two suitcases to the front door. She knocked and then peeked her head inside. "Hi, Ran."

Miranda's chest felt lighter. The cavalry had arrived. "I'm so glad to see you. I've missed you so much."

"I've missed you too."

Dragging her heavy suitcases through the doorway, Tanya set them down and went to her friend. They hugged.

"You can settle in the guest room," Miranda said. "My mom put on fresh sheets, and there are clean towels on the dresser."

"First, I want to get caught up."

"Nothing has changed." She patted the space on the couch beside her. "I told you about everything last night before you flew here. How was your flight?"

Tanya settled in beside Miranda. "It was fine. It's only four hours from Colorado Springs, including a layover."

"I can't believe you got a break from training."

"We've been training hard, and our coach thinks it's a good idea for us to take time off before we go at it again for the Olympic games. We're all tired." She faced Miranda and sat crisscrossed. "Let me look at you. You look pregnant. It's weird seeing you with a big belly. You've always been such a bean pole." She twirled her ponytail. "You're glowing."

"I feel like a blob. It's been hard doing nothing and lying around on the couch. But enough whining." She grabbed Tanya's hands and let go. "Lucky for me, you're here."

Tanya sat down and stretched out on the floor, straddling her legs. "I'm stiff from traveling." She reached forward and grabbed each foot. "Coach said we need to keep limber and stretch every day, so here goes."

"I miss moving my body. It's crappy staying still all the time. What I wouldn't give for a good, long run."

Tanya shifted into splits.

Miranda tsked. "Show off."

"Sorry, Ran, gotta stay limber."

"I know that. Maybe I can live through you." She smiled. "Could you go for a run for me?"

"Ha." Tanya grimaced. "You know how much I love running." She groaned. "But my coach told us to run, or jog, as he calls it, to stay loose and in shape." Tanya flattened both legs out in front in a pike and pressed her whole torso to her thighs. "You said Nash was coming to help too."

Miranda lifted an eyebrow. "You're wondering about Nash, huh? He *is* cute."

Tanya flicked her hand through the air. "Stop. I'm with Daniel."

Miranda wondered if Tanya really loved Daniel or if it was convenient that he was also an Olympian and they had similar interests. When she and Tanya had talked on the phone over the last few months, Tanya wavered between breaking up with Daniel and thinking he was the one.

Tanya crawled up in a chair and tucked her legs underneath her. She took a sip of Miranda's tea. "You got any cookies?"

"Mom made some chocolate chip. They're on the counter."

Tanya hopped up and scooted into the kitchen. She took a bite of one and closed her eyes. "Mmmm. These. Are. Heavenly. I haven't had a cookie in months. Sometimes it's so hard being a gymnast and always having to watch what I eat and counting calories."

Miranda scanned her friend's body. "You don't have an ounce of fat on you."

"That's because I eat carrots and lettuce." Tanya trotted over to the chair and sat down, facing Miranda. "When I get too old to do gymnastics, I'm going to eat whatever I want. I don't care if I get fat. It'll be worth it. Because I ate this cookie, I'll have to run a couple extra miles." She popped the last bite of cookie in her mouth. "Enough about my diet. Tell me what I can do to help."

"The horses need to be groomed. Hank fed them before he left." She chuckled halfheartedly. "If he didn't clean the stalls, you could do that as well." Miranda recalled the two of them as adolescents throwing straw at each other while doing chores. It took them twice as long because they had so much fun goofing around. On one occasion, they went to school afterward, and a boy who sat behind Miranda in math class picked straw out of her hair.

Tanya scrunched her nose. "Yes, boss."

"Very funny, friend." Miranda bent her legs to her chest, resting her hands on her knees. "Thank you, Tonny. You're the best, helping us out."

"Anything for you." Tanya winked. "Can't wait to see my niece in a couple months."

"Oh, and Tonny."

"Yeah?"

She giggled. "Nash is single."

A flash of pink spread over Tanya's face. "I'll move my stuff to the guest room." She dragged her two suitcases to the bedroom at the end of the hall.

Miranda was lucky to have such a good friend. She wished Tanya could find someone to share her life with. Someone other than Daniel. Miranda wished she could convince Tanya that she needed to let Daniel go and move on. He may be a high-class athlete and all shiny on the outside, but inside, there was an insecure, controlling man who was going to make Tanya's life miserable. He was the same as every other boyfriend Tanya had picked. She couldn't see what Tanya saw in him.

But Miranda was trying hard to accept the decisions the people in her life were making. She would be supportive and just listen. At least for now.

"Ready to work." Tanya came out of the bedroom dressed in tattered jeans and an old sweatshirt stained with paint. Her hair was pulled back in a ponytail beneath a navy baseball cap, and in one hand, she carried old riding boots. "I'll see you in a couple hours. I'll make dinner then."

"Mom brought some food."

"Hallelujah. Then *I* don't have to cook. You know that's not my thing, cooking." As she put her hand on the doorknob, she turned. "Call the barn phone if you need anything."

Miranda gestured to the phone on the table beside her. "Will do. Thanks again, Tonny."

Tanya shoved her boots on and headed to the barn. Inside, she made her way toward the tack room. She pawed through the box of grooming tools and picked out a curry comb, brush, and pick for the horses' hooves. Tanya decided to brush her favorite horse, the one she used to ride when she came to the Graaf's, Rocko.

The chestnut quarter horse gelding nickered when she came to the stall. He threw his big head through the stall door opening. "Hey, buddy. Good to see you." Tanya swallowed a lump in her throat and held an apple she'd grabbed from the tack room. It had been a long time since she'd seen Rocko. He scooped the apple with his mouth and chewed. Tanya scrubbed his velvety nose and remembered she had to groom each of the horses before she spent time with Rocko. She gathered her grooming tools. "I'll be back."

Tanya pivoted and headed for the other horses. At the end of the aisle, Nash was walking toward her. A pleasant shiver ran side to side from her head down to her toes. When he approached, her voice crackled. "Nash?" She stepped back, leaned on a stall door, and ran her hand over her hat until her nervous fingers found her ponytail.

"Nice to see you too."

Nash's deep base voice motored throughout her body, filling every cell, every muscle.

She knew that Nash was coming to help. Her heart had tripped over itself when Miranda told her, but she didn't think she'd feel the way she did now. Words stuck in her dry throat. Nash was good-looking in a rugged, cowboy-on-the-range kind of look with a few days' growth on his black beard. His broad shoulders filled out his denim shirt, narrowing to a vee at his waist. Her eyes locked on his shiny belt buckle and followed his long legs that poured into faded black Lee jeans. He wore dusty black cowboy boots. She felt his steel gray eyes on her and quickly diverted her attention to the grooming bucket she carried. "I … I … need to groom the horses."

One side of his lips lifted slightly in a slow, sexy smile. "I can help with that."

Tanya hadn't seen Nash in a few months. She'd thought about him. And maybe even fantasized about what it would be like to run her hands over his muscled arms and wrap her arms around his lean body. But that was just her thoughts getting intoxicated. She was committed to Daniel. Yes, he could be controlling at times. And yes, they argued some. But what couple didn't occasionally disagree? Plus, they were meant to be together. They both were obsessed with their sports, and who else would understand their training schedules?

Nash stood there, seemingly cool and calm, as Tanya felt flustered, trying to gain her composure. "Um. Sure. There're more brushes in the tack room." She picked up Rocko's halter and lead rope from a hook near his stall.

Nash hesitated and continued to give Tanya a once over with his clear gray eyes.

His eyes reminded her of a break in the clouds on a rainy day, giving a glimmer of hope on the horizon. He smiled his crooked smile once again, and to keep herself busy so she wouldn't come unglued, Tanya unlatched the door of Rocko's stall. What was she doing? She'd been on her way to groom the other horses first. Nash had her reeling as she tried to gain her equilibrium.

"I'll leave ya to it, then." He walked to the tack room.

Tanya slipped Rocko's halter over his head and led him out of his stall. She whispered to herself, "Get a grip, girl."

Rocko nickered as she gave him a cube of sugar from her pocket.

Tanya led him to the grooming station, where she hooked a rope on either side of his halter. She steadied her thoughts as she took a hoof pick and lifted one of Rocko's front hooves between her knees and flicked out stones and grime from the center of his hoof.

As she crouched, her quads screamed from the repeated dismounts and landings in practice. She enjoyed training for the Olympics but needed a break from the scrutinous schedule. Her body ached from the grueling eight hours, six days a week. She didn't remember the last time she wasn't sore. It became a familiar feeling to be hurting somewhere. She had always had at least a bruise or two from falling or continuous practice on the same routine or movement. The goal was to get it perfect. And some days were easier than others. Her intense drive kept her going. She didn't need a hotty like Nash to derail her. She was a professional athlete.

Her coach even said to the team before their break, "No. Distractions."

After Tanya finished brushing Rocko, she led him back to his stall, where Nash had filled his water bucket. Rocko went straight to it and drank long sips, satisfying his thirst. Tanya glanced down the line of stalls as she returned Rocko's halter to the hook outside his door. Nash worked, hose in hand, his tight jeans hugging his long legs. Those long legs sent a quick shiver up her spine. How she'd like to wrap her hands around his waist and bring him close to her. Run her fingers over his taut back muscles. Heat flowed over her body like a jolt of summer sun on a brisk spring day.

Tanya shook her head to clear these thoughts. Why didn't Daniel do the same thing to her as Nash did? She never had those feelings of desire with Daniel. They'd been together over a year, and she enjoyed him, but thoughts or feelings like she'd had in the last hour had never come to her with Daniel.

"No distractions," Tanya reminded herself out loud. "No distractions." She squeezed the lead rope tightly in her hand as she walked to the next stall.

"Aren't you guys adorable?" Penny and her foal stood inside the double-sized stall. The foal took a couple steps toward her, sniffing the air. When Tanya reached out to pet his nose, the foal backed up next to his mother.

Tanya put the mare's halter on and hooked the lead rope to it. "Come on, you beauties. Let's go get pretty." She led the mare down the aisle, the foal following close behind. When she reached the grooming station, she hooked up the mare on either side of her halter. Tanya settled in for an hour of grooming the rest of the horses in the barn and shoved thoughts of Nash far away in her mind. At least she tried to.

CHAPTER 52

Richard coasted his Cadillac into the parking lot of a strip mall in downtown Davenport. It was supposed to be the best bakery for wedding cakes, according to Justine's research. He pulled his big car into a parking spot. "Here we are, darling."

They faced a white store with a large window revealing yellow, pink, and chocolate cakes donned in elaborate decorations and positioned on pedestals. To the right of the cake shop stood a candle boutique, hair salon, and shoe store.

Her stomach fluttered. "Ready to eat cake?"

"I'm always ready for cake." Richard smiled. "Especially with you."

They walked hand in hand toward the building. A plump woman in her sixties greeted them when they entered the bakery. "Hello, Justine, welcome to Sweeties."

"Hi, Mrs. Sweetie." She gestured. "This is Richard. We have an appointment." She didn't know the Sweeties that well. They were acquaintances and went to the same church. Justine's skin prickled, and she wondered if the woman would judge her for marrying someone after Stanley. Justine didn't know anyone who had married a second time, and even though she had no reason to believe this, sometimes she felt as though she was under scrutiny in her community.

"We've got you all set up in the back room." The woman drifted toward the back of the building. "Follow me. My husband is all set up for you."

They were escorted through a curtain, and Justine scanned the table in front of them. Various slices of cake adorned small paper plates. The baker, Mr. Sweetie, a man in his sixties, came from an office on the side of the room. He said, "Please, take a seat, and we can get started." He took off his baker's hat and threw it on a chair in the corner as he sat across from Justine and Richard.

Justine and Richard settled in comfortable wooden dining room chairs. "This is our classical white-on-white cake." He gestured to a plate with two slices of cake.

Richard took a bite. "Mmmm. This one's good."

Justine said as she smiled slightly, "It *is* good." She tucked stray hairs behind her ears. The white cake reminded her of the cake she and Stanley had on their wedding day. A distant ache fell in her heart. "I'd like something a little different than the typical white."

After sampling several bites of chocolate, carrot, and red velvet cake, they chose a vanilla chocolate marble. "Let's wrap some cake up for Miranda and Hank. Oh, and Tanya will be there too. She has such a sweet tooth. She'd love some."

After packing several slices, the baker handed the box to Richard. Justine put her coat on, and they headed for the door. Once outside, Richard went around the car to open the door for Justine. One of his penny loafers tripped on the curb, and he tried to catch himself on the hood of the Cadillac, but the box of goodies fell out of his arms and onto the pavement. Cake flew everywhere, including on his white polo shirt. He had blotches of brown, green, blue, and pink gooey frosting all over his front.

Justine put her hand to her mouth. She skimmed his body and stifled a giggle.

Richard looked like a blue moon ice cream cone with his multicolored shirt and beige slacks. The look on his face did not share her sentiment. His brows furrowed, and he slapped at the sticky mess on his shirt as he tried to rub it off. The more he rubbed the frosting and cake, the more it smeared into his shirt.

"Here, Richard. Let me help." Justine found a Kleenex in her purse and stepped off the sidewalk toward him.

"It's fine." He grimaced. "I think I have a sweater in the back." He marched to the back of the car and opened the trunk. He yanked the messy shirt over his head. Then he took out a brown and gold angora sweater and slipped his arms through the holes, buttoning the front.

"I'll be right back." Justine returned to the store and asked the woman if they could have more cake samples. She explained what had happened to Richard. The woman went back to the baker, and he went about fixing another box of samples. As she waited, Justine thought about Stanley, knowing that if he got smeared with cake, the two of them would be roaring with laughter, having a good time. He'd probably scoop some frosting with his finger and lick it off.

Once Mrs. Sweetie finished, she handed the box to Justine. She said with a smirk, "I should have given it to *you* in the first place."

"Thank you. You have my number for any questions, right?"

The older lady placed her hand on Justine's arm. "Yes, dear. Don't you worry about a thing." She hesitated. "Just as nervous the second time around?"

"Maybe even more." Justine tucked the box of cake samples tightly in her arms. "It seemed so natural and easy with Stanley."

"He was a good man, that Stanley."

Justine's eyes filled. "He was for sure." She turned and dashed out the door. She saw Richard waiting for her in the car. Her stomach flip-flopped. But not the nervous excitement kind of belly roll. The "am I doing the right thing" flip flop. What if she was making a big mistake? She had always thought Stanley was the only one for her. And he was. Then. But she didn't want to live her life alone. It was too lonely.

She approached the door of the car and opened it. Was it worth it? Giving her heart to someone else with the possibility of getting it broken again? Her heart broke when Stanley died. She didn't know if she'd ever recover. She'd healed, but had she recovered? She still missed Stanley.

"Could you hold this?"

"What is this? More cake?" Richard's face was covered with "grumpy" as he took hold of the box. "After what just happened?"

She buckled her seat belt, turned, and looked at Richard with a smirk. "It was kind of funny, wasn't it?"

He scowled.

She settled the box in her lap and nudged his arm with her fist. She smiled. "Come on, Richard, lighten up just a little bit."

He forced a smile, then changed the subject. "Where to now, back home? Or do we still have that appointment with the caterer?"

"I changed that to next week. It seemed like a lot to do in one day." Justine didn't know if she wanted to have another appointment, seeing as Richard was in a mood. It wouldn't be fun, anyway. "Besides, Miranda needs our help."

"I thought her friend, Tammy, was arriving today."

"She is. And her name is Tanya." She fixed her eyes out the window as they traveled on the main street in Davenport. Several colonial houses, a jewelry store that had been owned by the same family for generations, a local bar, and Palmer

College of Chiropractic: buildings that had been familiar sights of the largest of the Quad Cities. A new house caught Justine's eye, contrasting with the old structures that had stood for over a hundred years. One thing was for sure, things never stayed the same. They rode in silence.

CHAPTER 53

A few days later, Hank drove his truck down the driveway, one hand flopped over the steering wheel, his body slumped and leaning to one side from the many long days of shoeing horses and trimming cows' hooves as a farrier, and then feeding and grooming horses at their farm. He was glad Nash had come to help. Cowboys were low maintenance, used to sleeping under the stars on the ground. Hank asked Nash to stay in the house, sleeping on a mattress in the living room, but Nash insisted on staying in the barn, going inside the house only to shower.

Hank wished he could have a quiet evening with Miranda. But Tanya had been staying with them, and she was helping a lot with the animals and chores around the house. He was grateful for that; still, he'd like an evening alone with his wife, eating dinner and talking about their future as parents. Ever since he and Miranda had shared the experience of bringing the foal into the world and witnessing his birth, he was overjoyed about becoming a father.

His father hadn't been a good role model. He abandoned the family when Hank was young. It nearly destroyed his mom. She was rarely home because she was always working, trying to keep the family afloat. His grandma did a good job of raising him, but he never had a male relative teach him how to be a man. Hank had done the best he could, but he had to admit he was nervous about being a dad. He didn't want to screw it up.

Before Hank got out of the truck, he stretched his stiff arms and glanced at the mail he'd grabbed from the mailbox. His eyes fell on an envelope from the District Court in Cheyenne, Wyoming, and his heart felt like a woodpecker rapping the inside of his chest. He'd gotten hold of an attorney from the list the caseworker had given him a few months ago.

His new lawyer told him to sit tight and that it sounded like the attorney for the plaintiff was fishing for money, suing Hank for bashing his nose at the bar in Wyoming two years ago.

Hank trusted his attorney had taken care of things but should have known that getting a court-appointed attorney was a bad idea as they had huge caseloads, and his case was probably on the bottom of the pile. Hank hadn't wanted to spend money on an expensive attorney. Besides, he'd paid his fines two years ago before he left Wyoming.

A bolt of lightning went through his body. What was he going to tell Miranda? He thought she'd never have to know about his felony and criminal record. He didn't want to alarm her and cause her anxiety, especially when she was on bedrest with the baby.

Hank sighed and stashed the envelope in the glove compartment. He then got out of his truck and headed for the door, his heart heavy.

"Hey, Hank."

He shoved his hands in his jean pockets and looked to his side, and then snapped his gaze away as he saw Nash walking from the barn, carrying a saddle.

Nash said, "Why the long face?" He hoisted the saddle onto one shoulder, the stirrups dangling along his leg.

"Just a long day."

Nash studied Hank. "Something tells me otherwise, but if you say so. My advice is you'd better put on a face of sunshine, or your wife is going to guess the same as me."

"I got a letter from the courts in Wyoming."

"I thought you'd taken care of that a long time ago."

"I did too."

"You haven't told Miranda, have you?"

"Now wouldn't be a good time. I don't want to upset her. The baby and all."

Balancing the saddle on his shoulder with one hand, he wiped the sweat from his brow with the other. "You gotta take care of it, man. You want the first time you meet your baby to be from jail?"

"I'm not ready yet."

"At least go to Wyoming and talk to them. Don't be an idiot. It won't go away if you ignore it."

He adjusted his Carhartt baseball cap. "Just don't say anything."

"I got your back, brother. I don't agree with how you're handling this, but I got ya." Nash thumped Hank's shoulder. "Let's go inside. Miranda invited me for dinner. I'll be right there." Nash hauled the saddle to his rig alongside the barn and stored it inside the trailer. He jogged back to Hank's side.

Before they opened the door to the house, Hank turned to Nash. "I'll take care of it."

Miranda looked up from the book she was reading and blinked. "Hi, honey. You're a sight for sore eyes."

Tanya pulled a casserole from the oven. "Dinner will be ready in five minutes."

Nash said, "Smells good." He tugged off his boots and put them to the side wall by the door.

"You can thank Justine. I can't cook like this."

Nash smiled. "You could have kept that to yourself. I would have been none the wiser."

Tanya sliced the lasagna into large pieces as steam rolled upward from the pan. "I could have." Disapproval gleamed in her eyes as she shot Miranda a sly look. "But I don't like secrets."

He harrumphed and padded across the living room in his stocking feet. "I get that." He threw a sharp look at Hank. "I don't like secrets either."

Tanya eased the hot pan onto a potholder at the table. "Yep. Secrets just make things worse and cause problems."

Miranda wrapped a curl around her finger, and her head waggled back and forth. "What's going on with you two? What are you talking about?"

Hank leaned in and gave Miranda a kiss. "They're just babbling. Sometimes, my buddy, Nash, doesn't make any sense. I think he's gotten kicked in the head too many times."

"I think you're the one that's been too close to the horses' hooves, pal."

"Ok, you guys. Let's quit acting like preschoolers and eat." Miranda gestured to the kitchen. "I'm hungry. My mom's parmesan chicken casserole is to die for."

"Let's eat family style," Tanya said. She slid a large spatula in the casserole. The plates and silverware were already on the table. "Miranda, can you join us, or do you have to sit on the couch?"

"I've got to move. I'm going crazy sitting on this couch all day. When we have this baby, we're burning this couch and getting a new one."

Hank chuckled. "Whatever you need, my love." He pulled out a chair for her. "Whatever you need."

They all sat and began filling their plates with casserole and salad. Tanya stood again. "I almost forgot." She went over to the oven. "We have garlic bread."

Miranda smiled. "I love garlic bread."

"Last week, it made you nauseous," Hank said. "Just the smell of it."

"This week, it's coffee that makes me want to hurl."

Nash added, "I'm glad I'm not a woman."

Tanya's eyebrow rose as she took a quick look at Nash. "Me too."

When they finished eating, Tanya started clearing the dishes off the table.

Nash sprang to his feet. "Let me help."

Nash rinsed the dishes off in the sink, and Tanya loaded the dishwasher. While they worked, Miranda and Hank snuggled on the couch in the living room.

Tanya smiled. "They look happy."

Nash glanced at them. "Indeed, they do."

They stood watching their friends for a few moments. Nash said, "It's going to change their lives when the baby comes. Having kids is a big thing."

"You want kids?" A plate clanked against a bowl as Tanya placed it in the dishwasher.

"You always ask such personal questions?"

"An innocent inquiry is all."

"Maybe." Nash scraped tomato sauce off a plate with a fork. "My sister has a couple kids. They're pretty cute." He smiled. "Thing about being an uncle is you can get them all jacked up with sugar and fun, then give them back when you're tired of playing hide and seek."

"My brother has a three-year-old son. Haven't ever met him."

He handed her a plate. "Why's that?"

"Haven't seen either of my brothers for a few years. Since they left after high school in the late seventies. They're a year apart."

"Must be a lot to that story." Nash gave her the last dish from the sink, and Tanya started the dishwasher.

"I'm going out to the barn to feed the animals."

Nash nodded sideways. "I think those two need some time alone. I'll help."

They grabbed their jackets, put their boots on, and headed for the door. Tanya said, "We'll be in the barn."

A pang of jealousy ran through Tanya like a rank gust of icy air as she viewed Hank and Miranda snuggled on the couch. She wished she could have what Miranda had. A great guy and a baby on the way. Even though the last few years she'd been consumed with training with the goal of the '88 Olympics in mind, deep down she'd always wanted the family she hadn't had as a child.

CHAPTER 54

Once Tanya and Nash had left, Miranda looked at Hank. "What's up, honey? You don't seem yourself." Hank studied his wife's concerned eyes. What would he tell her? Would he even tell her? He didn't want his bad news to be the reason she went into premature labor.

Yet maybe Nash was right. If he didn't tell Miranda about his legal issues and he went to jail, would his daughter's first sight of him be a picture of a mug shot or his face behind bars? Or worse yet, visiting him in prison with a bunch of other prisoners, only getting a few minutes to get to know his child.

What if he was sent away for a few years? His daughter would be in school already, and he'd have missed out on her early childhood. What could he do? He didn't like keeping this from Miranda, but he didn't want to upset her either.

"Honey? Where'd you go?"

"Huh? What?"

"It's like you're here, but your mind is somewhere else tonight. What is going *on* with you?"

"It's been a long day." Hank stretched. "I just need a good night's sleep."

"Is all this?" Miranda circled her belly. "Getting to be too much?" She put her hand on his. "Then we need to talk about it."

"No. It's fine. I'm going to take a shower." He kissed her on the forehead and headed for the bathroom. He knew Miranda would have more questions. She was very perceptive. But he didn't know how to answer them right then. He just needed to clear his head. He would have liked to take a walk in the evening air, but he didn't want to leave her alone, and she would be upset if he left. Maybe his worried thoughts would be washed away in the hot, soapy water and circle down the drain, clearing his mind and allowing him to find the answers to his problems.

CHAPTER 55

The next morning at Justine's house, Richard poured himself a second cup of coffee. "I don't know what makes this so hard." He added cream, clanking the sides of the cup with a spoon as he stirred his coffee. Justine sat at her kitchen table, arranging daffodils in a vase from her garden. "I don't want to be away from Miranda when she's so close to having her baby."

He leaned against the kitchen counter, holding his coffee mug. "We've talked about going abroad for our honeymoon. I thought we'd made the decision to go to Paris. I already called the travel agent and made reservations." The spoon made a sharp clatter when he set it down on the counter.

Justine clipped the end of a daffodil and tucked it in with the rest of the flowers. "Couldn't we go someplace closer? Colorado or Michigan would be nice. On Lake Michigan, we could rent a cottage on the beach."

Richard ran a hand through his salt and pepper crew cut. "It's starting to seem like you care more about your daughter and grandchild than about our upcoming nuptials."

Justine gathered some peanut butter cookies from the cookie jar. She set the plateful on the table and nudged them toward Richard.

"I don't like peanut butter. Remember, I told you that when you were baking them."

Justine recalled him saying that but absentmindedly thought they were someone's favorite cookie. Then she remembered. They were one of Stanley's favorites. She scooted the plate back toward herself and took one, chewed, and thought for a moment. What *was* Richard's favorite cookie?

"You can't make me choose between my daughter, her baby, and you. It's not fair."

"Do you even care about our wedding plans?" His eyebrows scrunched. "*Or* about *us*?"

"You're really asking me that?" Justine grabbed the plate of cookies and went to the counter, slamming them down a little too hard. One of the cookies fell off the plate and onto the floor. "I'm going for a walk." She shoved her boots and coat on and slammed the door on her way out to the porch. After she took her hat and gloves out of her pocket, she put those on too.

As Justine marched her way across the yard toward the barren cornfield, she breathed in the damp, earthy smell of the stagnant field awakening from a dormant winter underneath the snow. She took a step onto the squishy field, and her boots went *thck, thck* with each step in the black soil.

Was Richard that selfish that he couldn't realize the position he'd put her in? Miranda wasn't pregnant when they'd made wedding plans months ago. How could she not be here when her grandbaby was born? Her first grandchild. Or was she being selfish? Maybe she was only thinking of herself.

Justine marched right into the middle of the field as her mind swirled around the words and thoughts of the day. A slow burn formed in the center of her forehead and caught like a hot coal simmering in the bottom of a backyard barbecue. Richard was so different from Stanley, who would have been understanding about the whole situation. If they had planned a trip, he would have wanted to stay too. He'd be excited about his new grandchild.

But this wasn't Richard's grandchild. This was different for him. He didn't even get along with Miranda. How could Justine expect him to be excited like she was? On the other hand, why was he being so stubborn and selfish?

Justine fixed her gaze on a flock of starlings in the air. They were a nuisance, just like the past few days were. Just a big nuisance. From the cake incident to the quiet ride home to the tiff about changing honeymoon plans. Why weren't things going well between them?

She knew she had to return to the house and talk things through because their marriage wasn't going to work if there wasn't give and take and more understanding between them. She and Stanley always cleared the air. Ugh! There she went again, comparing Stanley to Richard. They were two different men. And their marriages would be different also. She couldn't expect to have the same marriage. She'd have to expect something different.

She looked up from the muck and realized she had walked across the field to the edge of their property. When she turned, she spotted Ben and Petey trotting toward her. She smiled and bent over to cuddle Ben. "You're a good dog. You always know when I need a sounding ear." She knelt and rubbed his face. "You were always there for Stanley, too, weren't you?" She stroked his smooth black and tan fur as he leaned into her.

"And you, his pal, Petey." Justine patted his gray neck and caressed his long ears. "Such a special friendship." The animals strolled beside Justine as she headed back.

She'd get it all sorted eventually.

CHAPTER 56

A few days later, Tanya picked up the ringing phone on the wall of the barn. "Hello, Graaf residence. Tanya speaking."

"Hi, babe."

Her heart fluttered, not because she was excited to hear from Daniel but because she had just been helping Nash clean the stalls. They had been laughing and goofing around. She had thrown some straw at him when he teased her about wrangling cows and breaking horses and how it was harder than being a gymnast. He had thrown straw back, and it got stuck in her hair. He had moved closer and reached toward her and was about to take the straw out of her hair when the phone rang.

"Hi, Daniel." She absentmindedly did a plie squat and twisted the phone cord in her hand while she was talking.

"You're out of breath. Whatya been doing?"

"Just cleaning the stalls, ya know, helping Miranda and Hank out?"

He sighed. "How much longer will you be there?"

"I don't know." She twisted the phone cord until it tangled around her hand. "Miranda is still on bed rest. I can't just leave. I have another week off from practice."

Daniel grunted on the other end of the line. "I was hoping we could spend some time together before you have to go back in training."

She watched as Nash went out the side door of the barn, pushing a wheelbarrow full of horse manure. "Me too. Babe. Me too. But we'll have to see how Miranda does in the next few days."

"Why do *you* have to do all the work for them?"

"I'm not. Hank's friend, Nash, is helping too."

Silence.

"Daniel. Babe?"

"That *cowboy* I saw when I was there this fall?"

"Yes. Nash is a cowboy."

"Hmm."

"What's wrong with being a cowboy?" She found herself defending Nash even though she was sure he could handle things just fine on his own.

"Are you working together?"

"It makes things go quicker when we can work as a team." Tanya could hear Daniel breathing, but he didn't say anything. After a couple minutes Tanya asked, "You still there?"

He grumbled, "Yes."

"What's wrong?"

"You really have to ask?"

"Yeah, I do." She sighed. "*What* is bugging you?"

"It's that *cowboy*. Why does he have to be there at the same time you are?"

"Really, Daniel. You're jealous of Nash? He's Hank's friend, and Miranda needs help. She's in a serious situation with her pregnancy. If she moves around too much, she could lose the baby."

"I'm not jealous." His voice rose. "I just don't like him being there the same time you are."

"Ugh. Quit being so selfish." Her voice took a sarcastic turn. "Maybe you should come and help too. Then you wouldn't have to be worried about me going out on you or Nash making a pass at me."

"You know I can't come right now. I'm in the middle of training. Track is different than gymnastics. Our coach won't give us a break. He's brutal. And it's tough competition. I want to win. Same as you."

"Oh. So now you think gymnastics is a fluff sport, huh? And our coach is soft on us. Well, let me tell you, maybe he's just smarter than your coach. He knows if we don't take time off, we could get hurt." She paused, and the phone went silent. A few moments later, she said, "Besides, who beat who in arm wrestling? Huh?"

Daniel forced a laugh. "That was one time. And I was tired after a long run."

"You keep telling yourself that. But you know darn well it was your girlfriend, the gymnast."

"I'll see if I can get plane tickets for this weekend."

Tanya's jaw clenched. "You think that's a good idea?"

"I'll tell my coach I have a family emergency. He'll let me go. Just for a couple days."

"You coming because you miss me or because you don't trust me?"

He barked into the phone. "Give me more credit than that. I haven't seen you in two weeks. Of course, I miss you."

"Hmm. You didn't say anything about coming or missing me until you found out that Nash was here."

He reeled his voice back in. "Look, babe. I love you. I don't want to fight."

She hesitated, then said in a quiet voice, "I love you too, Daniel. I just wish you would trust me."

"I trust you, babe. I do."

"Sometimes it doesn't feel like it."

"Do you want me to come or not?"

"I do. I'll pick you up from the airport. Let me know your flight details when you get tickets."

"I miss you."

Her heart swelled. "I miss you, too."

Tanya untangled the phone cord and hung the receiver on the wall. She rubbed her forehead. When they were first going out, he drove five hours in the middle of the night just to give Tanya a bouquet of her favorite flower, gerbera daisies in an array of bright yellow, coral, and deep red. They were at separate training camps in Colorado. She was so surprised when he knocked on her door. He stayed for a half hour, then drove the five hours back just in time to work out with his track team. Her roommates went on and on about how he must really love her to go to all that trouble.

Another time, when she had a bad cold and was in bed for a couple days, he paid someone from a local restaurant to deliver chicken soup and orange juice to her apartment.

He could be so thoughtful but, at other times, so demanding and controlling. Sometimes, he yelled at her and called her names. He always apologized the next day when she got upset. Her tendency was to leave him when he became rude. So that was something, wasn't it? Their relationship was complicated, for sure. But it seemed that it was the best one so far in Tanya's life. And they had a lot in common. She'd never been with anyone who liked as many things as she did.

Yet she felt confused, irritated, and anxious. Her chest constricted and tightened into a ball. When Daniel arrived this weekend, would he be mad if Nash was still here?

CHAPTER 57

After she and Nash had released the horses and two Guernseys into the fields, Tanya strolled to the house to check on Miranda. Miranda lounged with her eyes closed, head resting on the back of the couch.

Tanya said, "How ya doing, Momma?"

Miranda opened her eyes and sat up. "I'm bored. This is driving me crazy. I've read three books and watched several TV shows, and I'm about to ask my mom if she'll show me how to knit. She taught me when I was a kid, but I hated it. Right now, knitting is looking pretty darn interesting. How pathetic."

"Need anything? I'm thirsty. Want some ice water?"

"Sure. Sounds good. Could you put lemon in the glass?"

Tanya nodded and walked to the kitchen. She got out two glasses and some ice from the freezer. She grabbed a lemon from the counter and began slicing it. As she plopped a couple pieces of lemon into the glasses, Miranda groaned.

"Ran? What's wrong?" Tanya scooted over to the couch and sat next to Miranda.

Miranda shut her eyes and rubbed her belly. "My doctor said this was Braxton Hicks contractions." She started taking deep, slow breaths.

"This early?" She rubbed her forehead. "Aren't you eight months along?"

Miranda stopped her deep breathing and settled into the couch. "I think it's passed, hopefully."

"It looked painful."

"It's not fun, for sure." Miranda patted Tanya's hand. "Nothing to worry about, Tonny."

"It's hard to see your best friend uncomfortable."

"Thanks, Tonny. And thanks for everything."

"Wouldn't have it any other way."

"Getting along ok with Nash?"

"We've been working just fine together out in the barn." Her emotions flitted across her face like ripples on a pond.

Miranda's eyes narrowed. "What aren't you telling me, Tanya?"

She opened her mouth, then paused.

Miranda leaned in. "What is it?"

"Daniel called."

Miranda pressed her fingers to her lips.

"He's not too happy about Nash being in the barn helping out while I'm here."

Miranda rolled her eyes. "He gets so jealous."

"He does, I know. But there are so many good things about him too."

"Are you trying to convince me ... or ... yourself?"

"It's just that he can be so sweet ..."

Miranda doubled over.

Tanya shouted. "Ran." She jumped up from the couch and headed toward the door. "I'm going to get your mom."

Tanya sprinted the fifty yards to Justine's porch. She pounded on the door with her fist and yelled, "Justine!" She kept pounding, but nobody came to the door. Her chest flooded with fear. Justine wasn't answering. What would she do? She didn't know anything about having babies.

CHAPTER 58

Meanwhile, Hank searched the aisles in Farm and Fleet for a farrier driving hammer that he used to drive the nails into shoes on horses. The wooden handle had broken off on his last farm visit. Walking through the Carhart racks, the jeans, and then the horse feed supplies, he heard some commotion at the customer service counter. He looked up and spotted two state troopers in olive green shirts and khakis. One of them tipped his olive-green hat as he talked to Miranda's cousin, Larry. Hank recognized the men as officers from Wyoming. He set down the hammer in his hand and dashed to the back of the store, passing horse blankets, bridles, and then saddles as Hank made a break for the side door. He fled across the parking lot as fast as he could. On his way, he passed Mrs. Brown. She held up her hand and tried to say something, but Hank dismissed her with a nod.

Inches from his door handle, he was too slow. From behind, he heard a deep voice booming, "Hank Driskill?"

Hank stopped cold. A dropping sensation swept through his chest. Hank turned slowly and watched as one Wyoming cop removed his handcuffs from his belt. He said, once again, "Hank Driskill?"

Hank nodded.

"There's a warrant out for your arrest in Wyoming. You need to come with us." The cop moved behind him, took both his arms, and cuffed his wrists. While the cop was securing the hand cuffs, the other Wyoming cop read Hank his Miranda rights.

Hank dry swallowed. "Why am I being arrested?"

The cop said, "There's been a warrant out for your arrest for leaving the state. One of the terms of your probation is you're not to leave the state of Wyoming."

Hank grimaced. "Are you sure? I was never put on probation."

"That's something you've got to take up with the DA's office in Wyoming when we get there."

Hank kicked the side of his truck. "You're taking me to Wyoming?"

The officers led Hank to the green cruiser and placed him in the back seat. They removed his cuffs and shut the door. When the two cops got in the front, one turned and said through the glass, "We've got a fourteen-hour drive. We'll make a few stops along the way. You'll get one phone call when we get to a phone. So, you'd better settle in."

As they were leaving the parking lot, Hank glanced at two cars over where his neighbor, Mrs. Brown, watched the whole scene. On their way to Cheyenne, heaviness spread throughout Hank's body as self-loathing consumed him. His head pounded as his thoughts circled around, neglecting to take care of the subpoena that had come in the mail a month ago. He'd called an attorney in Wyoming, and the guy reassured him it would be taken care of. Hank should have followed up, but he pushed it away in his mind and foolishly thought it'd be taken care of. But deep down, he knew that his decisions over the past several months had gotten him to this place.

Hank shook his head slightly, unable to comprehend that the fool he'd gotten into a fight with two years prior was pressing charges, and Hank was the one going to jail. The guy who beat his girlfriend, the waitress at the bar, should be the one in jail, not Hank, for trying to help the woman. This was what he got for being a nice guy.

*

The phone on the wall in the barn kept ringing and ringing repeatedly. Nash plopped another scoop of grain into one of the horses' feed bins. He patted the mare on her back and walked toward the phone.

"Graaf residence."

"Nash, glad to hear your voice."

"What's up, bud."

"I'm in jail." In the hallway next to the payphone used for inmates, Hank flunked against the wall. The silence was way too loud on the other end. "Nash. Say something."

"I'd say I told you so, but that wouldn't be a very good friend, now would it."

"I need you to help me out, buddy."

"Need me to come get ya?"

"They won't let me go. They're transporting me to Wyoming, and I'll be held without bail in Cheyenne."

Nash sucked in a breath. "Wow. That's a low blow."

Hank knew what he was about to ask his friend was a lot to ask of anyone. But he had no choice. "I need you to lie to Miranda. She can't get upset right now. I don't want her going into early labor."

Nash paused for a few beats. "Are you sure you don't want to call her yourself and come clean?"

"Now's not the time. Can you do this? The cop is motioning for me to get off the phone."

Nash exhaled. "I got your back, bud."

With a quick thanks, Hank hung up.

CHAPTER 59

After one last knock on Justine's door, Tanya ran back toward Miranda's house. Just then, Nash came out of the barn. She practically ran into him as he walked across the barnyard.

"Something's wrong with Miranda. We gotta get her to the hospital." Tanya dashed back to Miranda, and Nash followed right behind her.

Miranda was still doubled over on the couch. Tanya knelt beside her. "Honey, I think we'd better take you to the hospital."

Miranda nodded.

Nash's face paled. "Shouldn't we call an ambulance?"

"I think it will be quicker if we just drive her. Can you carry her to your truck?"

"It's hooked up to the trailer."

Tanya grabbed keys off a hook in the kitchen and threw them at Nash. "These are Miranda's. We'll take her truck."

With a strained voice, she said, "Call Hank."

Nash motioned to the hallway near the bathroom and bedrooms. Tanya's brown eyes shot Nash a look as she followed him.

Nash whispered, "We can't call Hank right now."

"Why not?"

"I can't tell you, but he won't be able to be at the hospital."

Tanya's nails dug into his forearm as she glared at him. "Tell me what's going on."

Nash hesitated, and Miranda groaned in the living room.

Tanya squeezed his arm harder. "Tell me."

"Geez. You gymnasts have muscles, man." Nash whispered something inaudibly.

Tanya bent her ear toward his mouth.

"Hank is in jail."

Tanya started to screech and slapped a hand over her own mouth. "What? What for? What did he do?"

Miranda moaned again.

"I'll tell you later."

She looked him straight in the eye. "Not a word to Miranda."

"Agreed."

As Nash scooped up Miranda, she stuttered, "Tanya, call Hank and my mom. There's a number where he can be reached. And my mom is at Richard's in Chicago. Both numbers are on the wall next to the phone."

Nash carried Miranda through the door and out to the truck.

Tanya couldn't believe she had to keep Hank's whereabouts from her best friend. What could he have possibly gotten himself into? Miranda didn't need this right now. She'd have to be there the best she could for her.

Tanya dialed Richard's number. Richard answered the phone, and she relayed the message about Miranda. He said Justine wasn't there then, but he would get her, and they'd come straight away to Davenport.

Tanya sprinted to the truck where Nash had put Miranda on the passenger seat. Tanya went to the driver's side of the truck and leaped to the middle. Nash hopped in and started the truck.

Miranda whimpered, and Tanya took her hand. "It'll be ok, Ran. We'll be at the hospital real soon."

Nash flashed her an anxious smile. They sped down the driveway, dirt spewing from beneath the tires and scattering sparrows into the air.

CHAPTER 60

Justine felt pampered in a way she'd never felt before. Richard had treated her to a spa outing in Chicago at a resort a few miles from his house. He had dropped Justine off in the morning and would pick her up in the afternoon. She'd had a massage, a mud wrap, and she was getting a facial, and then to finish her luxurious day, a pedicure and manicure. She was thinking about what nail color she'd pick and was torn between a coral and deep red when the receptionist peeked her head into the treatment room. She said, "Mrs. Graaf? There's a call from your fiancé. You can pick it up on Line One."

Justine's jaw tightened. Why was Richard bugging her? Sure, he'd given her this wonderful experience as a gift, but he couldn't even leave her alone for a few hours. She felt guilty about feeling irritated and looked at the technician. She said, "Excuse me, Sally. I'd better get this." She flipflopped her way to the phone on a corner table. "Richard? What …?"

"Justine," he boomed. "Your daughter is on her way to the hospital. Tanya and Nash are taking her. She's having a lot of pain."

"What? Where is Hank?"

"They can't get a hold of him."

"Come pick me up, Richard. We've got to go home."

"I'll be there in a few minutes."

Justine hung up the phone. Numbness circled inside her, filling every nook and cranny in her body. "I've got to go. My daughter's in trouble. Where is my coat?"

The technician left the room and came back shortly with Justine's shoes and coat. In a couple minutes, Richard parked next to the building. Justine ran out and got into the car. "Go!"

He sped onto the road.

"What did Tanya say?" Justine took out a handkerchief from her purse and wiped off the green goop from her cheeks and forehead.

"She just told me Miranda was in a lot of pain, and they were taking her to the hospital. Miranda was asking for you."

"Did she think she was in labor? It's too soon. She's got one month to go." Justine fiddled with the collar on her coat, trying to straighten its edges. "And why isn't Hank there?" Her voice rose. "Where is he?"

"I don't know the answer to any of that. As soon as we get there, we'll find out."

As they drove down the freeway, the reality of what was happening sank in. "Can't you go any faster?" Justine panicked and started hyperventilating.

Richard took her hand, saying, "Slow, deep breaths, honey. Slow, deep breaths. Follow my breathing."

Surprisingly, she took comfort in his rhythmic breathing and started to breathe somewhat normally. "Go faster, Richard."

"I'm going ninety. I hope we don't get pulled over."

CHAPTER 61

When they reached the emergency room, Nash hopped out of the truck and ran to the entrance. He hollered at an attendant, and she followed him out to the truck with a wheelchair. Tanya jumped out of the driver's side. She and Nash eased Miranda into the wheelchair, and the group went inside the hospital.

The attendant said, "Bring your wife this way. I'll show you where the maternity ward is."

Tanya and Nash stared at each other. Miranda held her belly and said through gritted teeth, "Somebody, *do* something."

Nash said, "I'm not the father."

The attendant said, "I won't judge," as he put his hand up. "Just follow me."

Tanya spoke up. "We can't find her husband."

Miranda shot her a look like a horse in the middle of a fire.

"I mean, we left a message. He should be here soon."

Miranda bent over, and by the time they reached the elevator, she shrieked, "Hurry!"

When they reached the maternity ward and the elevator door opened, Nash put his hand up and shook his head. "I'm not going in there." He backed up against the elevator wall as the attendant pushed Miranda into the hall. "I think I'll go back to the farm and take care of the animals."

"No, you're not. You're coming with me." Tanya yanked his shirt, pulling him through the door. She nudged him into a chair in the waiting area and shook her finger at him. "You wait here. Don't leave."

Nash grabbed a *TIME* magazine and held it in front of him so it blocked his view.

Tanya looked at all the men scattered in the waiting area. She whispered under her breath, "Wimps." The thought of those poor women pushing out humans into the world and their husbands couldn't even be bothered to help. They just sat there and waited like the cowards they were. She shook her head.

When the attendant was finished talking to the nurse at the reception desk, he pushed Miranda toward a room.

Tanya followed. She turned, looked at Nash, and pointed her finger. "Don't move."

As they were getting Miranda settled in a room and Tanya was helping her change into a light blue hospital gown, her thoughts diverted to Hank. What was that all about? Is her best friend's husband a criminal? What did he do? What. Did. He. Do? She always thought Hank was a great guy and perfect for Miranda, but this was so out of the blue. Why was he being taken away in handcuffs? And at the worst possible time.

Tanya and a nurse who had come into the room helped Miranda into a bed and propped some pillows against her back. The nurse took Miranda's vitals and said that the doctor would be in shortly.

When the nurse left, Tanya held Miranda's hand. "How're you doing, sweetie?"

"It hurts bad." She squeezed Tanya's hand and looked at her with pleading eyes. "Can you go find Hank?"

She had never lied to Miranda and didn't want to start, but she had no choice. She didn't want to add stress to her already full plate. "Ran, I left a message with him and your mom. Right now, you focus on your baby and you."

"But what if it's time?" Miranda groaned and curled into a fetal position on her side.

"Maybe it's more Braxton Hicks. And then we can all go home and figure it all out."

"This feels different."

Tanya rubbed Miranda's back.

Just then, a tall man in his sixties walked in wearing a white coat. A stethoscope hung around his neck. "Hi, Miranda. The nurse tells me you're having some pain."

In a shaky voice, Miranda said, "Hi, Dr. Cleary."

His easygoing manner and kind blue eyes sparkled as he looked at her. "Let's see if we can find out what's going on." He placed his hand on her belly and palpated. His shoulders dropped, and a thin line formed across his lips. "I'd like to do a pelvic exam too."

Dr. Cleary washed his hands at the sink and then rolled a stool around the end of her bed and sat. The nurse returned and stood beside him. He slipped on gloves, and while he was conducting the exam, Miranda clenched her teeth, and Tanya held her hand.

He finished his exam and stood, rolling the stool over to the corner of the room near a small counter. When he turned around, he looked at Miranda. "Well, dear." He smiled a slight smile. "You are in labor."

"But I'm a month early."

"You *are* early. But you're dilated to seven centimeters, and this baby is getting ready to be born." He nodded to the nurse standing by the bed. "Prep mom for labor." He looked at Miranda. "See you shortly." Then, the doctor left the room.

Tanya smiled and said, "We're having a baby."

Miranda rubbed her belly, looking straight ahead. "Where's Hank?"

"I'm sure he'll be here soon." More lies to her best friend. At one point, Miranda was going to find out that Tanya was lying. She'd have to tell her the truth, but not now. "Hank wouldn't miss it."

CHAPTER 62

For two more hours, Miranda, restricted to the bed because she was high risk, panted Lamaze breathing, as Tanya coached alongside. Miranda continued to ask for Hank, and Tanya continued to lie to her, telling her that he'd be there soon. The more she lied, the more Miranda cussed Hank out for not being there.

"How could shoeing a horse be more important than seeing his baby being born?"

When Miranda lay on the maternity bed, about ready to start pushing, the door burst open, and Justine stood there, decked out in a medical gown. She sang out, "Miranda, oh, Miranda, they told me you're about ready to have a baby."

In a shaky voice, Miranda said, "Mom. I'm glad you're here. Do you know where Hank is?"

Justine looked at Tanya. Tanya shrugged.

"Argghh." Miranda's face turned red as she began to push.

"It's time," the nurse said as she went to get the doctor.

When the doctor returned and positioned himself at the foot of the bed, Justine and Tanya each held a hand as Miranda pushed, groaned, and grunted, and within minutes, a beautiful baby girl was born.

Justine gave a small yelp and fisted her hand against her lips as tears streamed down her face.

The baby, wailing in a high-pitched, intense cry, was placed on Miranda's chest.

Miranda, her eyes a waterfall, looked at her brand-new daughter and said, "You're here. You're finally here." She stroked her back and kissed her head filled with curly dark blond hair.

Through shining eyes, Justine said, "She's beautiful."

Tanya felt light-headed as she said, "She sure is, Miranda. Good job."

Back home at the Graaf farm, the phone rang and echoed against the walls of the barn. It kept ringing and ringing and ringing.

ACKNOWLEDGMENTS

Much gratitude to my wonderful readers that have stuck with me since the beginning. From the first pages, when Miranda meets Hank, Justine grieves the loss of her husband, and Tanya takes her gift as a gymnast to the next level. Thank you for being patient waiting for Secret Dreams!

Thank you to Geoff Affleck for guiding me on the path to publishing my second book.

Thank you, thank you, thank you to Alissia J.R. Lingaur, for your friendship, and editing my book once again. Your wisdom and talent as an editor are priceless.

To Peter, the love of my life, thank you for your continuous support and encouragement of my creative endeavors. With you by my side dreams really do come true.

ABOUT THE AUTHOR

Elizabeth Ann Thompson lives in northern Michigan with her husband. She enjoys hiking, running and riding horses. She pairs listening to music and eating comfort food with writing stories about love and relationships. Elizabeth Ann is passionate about encouraging others to follow their dreams.

Follow Elizabeth Ann Thompson on social media and be the first to know when book three in the *Dreams* trilogy is available:

Websites: elizabethannthompson.net & pursueyourdreams.net

Instagram: elizabethannthompson20

Facebook: Elizabeth Ann Thompson – Author